SKYWARD

SKYWARD

A Novel

PHILIP DAVID ALEXANDER

NON CANADA

Library and Archives Canada Cataloguing in Publication

Alexander, Philip David, author
Skyward / Philip David Alexander.

ISBN 978-1-988098-21-0 (paperback)

I. Title.

PS8601.L345S59 2016   C813'.6   C2016-905032-7

Printed and bound in Canada on 100% recycled paper.

Now Or Never Publishing
#313, 1255 Seymour Street
Vancouver, British Columbia
Canada V6B 0H1

nonpublishing.com
Fighting Words.

We gratefully acknowledge the support of the Canada Council for the Arts
and the British Columbia Arts Council for our publishing program.

For Matthew Firth, known to many for his visceral and truthful short fiction, but who has also spent decades publishing and editing magazines like Black Cat 115 and Front & Centre, giving a voice to hundreds of writers.

Chapter 1: Sharp

"Central, this 616, we are in pursuit."

Sharp tapped the mic on his knee and waited. The radio room was busy with a train derailment to the south, near Courtland: twenty cars overturned, some of them on fire, three of them contained phenol. The Ministry of the Environment was on scene. Sharp had been talking to Sergeant Glendon this morning at the coffee shop across from the station. Glendon said it was a mess. They were evacuating the subdivision—motels, sleeping bags in church basements, the whole nine yards. Glendon said a Ministry of the Environment guy had arrived, climbed into a pair of coveralls and talked to the fire crew, wandered the scene, and then trudged to his car, shut himself in there with his laptop. Within an hour there was a swarm of Ministry people there, and the Fire Chief, and a TV truck.

Sharp took a breath, pressed the trans button again, held the mic closer to his mouth.

"Central, 616 is in pursuit."

"*Take* your time, don't mind us," said Ryan.

"She'll get us. They've got that derailment. They're calling in more support."

Sharp looked at Ryan. He'd been complaining he was tired and bored a few minutes ago. Well he was wide-eyed now, and had the cruiser's nose right up the back of a silver Mercedes that had refused to stop.

"He slows and you'll rip right through him," said Sharp.

"He's *not* slowing."

"Just the same, Ryan, hang back a little."

Ryan rammed his palm against the steering wheel like he meant to hurt it. The growler blared, but the Mercedes kept on. Ryan eased back and the Mercedes seemed to catapult ahead.

"Idiot," said Ryan.

"616, this is central, go ahead."

Sharp keyed the mic. "Central, we're in pursuit of a silver Mercedes, marker number Bravo, Bravo, Alpha, Kilo, 2–1–9, northbound Highway 6, just through Allan's Corners, be advised the occupant was observed drinking liquor in the vehicle, refused to stop."

"10–4, 616, stand by."

Ryan flicked over to the yelp and pressed the horn again. The cruiser's siren started strong, but vanished, swallowed by a massive and dull winter sky. Sharp was glad it was Sunday. Traffic was light. The roads had been plowed and salted. Some snow had started falling as they pushed north and the highway narrowed to two lanes; big, wet flakes that hit the windshield with a splatter.

"Hopefully just flurries," he said, thinking aloud.

The Mercedes had pulled away. Sharp watched the sedan's back end. It stayed firm on the road, not a slip or a shudder.

"He can drive, and he's got good tires on it," said Sharp.

"He's an idiot," said Ryan. "Buddy, give it up, there's nowhere to go!"

"616, this is Central."

"Central, 616, go ahead."

"2009, Mercedes E-Class, silver, registered to a Donovan McAllister, 21 Marlborough Drive in Dufferin. DOB: five, June, nineteen–sixty–five. That subject is 10–60. Confirm your speed and 10–20."

"Central, we are northbound Highway 6, approaching Gibson, one–hundred and sixty K."

"10–4 616, stand by."

"Must be the 4.7 turbo. He's rolling," said Ryan.

"Could be," said Sharp.

Sharp watched Ryan's hands for white knuckles, but he was fine. He sat confidently in the driver's seat of the Taurus. He was hanging back now, keeping the Mercedes at a safe distance. Wind blew across the highway from cornfields either side, bringing snow and grit that whirled just above the road's surface.

"He *did* have a bottle. I wasn't seeing things," said Ryan.

Sharp nodded. He'd seen it too. They had just stopped at the Sitko Station. Sharp was catching up his notes from a neighbour dispute south of Allan's Corners. The Orchard Estates: executive homes on half acre lots, lined with apple trees. A squabble and a threat of violence over a snow-blower stored between luxury homes.

The bigger the lot, the lower the tolerance. The larger the home, the smaller the heart. Sharp smiled. That was something his grandfather had said. His grandfather was probably playing shuffleboard, or eating lunch right now. Sharp wanted to talk to him just then, and promised himself he'd visit next weekend.

"Why not wait until you get home. Idiot," said Ryan.

"Needed a drink, I guess," said Sharp. He chuckled.

"Well, that drink's gonna cost him."

The Mercedes had cruised through the Sitko Station like a predator with its silver halogens and tinted glass. The driver's side window halfway down, driver's head obscured, wearing a hooded sweatshirt pulled up. Middle-aged, middle-class geek trying to look gangster, a glass flask tipped to his lips—whiskey or rum judging by the amber colour—and then he made the police cruiser and probably made Ryan's face contorted to ask: *What the hell are you doing?*

Ryan slowed and the cruiser shuddered as the Mercedes made a fast and efficient left turn across Highway 6 and onto Concession 8. The pursued indeed knew his car. He timed it perfectly. Not a slip or a skid. He left 616 in the lurch. They blew by Concession 8 and had to pull a U-turn and come back to it. Ryan hitting the yelp and yelling such a string of profanity that Sharp could see a mist of spit flying from his young partner's mouth.

"Easy, Ryan, easy."

"Central, 616 we are now westbound Concession 8 just north of Gibson headed towards the fairgrounds."

"10–4, 616, be advised our Dufferin and Courtland cars are tied up on the evacuation. I am freeing up a car to check on the registered owner's address on Marlborough—will advise."

"10–4."

"He might be low on gas. He was probably in there looking to fill up and then saw us," said Ryan.

"Give him space, we're doing alright," said Sharp.

Ryan nodded and eased off again. The snow seemed worse on the concession, more of a pest than a hazard, but Sharp did not want to wind up in a ditch, their cruiser rendered a fridge with flashing lights. The two of them shivering and waiting for a tow truck.

Sharp thought again of his grandfather, Victor Sharp. He was eighty-two years old now and in the Crestview Nursing Home, and he did not get along with his own son Edward, Sharp's officious father, or his youngest grandson Daniel, Sharp's know-it-all brother. Father Edward proudly told people, anyone who'd listen, that they were a "police family."

Granddad Victor would chuckle at this and say, "We are just a family, many of whom happen to be policemen."

Granddad Victor had been a police officer over in the UK and also here in Canada, once he'd immigrated. Father Edward was an Inspector now, Sharp's brother Daniel was a provincial police tactical officer. Brother Daniel and father Edward lived and breathed their jobs. It was police *everything* when they got together. They stretched out on reclining chairs, or couches, wearing police baseball caps and yammering about cop politics, culture, equipment and maneuvers. They seldom talked about life: holidays, good wine, or art. Brother Daniel didn't know anything about art. He had a lurid photo of a pick-up truck over the imitation fireplace at his apartment. It hung where a nice painting ought to have been. There was a switch at the base of the truck photo that turned the truck's headlights on. Father Edward would stand with his hands crossed over his chest and say, "That's a beauty. When I retire I'm buying one just like it!"

"Me too," Brother Daniel would say.

Sharp seldom went over to Brother Daniel's place, but when he did, he studied that truck and its little twinkling headlights, and he wanted to shove his brother right out the window. Brother Daniel and Father Edward drank the same brand of beer. They cheered for the same hockey and football teams. They wore their hair in the same flat-top style, and both of them sported the same conservative mustache worn only by cops or 1970s porn stars.

Sharp was the black sheep. He knew it and he was thankful for it. He seldom talked about police work. His closest neighbour, Tim, didn't even know he was a cop until Sharp and Ingrid had lived in the area for over a year.

Sharp thought of his wife, Ingrid. He was still in love with her. Sharp had a couple of Boss suits and stylish dress shirts and he and Ingrid liked to dress up and go to a play in Stratford, or go to Toronto and sit in the King Edward Hotel and have cocktails and talk about jazz, their favourite poets and playwrights, and their future: *The plan*.

He was saving his money to take an early retirement from the department, and he and Ingrid would then buy a bed and breakfast. Father Edward and Brother Daniel did not know about this plan. They did not know that in five years—if Sharp's investments remained stable—that Sharp would quit and move away and seldom think about the police department. If they tried to visit the bed and breakfast, Sharp would tell them, *Sorry, we're all booked up*, even if they weren't. Sharp had shared his plan with Granddad Victor and after he'd done so, Granddad Victor had chuckled, reached out and taken Sharp's hand and squeezed it. They did not say anything else to each other and Sharp felt a lump in his throat and wanted to say something, but couldn't think of what to say.

Sharp thought of Ingrid often when he was away from her, and imagined her at home, in their picturesque bungalow, with her acrylic paint tubes and brushes strewn about the kitchen, standing before a large canvas in her T-shirt and underwear. She didn't wear much around the house and that suited Sharp just fine. She was slim, sinewy and had beautiful legs and unblemished skin. They had been together since college. Ingrid *had* been Brother Daniel's girlfriend at first for about six months, and then she'd broke it off. A month later Sharp had asked her out. That hadn't gone over well with Brother Daniel, or Father Edward.

"You don't pull a stunt like that. There's plenty of fish in the sea," Father Edward had said.

But Sharp had always liked Ingrid and she confessed that she had always been attracted to him, but had found him difficult to read. But she had quickly felt at ease with him. She referred to him as communicative. She liked that he was artistic and fashion-conscious. And while she wasn't initially keen on dating another cop, she said he seemed different. She had also told Sharp, on a few occasions, that his dick was bigger than Brother Daniel's. Much bigger, apparently. Sharp couldn't recall a difference back when they were kids, growing up. But then again, they were just kids. Sharp liked to think of himself and Granddad Victor as being hung like stallions, while Father Edward and Brother Daniel were just pencil-dicks who liked guns and pick-up trucks. This he had *not* shared with Granddad Victor, but thought perhaps he would. Sharp chuckled at the fact he was having these thoughts as they tore along the concession after this Mercedes while the light snow appeared to be changing to freezing rain and slicking the tarmac.

"What's so funny?" said Ryan.

"Nothing. You're right, this guy is an idiot."

"You do that a lot, laugh to yourself. I hope if I'm fucking-up you'll just tell me and not laugh about it."

"I'll tell you if it has anything to do with you."

The Mercedes moved like it was on a cable being frantically dragged to its destination. It was a sleek package of speed and danger that should have been hampered by the freezing drizzle, but moved without a hint of instability. It forged on with a cloud of frozen mist around it, and looked as if it might take flight.

Sharp keyed the mic. "Central, 616, we are now northbound on Timberland from Concession 8."

"10–4, 616."

"Looky here," Ryan said.

Sharp saw an OPP cruiser slow and glide off a county side road up ahead and join the pursuit. A blast of exhaust hit the air as the cruiser accelerated and surged at the Mercedes.

Ryan backed off, glanced at Sharp and nodded. Sharp wasn't certain if his partner was acknowledging the wisdom of keeping a safe distance, or that the provincial police were now in the game.

"616, this is Central, be advised the OPP are now also in pursuit. They will also parallel on County Line 6. We are in contact with their communication centre."

Sharp keyed the mic. "616, 10–4, we see them."

"616, this is Sergeant One. Keep up your 10–20 and report your speed."

Ryan sighed and checked the dash. "Is that Whitney?"

"Yeah, it's Whitney." Sharp keyed up the mic and replied, "Sierra One this is 616, we're northbound Timberland at 145 clicks."

They were doing 170. Ryan smiled at Sharp's white lie.

"He'll call it off. He'll tell us to let the OPP take it," said Sharp.

"He'd *better* not," said Ryan.

Sharp glanced at Ryan's knuckles and then at his neck and jaw.

"Remember to breathe. You're doing good."

Ryan gave his head a slight shake and inhaled. Sharp kept an eye on him for a moment and then turned his attention to the road. He couldn't see the Mercedes. The provincial police cruiser's lights seemed to rush into the dreary sky and ruin what had been a simple and linear pursuit. Ryan looked tense. The involvement of the second cruiser had somehow introduced some panic. Panic had no place in police-work. You had to fight nerves and panic.

"You have to condition your mind to watch for panic and chase it off before it manifests."

That's what Granddad Victor had told Sharp. Victor had walked a beat and rode a bicycle in the UK. He had policed a town with very few streetlamps.

"You don't know if you're scared of the dark until you've walked a beat like that," he'd told Sharp.

When night fell it was pitch black in most places. Granddad Victor patrolled those streets and gas-lit parks alone, without a gun, pepper canister, or radio. He carried a flashlight (that he called 'a torch'), a truncheon, handcuffs and a key for the call-box—his only lifeline to the station. Sharp liked Granddad Victor's stories of walking the beat in England. They were like something out of a Dickens novel. Sharp liked the stories so much, Granddad Victor would tease Sharp that he was born in the wrong era. He'd tell Sharp that policemen were actually *policemen* back then. They knew the community and its people, and the people knew their local constables. There was a respect and understanding that trumped any law on the books. There was a lot of wisdom in his grandfather's tales. Sharp liked to sit and listen closely, and pull out those strands of wisdom.

"You'll be a good copper. You're already the best of the lot," Granddad Victor would say.

Sharp enjoyed it when Granddad Victor raised the topic of Sharp being the superior police officer in front of Father Edward and Brother Daniel. Granddad Victor would peer over at Sharp and flash a quick grin because he knew he was causing trouble. Father Edward, completely backed up by Brother Daniel, would vigorously defend what he called "modern police methodology" and give a speech about how Sharp is not progressive enough.

Granddad Victor would sip his Scotch while his son and second grandson gave a tag-team rebuttal, throwing stats and terminology around the room. Granddad Victor would listen impatiently and would then say something like, "But all I'm hearing are these terms like *conflict management* and what you actually mean by that is shocking some poor bugger with an electric gun. Whatever happened to a wrist-lock or throw? All of your new tactics seem to involve five coppers standing around taking notes and watching the perp, and then suddenly you rush in and blast him with a million bloody volts! Get in there right off the bat, grab the bastard, toss him in the muck and arrest him! That's your bloody job!"

Granddad Victor would then put his head back and laugh, drowning out Father Edward and Brother Daniel. He once put his fingers in his ears and shut his eyes while he laughed, and Father Edward had left the room and slammed the door. Brother Daniel looked at Sharp as if the debate had been his fault. He said something like, "You're outdated. Too old school. If you joined my department, and joined the tactical team, you'd have to get with the program."

Sharp did not reply. He sat back and enjoyed the show, thinking to himself: *Well, I'm not joining the tactical team. In just a few years I'll be living by a lake with a woman you couldn't keep, and you can stay down here and play with your camouflage, ropes, and your M4.*

"616, this is Central, be advised that the suspect vehicle is stolen. A Courtland unit has attended the registered owner's address and reports that the owner is home. The vehicle had been on the driveway when the owner last saw it."

"616, 10–4."

Ryan sighed and said something under his breath. Up ahead Sharp watched as the OPP cruiser stayed on the Mercedes and ripped past a short row of homes and a church. Sharp could see cars in the parking lot of the white clapboard church. He could see movement, perhaps one of the cars attempting to leave the lot, edging toward the concession. Whatever was happening, it spooked the OPP. His cruiser wobbled. The brake lights flared, and the back end of the car swung like a pendulum before jumping the road and plunging into the ditch. Sharp could see people running, hands waving, a plume of snow.

The Mercedes was through the hamlet and gaining. Sharp imagined the driver glancing in his rearview and laughing. Sharp felt a twinge of anger, but tamped it down.

"Slow down," he said to Ryan.

"Okay, okay."

"Slow, pull back, we have to check on him. He ditched it pretty fast."

Sharp keyed the mic. "Central this is 616, be advised we have an MVA with the OPP involved, stand by."

The dispatcher acknowledged as Ryan pulled onto the shoulder and slowed. Sharp saw the concerned faces of ladies, a small group of them arrayed in their floral dresses at the edge of the church parking area. They were holding their coats closed and their hats on their heads. He didn't want anyone falling on the icy road, or getting hit.

"Stop for just a second."

"616, this is Central. Is the suspect vehicle involved?"

Ryan took up the mic while Sharp jumped out of the car and pleaded with the ladies to stay on the church property. They nodded and chattered and moved back from the road. Sharp jumped back in and they rolled toward a cluster of men doing their best to climb down a snowy embankment in their dress shoes or galoshes. Their suit coats flapped and one man's Fedora blew from his head and sailed away like a virgin wool Frisbee. The officer appeared unharmed. He was out of his cruiser and climbing up towards them. Sharp called down to him and he waved and pointed north with a look of determination on his reddened face.

"You alright?"

"I'm good. Black ice," said the officer.

Ryan stamped on the accelerator and they spit slush and grit towards the group of men as they got back onto the concession.

"We might get some dry-cleaning bills," said Sharp.

Ryan smiled, but the grin quickly faded, knowing that a minute was an eternity in a high-speed pursuit.

"Damn it," said Ryan.

Sharp scanned the road ahead. They passed a snow-covered side road to Sharp's right. He looked down it, but with the freezing rain it was difficult to tell how fresh the tire tracks were. He continued looking over his shoulder and told Ryan to slow a little.

"You think he went down there?"

"I'm not sure."

They passed a second side road on the left. There was a tractor chugging along, a lone yellow light flashing on its back end. Ryan groaned and thumped the top of the steering wheel.

"We would have had him."

"We were doing alright," said Sharp.

Sharp thought again about Ingrid. He wanted to call her. He checked his cellphone and the battery was down to a single bar, so he dropped it back in his pocket. She wasn't herself lately. She was distant, easily aggravated.

"Were you gonna call the station?" said Ryan.

"Yeah, but don't worry about it."

Sharp keyed the mic and advised that they'd lost the Mercedes.

"Pull a U-turn and go back to where that tractor was," he said.

"I was thinking the same," said Ryan.

They bumped and slid along the broken concession. It was tough going and Sharp actually wondered if they might blow a shock or damage a strut.

"He's not here. This road would have shredded that car. Let's go back."

Ryan pulled a three-point turn. His disappointment filled the cruiser's cabin.

Chapter 2: The Pursued

When he shook them he felt both relief and disappointment. He was split inside. Nothing unusual about that. He hoped that the cop who'd joined the chase was okay, but also didn't mind the idea that he might have gotten banged up just a little—a fractured collarbone or bloodied nose. The original car had played it right, stayed back and seen the big picture, allowed time and space to stop if the pursuit went sideways. They were ripping along well, hunter and the hunted on slick asphalt. It had been dangerous, exhilarating, *and* stimulating. And then the provincial unit showed up out of nowhere and followed too close, dashed everything. He could see the officer moving around behind the wheel, as if trying to control a wild horse. The churchgoers and their Sunday driving had obviously rattled him. He must have touched the brakes, and the wet, glassy pavement took over. The thrill of leaving them all behind was incredible, but the end of the pursuit left a rotten disappointment inside.

He thought about taking a right, but the road was too narrow. He took his foot off the gas and considered a left, loved the idea of squeezing in a nearly impossible turn, at the risk of spinning out. He licked his lips in anticipation and then aborted when he saw a tractor bouncing along the broken road. The old tractor dipped and wobbled like a moon-buggy. He floored the accelerator, demanded all the car could give. He reached 190 before there was a slight moaning, a subtle shudder from the back end. It was a nice car. Well-tuned with an immaculate interior. The owner likely knew by now that it had been taken, *borrowed*. He snickered at that. It felt good. It had been a while.

He slowed and made a right onto a concession with a large blue barn and matching farmhouse tucked into the northeast corner. There were cows scattered in the neighbouring field and a man in a beige coat and bright red cap walking among them. He felt the urge to pull onto the farm's lane and drive up, say hello to the man, perhaps get himself invited in for coffee. He could do that. He could make friends with anyone when it suited him. He drove past the farmer's field at a leisurely speed—like a regular man in his Mercedes out for a drive in the country. The windshield wipers whined against the glass so he switched them off.

He found a hamlet down the road: Pollard.

"Hello, Pollard," he said.

He'd been here once or twice before. The place was something you'd see on a postcard. There was a post office; a place called Dale's Dairy and a few other old-world storefronts, the type with soap and paint lettering in the windows. There were lovely, well-kept Victorian homes, and a gas station with only one island and two oval, vintage pumps. The sign read: OPEN and WE SERVE. He cruised in and the Mercedes tires ran across a rubber hose that rang a bell to alert the station's attendant.

"How moronic and charming," he said.

The attendant was a teenage boy. He was skinny and narrow-faced and his retro gas station uniform hung from his body.

"Can I help you?"

"Yes, fill it up, please."

He watched for reinforcements as the boy filled the tank. He could spot red and blue lights from miles off. *I can see faster than the speed of light when it comes to those police red and blues,* he thought.

"The cavalry is coming, if they can find me," he said.

He laughed and pulled out his wallet and had a thought. It was a seed and then it sprouted and blossomed all at once, and sat there, a gnarled and twisted plant, perfectly formed. He pulled out a stack of cash. The boy came to the door and he lowered the window all the way.

"That's forty-seven please, sir."

He handed the boy a fifty. The kid took it and began digging into his baggy pockets for change.

"It's alright, I don't need the change."

"Oh, okay, thank you, sir. Did you need any washer fluid, can I check that for you?"

He looked down the road for signs of the police and checked his rearview as well.

"That would be perfect."

He pulled the lever and popped the hood, peeled off a ten while the boy opened it up and stuck his narrow head in there. He watched the boy wander into the station. His long face and unusual gait gave him an equine quality.

"If you were my son I'd keep you in a stable," he said. He laughed and reached under his seat for his gun. He lifted his left leg and tucked the pistol under his hamstring.

The boy emerged from the station with a jug of blue washer fluid. He fumbled around for a moment, but finally got the spout lined up with the car's reservoir and emptied the jug in several loud glugs.

"That's three dollars, sir. I can take it out of the left-over cash, if you want."

"Absolutely not. Here, here's ten, you can keep the change."

The boy smiled and revealed a row of giant, crooked teeth.

"Do you like danger?" he asked the boy.

The boy crouched a little, to make sure he'd heard correctly.

"What do you mean?"

"Danger, or not necessarily *danger,* but something that gives you a thrill. More often than not the thrilling things in life carry some danger, don't you think?"

"I guess. I've been skydiving twice."

"And how was that? Scary, I'll bet."

"Yeah, but a good kind of scary, if that makes sense."

"Oh, it makes perfect sense. That's exactly what I'm talking about."

He handed the boy a fifty.

"Take this."

The boy's filthy hand reached out slowly. He was clearly uncertain of what he was getting himself into. His eyes went a little hazy as his thumb and finger closed like greasy pincers on the bill. He was rapt as the boy gently tugged the bill. It was like the boy's grubby hand was asking: Is this *really* for me? May I take it? He sighed as he released the bill and watched the dirty hand tremble ever-so-slightly and tuck the money into a pocket.

"Are you okay, sir?"

"I'm just fine, thanks."

"No one ever gave me fifty bucks before."

His tone wasn't exactly accusing, but it wasn't grateful either.

"Do me a favour, would you?"

Now, the boy backed away from the car—just a half-step.

"What a perfect day."

The boy glanced up at the dull sky and then at the freezing drizzle collecting on the car's hood. He nodded, but did not reply.

"So, this favour that I need, you can step closer, I won't bite you, and I don't want to yell this out for the entire hamlet to hear."

"I don't have any drugs. I don't know anyone who deals, either."

The boy's hand was back in his greasy pocket, about to pull the fifty back out.

"No, no it's not about that. I don't do drugs. I want your word on something." He waved the boy closer. He smiled brightly and said, "It's alright. I'm not looking for anything other than your word on something."

He kept smiling and winked, and the boy's face relaxed as if under hypnosis.

"If the police come around, and they just might, I want you to tell them you never saw me or this car."

The boy blinked a few times. And he then looked at the dash and steering wheel.

"I guess, but I don't want to get involved—"

"I *thought* you liked danger. You said you were a skydiver."

"Yeah, but I don't want any trouble."

"What trouble? I've given you some cash. All you have to do is tell the police you haven't seen me."

The boy looked down at the ground to consider this, and by the time he looked back up, there was a Sig P226 leveled at his face. He flinched and said, "Oh, uh, please, sir."

He held the gun steady, its barrel pointed right between the boy's eyes.

"I'll tell you what. If the police do come around, and you tell them you saw me, or this car, I'll know, *believe me* I'll know, and I'll come back, find you, and put a bullet in your head. How does that sound?"

The boy stared at the gun. His mouth was open and his pupils like two black buttons.

"Okay, okay."

"Okay what?"

"I'll tell them I didn't see anyone."

"Good. Enjoy the money. Spend it wisely. Buy a bucket of oats."

The boy watched the gun as it was tucked back under the driver's seat.

"I can go now, right?"

"Yes, back to work. Enough of this horsing around!"

He pulled out of the gas station stifling laughter like a school-boy with a dirty joke lodged under his tongue. He drove past Dale's Dairy and shook his head, wished he hadn't needed gas so badly.

If he'd arrived in town with enough gas he could have scared the shit out of the counter help in Dale's and come away with both a thrill *and* something sweet. A chocolate bar, one with shredded coconut, would be just the ticket right about now.

He found a small factory with two snow-covered trucks and a small mountain of wood pallets along one side. He pulled the Mercedes in behind the last truck, opened the window, turned up the heat and unscrewed the cap on his whiskey. There had been a time, not long ago, when he would have sat and savoured the stunt with the human horse at the gas station. There had been a time, not long ago, when he would have had larger, more incredible conquests to savour. It hadn't been easy this past year. The thrill seemed to be diminishing. He was entirely disappointed in himself and it was becoming increasingly obvious that he might be stuck with one life. He'd always had two. He'd nearly convinced himself, over the years, that the two lives were because of his father. But then he'd recall something, a vivid memory from when he was just a little boy, and he'd wrestle with the possibility that he'd always had two minds, two sets of completely different motivations, stuffed into one unusual brain. It had *nothing* to do with his father. He took one more sip of whiskey and spun the cap back on the bottle.

He remained at the edge of Pollard, parked at the factory, which turned out to be a feed mill. He played with the seat controls and windshield wipers. He moved back and forth and up and down, and kept the windshield drizzle-free while he waited for the police to drive past in search of him. He had concealed the car well and felt confident they'd cruise by and he'd simply chuckle and thumb his nose at them. The car's interior really was beautiful. He now had the chance to sit back and admire it. He liked the German luxury sedans best. The Swedish cars were nice too, but they had gotten cheap and plastic inside over time—cursed by platform engineering. The Brits made a nice car as well, but it was tricky getting the keys duplicated for a Jag or a Land Rover, and if you did steal one, the NAV and voice system talked to you in an English accent, which was enough to get on anyone's nerves.

The Mercedes seats were done in a black, perforated leather, and they cradled you. The dash was trimmed in lacquered wood, and the stereo was perfect, six speakers and deep bass. The owner had placed a bottle of air-freshener on the dash—a strange little trinket made of glass with a little sponge cork for a stopper. *Heavenly Lavender Mint* was printed in calligraphic writing on the air-freshener's label. He never felt bad about taking expensive cars. They belonged to people who never missed them anyway. People who had enough money that they left $100 gift cards in the glove-box; $50 bills tucked in the sun visor; Visconti pens in the console, or fancy glass bottles of air-freshener fastened to the dash. He snatched up the bottle with a ripping sound and tossed it out the window into the melting snow.

He took car keys and fobs quickly and deftly. He tried not to overdo it; kept it to one theft every couple of months. He'd scoop them off the hallway table and pocket them; he'd casually reach into a handbag when the lady of the house had trotted off to get something or answer the phone. He'd dig into the pocket of a coat hanging in the hallway when the owner had turned his back for a moment. He had a mechanic over in Niagara, Rick, who was not exactly suspicious, but had become curious. He'd begun to make comments.

"I am assuming this is all legit. You're not gonna bring me any trouble . . ."

He had simply stared into Rick's eyes and, at that moment, could have killed him. Shot or strangled him without hesitation and without a vapor of an afterthought. Rick gave him a weak smile, took the $500 and the key and slipped them into his overalls. It usually took five or six days. When he went back the new key and the original were waiting for him in an oil-smeared envelope in the office. There was a skinny woman in the office who chain-smoked and had peculiar, ginger hair. It looked lopsided and he wondered if it was a wig. She had a lazy eye that seemed to drift out of alignment and then slowly drift back. She wore baggy, blue maintenance clothes with GRETA stitched over the left pocket.

"Rick left this for you," she'd say, and toss him the envelope.

One day, he caught the package and said, "It's rude to throw things at people. You know that, don't you, Greta?"

She squinted at him through a blue haze of smoke.

"It's just that a nice lady like you, with that lovely hair and striking green eyes . . . I'll tell you what, if you put on something classic—I know you're working in a garage, so nothing *too* nice— perhaps a pair of jeans and a nice blouse, a solid colour, let's say dark purple, or a middle green to match those eyes. Straighten that vibrant hair. Do you mind me making these suggestions?"

The anger that had rushed across her face had retreated. She touched her hair and her eyes twitched nervously.

"You think I have nice eyes and hair?"

"I do."

"You're not shitting me?"

"I would never."

She adjusted her rumpled blue work-shirt and began straightening up the mess on her desk.

"And if you put just a little make-up, not too much because you have nice skin, but enough to warm up your cheeks. You know, your skin is just the right side of porcelain, if you don't mind me saying so."

"Oh I *don't* mind, as *long* as you're not shitting me."

"Never."

"Porcelain, that's white, right?"

"Typically, and very smooth as well."

"Huh." She touched her face and grinned.

"Well, we'll see you soon. Tell Rick I said thanks. I feel as if I'm putting him out these days."

"I'll tell him, but you can deal with me from now on, if you want," she said.

Her finger was still tracing her face.

"Yes, I'd like that."

The next time he visited with a stolen key Greta was dressed in crisp blue jeans and a navy blouse with the collar fashionably turned up. She had fixed her hair and it looked miles better, and apparently wasn't a wig. Greta bent over the desk to take the key from him. Her new blouse hung from her pale chest. She was bra-less. He peered at her freckled breasts and she smiled and closed the office door. It took some effort. He was as interested in her as a house cat would be in a paddle-boat ride, but he dug deep and kissed her neck while she thrust her hips forward and blurted, "Oh yeah, pound it, that's the way," over and over, like a chant.

It was the *pound it* part of the chant that disgusted him, but he told himself, as he pumped away, that she *did* work in a garage, and that he would get his keys on time and when he wanted, and without dealing with Rick (which he did every visit after the *pounding*).

"That was fun. Was it good for you?" she asked.

He zipped-up, buttoned his shirt and prepared to leave the office. He nodded and gave her a smile, all the while thinking, *It was great, provided you like sex with an ashtray.* He desperately wanted a hot shower.

"Oh, someone's gotten all shy. Don't be shy now," she said, and laughed her smoky laugh.

He would take the original key or fob back to the owner's place late at night. It was simple. He'd toss it out the window onto the property, usually alongside the driveway. Sometimes he'd walk to the doorstep and drop the key near a flowerpot or lawn chair. Over the next few hours the owner would spot the key and think, *Damn, there it is. I must have dropped it.* He kept his newly coded key for use at his convenience. He'd often wait weeks before returning to the property, casually hopping in the car, and driving away.

He started the E-class and positioned it closer to the back of the mill, where the exhaust would not be as visible as it collided with the chilly air. He opened the windows just a crack and reclined his seat. He closed his eyes and waited for sleep—just an hour or so, to recharge himself before making his next move.

Chapter 3: Stan Hill

The cops around here have too much time on their hands. They cover a vast area and I've heard them complain about how stretched they are. And yet they have time to hound a dude like me. I've been in the backseat of their cars a few times—nothing serious, until recently. It was usually over a disagreement with one of the local neanderthals at a bar on the main street. They've come by the house a few times, especially now that my father has moved down south. If he was around they wouldn't dare drop in, asking questions that contain little shards of accusation. When they do come around I wind up telling them to fuck off.

My mother and the cops will tell me there's no need for that. But there's plenty of need for it.

My mother wants the cops around. She thinks they'll find my younger brother, Jarrod, who went missing last year. But they won't. And he isn't missing. Missing is when you disappear and the disappearance is unplanned, a surprise to those around you. My mother, stupidly, gave Jarrod a wad of cash because she felt sorry for him. He took off with it, and once he's burned through it doing God knows what, he'll reappear.

Jarrod is nineteen years old going on fourteen. He was last seen at the Skyward Fair, a huge county event that started years ago as an agricultural show, but has grown over time into a giant, twinkling freak-show with a big top, midway, quarter-horse races, musicians, clowns, and a casino—if you can call a hundred plaid-shirted, baseball-capped hicks cranking the handles of old slot machines a *casino*. It draws people from all over the region. It's a loud, damp, backward-ass event that reeks of horse shit and deep-fried food, courtesy of a battalion of chip trucks scattered all over the property. It gives the locals a point of pride and creates something that looks like tourism. I think it looks like a cross-breeder's convention. There are enough rebel flag belt buckles and wallet chains in that place to stretch around the earth's circumference at least once.

It would come and go each year, and *would* be forgotten the day after they shoveled up the last pile of horseshit and drove the last chip truck home, if it weren't for one little detail. A young man has disappeared each year since Skyward moved to its new fairground near Gibson. The cops and my mother believe Jarrod is one of them, and theoretically they are correct. I'm not sure what happened to the other two. The police believe the three missing people, Jarrod included, were taken. Abducted. All three were seen at Skyward at some point on the day they went missing. All three have completely vanished without any trace. There is a police hot-line that has turned up nothing. Zero. Wherever my brother and the other two guys went, they went quietly and completely unnoticed. The community is split on what happened to them. Some side with the cops and believe they were taken against their will, and robbed (or worse) and then murdered. I think my mother believes those folks, but hopes they are wrong. Others believe they went to Skyward packed and ready to go. There are hordes of people there; out-of-town people with cars and money. You could grab a ride or hitchhike your way to a new life. It's the perfect place to *meet up* and *get out* with anonymity, lost in the crowd. I side with this school of thought.

There's evidence to support it. The first guy that went *poof* was from up north. He was a martial artist; two different black belts and a room full of trophies and medals back home to prove it. As his father told reporters: *No one was taking him anywhere he didn't want to go.* The second guy was local and had mental health issues—big surprise. His parents received an email from him the evening he vanished. It told them that he needed to get away, to move on for a while. It promised them he'd be in touch. Granted, that was two years ago now, but the email was apparently sent from his laptop. And then there's my brother Jarrod: the laziest guy on earth. A guy who would shamelessly survive on welfare cheques that furbished him with an endless supply of junk food and a vat of root beer, if he could. Where did he go?

Who knows? In my mind he was a mystery even before he became a mystery.

My father left my mother when I was eighteen. Jarrod was around sixteen. My old man moved to Florida. He was born down in the States and he decided to pack up and head back. He has his own security company and a nice little condo setup within walking distance of the beach. I visit him down there every year and man, do I look forward to that. The end game is to go down there and join him, permanently. So I work as many hours as I can get at the plant. I pull double shifts and do Sundays in the spring when demand spikes and they throw on extra shifts. I take correspondence courses, university level, not at the backwoods college just outside town. They have a heavy equipment operators program here at our college. They also have a call-centre management program. What does that even mean? Forget that shit. I like sun. I like the college down there, where the profs wear shorts and golf shirts. I like my father. I like his life, and the way he rolls. Our family is strange that way; split into two teams. Jarrod and my mother with their phobias and secrets. And me and the old man. Give us a sunny day, a stretch of beach, a six-pack and a good book, and all is right with the world. And you can toss in a few string bikinis playing beach volleyball, too. We never complain about that. As he likes to say: We control the controllable.

CHAPTER 4: WARFIELD

Constable Sheila Warfield *knows* things. She has since she was a child. When she was thirteen years old she threw a tantrum: a crying, screaming, hissing fit, where her skinny body moved like a washing machine agitator. She put on a performance worthy of any spoiled and snot-faced toddler. They were at the airport. Her mother was incredulous and stood with her hand at her mouth. Her father gripped Sheila's arm until it stung, and dragged her over to a vestibule where there was an ATM and pay-phone.

"What's gotten into you?"

Sheila eventually stood still, but didn't answer him. She looked like a zombie. He tried to pick her up to carry her back to the boarding area. She kicked at his legs and grabbed the pay telephone, so that when he pulled her away the metal cord stretched and blocked the path of a lady in a wheelchair. A security guard came over. Her father let go of her, and Sheila hung up the phone and began to bellow at the top of her lungs. More security people arrived, along with a man in a blazer from the airline. The man in the blazer looked like a washed up rock star, tight curly hair loaded with gel. He had tattoos on his hands. He told Sheila and her parents they could not board the aircraft until she settled down. Sheila kicked the airline blazer man in the knee, and the airline blazer man said, "Ah, shit," and made a whistling noise as he grabbed his kneecap. Sheila snatched a flashlight out of a nearby security guard's belt. She threw the flashlight and it landed behind the counter of a coffee stand. The coffee lady screamed and some idiot with a loud, deep voice asked if it was a bomb. He kept saying *bomb* over and over and Sheila recalls the airline blazer man closing his eyes, shaking his head and saying, "I *hate* this place."

Sheila's parents lectured her all the way home. There would be changes. She would be grounded and there would be summer school if her grades did not improve. The shopping mall was now off-limits. Her father tapped his finger on the top of the steering wheel and said, "That's half the trouble, you run around in the damn mall with Andrea and Grace, and that other one, the older one, Grace's sister who's supposed to be watching you . . ."

"You'd better not be smoking pot," her mother added.

"She's *not* smoking pot," said her father.

"She acting like it," said her mother.

"*Pot* doesn't make you act like this. *Are* you smoking pot?"

"No!"

That night the news came that the flight they should have been on made an emergency landing and skidded off the runway. There had been a fire on board. There were no fatalities, but forty passengers were injured, three were in critical condition. Sheila's parents were quiet and whispered a lot. Her father's face was twisted into a funny expression, half fear and half curiosity, like he'd just seen a UFO.

Her mother came into her room and hugged her, but also questioned her about the tantrum and the fate of their flight. Sheila didn't want to talk about it and couldn't explain it, and wouldn't have even if she could. Her mother was a tornado of a person, a jovial, goal-oriented entity that sucked up everything in its path. So Sheila told her that she'd simply felt panicked. Her mother said they'd have to keep an eye on that. She was too young to be having panic attacks.

"Are you sure that's all there is to it?"

"Yes mum!"

"Don't yell, let's watch our attitude."

Go and bug dad, she thought, *nag and drive him insane.*

There was a boy named Jerry Plowman in junior high school. He was thin and anemic. He had bad acne and limp hair. The boys on the track team picked on him, and called him *preacher boy*. He had very few friends. Jerry always carried a dented guitar case. The athletic boys would tease and taunt him, question him about why he never played the guitar; why wasn't he in a band?

They would say things like, " 'Cause there is no guitar in there. It's probably an animal carcass . . ."

"It's a wig and a preacher's suit and he's gonna preach in the gym . . . "

"It's a blow-up sex doll . . ."

"Yeah, a male one, a bum buddy . . ."

That last one had them keeled over laughing. Rolling around in the hallway gasping for air.

Jerry played Sheila a song one afternoon, in private, at the back of the science lab when everyone had gone home. He strummed and picked the guitar incredibly well. Sheila was mesmerized as she watched him play. He sang too. His voice wasn't necessarily good, but it was unique—clear and papery. Sheila told him he'd be famous. She *saw* it and *knew* it. He'd have great success with his music. Jerry liked that, but hung his head and said he doubted it. His parents were religious and strict. His father wanted him in seminary. They didn't have much money and when there was some extra it went to the church. Sheila told him that none of that mattered. She told him it was a certainty and when it happened, she said to remember her.

When Sheila was twenty-one and floundering in community college, she saw a TV interview with Jerry Plowman. He was bald and wore strange eyeglasses with white plastic frames. He had precision trimmed facial hair. The tattoos on his arms looked like the stained glass windows of a church. He was talking to the music reporter from a prime time entertainment show about his band The Sower & The Plow. They had a hit song that had crossed over from Christian radio to mainstream, and they were embarking on a European tour. Sheila waited until JERRY PLOWMAN - LEAD-SINGER - THE SOWER & THE PLOW ran like a ticker tape along the bottom of the TV screen. She aimed the remote and shut the TV off, and smiled.

Sheila did not have visions. There was no flickering film-loop of the future in her head. She didn't talk to friends or family about the things that came to her. As she grew older she thought about seeing a shrink, knew she'd eventually have to.

How would she explain it?

Sometimes, I observe shadows that interrupt the light, and my thoughts—something like when a night bird flies across the moon, or a moth flutters past a light bulb. The space around me darkens. Sometimes I go blind for a few seconds. And something sits in my mind, like a parcel, and I try to ignore it, but it pulls, like a vortex. I wind up going to it, opening it. And then I walk around shuddering and wondering what to do with the information. I am aware of potential damage to my reputation, how I will be perceived, and how difficult it will be to make friends and establish relationships—and I already have enough trouble with that. So I usually do nothing. I try to ignore it.

Sheila can see the shrink's confused face, especially when she explains that she doesn't *really* believe in any of it: clairvoyance, second-sight. She sees the shrink on the phone, arranging for her to participate in other tests, in the company of a whole team of shrinks. She has a competing scenario where she's in a shrink's office as he writes out a prescription and gives her a fact sheet that lists the various side-effects and complications that can occur while taking the drug, pills that dull her mind and dry her mouth. She once got to the door of the psychiatrist's office, her finger poised above the illuminated button, about to ring the bell. She looked over her shoulder at a brilliant autumn day, fire red and bronze-leaved trees. The wind was crisp and the sky clear except for the odd silvery cloud. She stepped out of the doorway and saw a hot dog vendor in the park across the street, steam rushing from the stack of his wagon. She left and never returned the doctor's call when he followed up with her to reschedule the missed appointment.

Sheila decided not to finish her college diploma, which was in fashion and clothing design. She did not fit with the other girls in the program. She did not look like them, either. Emma, the only girl with whom she made friends, wound up meeting a guy. She moved in with him.

"Don't worry, you'll meet someone. You're pretty! You need to get out there more!"

Sheila wanted a career that dealt with *facts*. She did not want to waste her life associating with women three times as attractive as her, and who would merely pretend to accept and include her, nor did she want to spend years navigating their catty behaviour.

She wanted a life where strange information that pulled at her from dark caverns in her mind was meaningless. She wanted to live according to facts. She thought about law and becoming a litigator, perhaps a crown prosecutor. People went to prison because they were charged with an offense. The justice system used facts to convict them. She would have to stick to facts in that world. She took a train to Toronto and collected brochures and booklets from U of T. She read the information and wondered if she had the patience to spend that much time in school. She certainly didn't have the money. She was also troubled, and amused, as she pictured herself in a packed courtroom, wearing a nice, flared Glen-check skirt and crisp white blouse with black buttons. She saw the judge asking her a question:

"And how, Ms. Warfield, would you know that the accused had written several threatening letters and kept them in a locked drawer in his office?"

"I saw them, your honor."

"Saw them?"

"Yes, I saw them in my mind."

"But you don't actually know they exist. You haven't read them."

"Correct."

"We'll take recess at which time, Ms. Warfield. I'd like to talk to you. Alone."

The courtroom would then break out in grunts and giggles.

Sheila was at a job fair arranged by the college student association a few years ago. The police were there. They had set up a large press-board display booth and the representing officer, Sergeant Glendon, was very friendly and took a shine to her. He told her that the department was on an initiative to recruit more female officers, as well as people from cultures that might not ordinarily consider policing as a career. Sheila had stood and talked to him for nearly an hour. She told him that she was very interested in a career where serving her community and relying on facts were the foundation for success. The two shook hands and Sheila left that day with yet more brochures and the Sergeant's fancy business card with its coat of arms and Staff Sergeant William David Glendon in dark blue raised letters.

Sheila joined the department and graduated as the top recruit in police college. Glendon took her under his wing and was like an uncle to her. She was well-liked among the rank and file and considered by the brass to be an up-and-comer. A good cop.

Chapter 5: Sharp

They drove to a little village, Pollard. Sharp hadn't been up this way for a while.

"What is this, a time-warp or something?" said Ryan.

"You've never been up here before?"

"Never."

"Ingrid and I used to come to the tree farm and buy our Christmas tree."

"I have a fake one with the lights built in," said Ryan.

"Yes, same here. She always felt bad about cutting down a tree. I like the smell of it."

Sharp pointed and Ryan parked on the modest main drag: five shops adorned with matching striped awnings. Ryan shut down the motor and went into Dale's Dairy.

"Coffee?"

"Sure," said Sharp.

Sharp stepped inside a tiny shop called Max's General Goods. There was a cluster of electronics symbols, decals, on the storefront, along with a hand-painted sign boasting new cell phones and laptops in stock. The man at the counter was ancient and rheumy-eyed. He was friendly, but immediately concerned at the sight of Sharp. Sharp could see it in the man's weathered face.

"Everything alright, officer?"

"Everything is fine, sir. Do you sell phone chargers? One that would plug into the car?"

Sharp handed over his phone. The counter-man examined it briefly and then rummaged around in a deep drawer, eventually coming up with a charger in a blister pack. Sharp paid up and turned away from the counter-man, taking out his knife. He flicked it open and pushed the short blade through the top of the plastic pack. He turned back to the counter and pulled apart the packaging.

"That's how to do it. I hate those blasted packages," said the man.

"Can you recycle this for me?"

The counter-man accepted the empty pack and looked out the window. Sharp followed his stare and saw a tall kid in a baggy uniform over at the gas station. The kid was standing away from the pumps, smoking a cigarette. Sharp figured he'd been watching the cruiser, but averted his eyes when he and the counter-man looked in his direction.

"Have a good day, officer," said the counter-man.

Sharp wished him the same and went to the cruiser. Ryan had arrived with two coffees. He placed them on the roof and unhooked the keys from his belt.

Sharp cracked the top of his coffee and sipped. Ryan put his in the cup-holder and turned the ignition key. Sharp watched and hoped the Taurus would fire up, considering how hard they'd pushed it chasing that jerk in the stolen Mercedes. The cruiser came to life and Sharp plugged his charger into the car's outlet. He looked over to the gas station; it was an old-school place, oval pumps with big, hooded incandescent bulbs overhead. The office was all glass, and sat beside two bays with wooden roll-ups. They appeared locked; the mechanic probably enjoying a Sunday off. The kid was inside the office, but still paying casual attention to the rare appearance of a police car in their little village.

"Do me favour, Ryan, and drive over to the gas station."

Ryan put his coffee down and checked the fuel gauge.

"We're good, over half a tank and we're heading back—"

"Not for gas. I want to see what's on his mind."

"Who?"

Sharp nodded towards the glass office. "Curious George over there."

Granddad Victor had always insisted that citizens who stare at the police will tell you something.

"They usually have some useless question or comment. There's a high percentage that believe that they should talk to you just for the sake of talking, just because you're there. But every now and then they'll tell you something, something useful, a thing that they've seen, or a thing that's been on their mind. Always talk to them. Give them the time of day."

Sharp had always remembered this and as he gained experience in a community patrol car, he'd found it to be true. Ryan cruised over to the gas pumps.

"We may as well fill it up while we're here," said Sharp.

"Roger that," said Ryan.

Sharp watched the exchange as the bell rang and summoned the kid out to talk to Ryan. He was a nervous, long-faced boy with shifty eyes. Sharp watched him in the side mirror as he disengaged the pump nozzle and fumbled with the cruiser's gas cap. Sharp got out and stretched, and then reached for his wallet and produced his fleet card.

"Miserable day," he said.

The kid looked over and smiled. No eye contact. Head down. Face twitching and lips moving the way a woman's will when she's just applied lipstick. Sharp thought of Ingrid just then. He saw her lips and pictured paint splashes on her opaque T-shirt.

"What time do you close today?"

"Six," said the kid. He did not look at Sharp. His lips kept moving.

He twisted the gas cap back on and docked the pump nozzle. Sharp could see that his hand, in fact his entire arm, was trembling.

"You haven't seen a silver Mercedes come through here today, have you?"

The kid jammed his hands in his pockets. Still, no eye contact.

"I'm not supposed to say," said the kid.

"Why's that?"

The kid tilted his forehead towards the office.

"I'll talk in there. Not out here."

Ryan took notes while the kid told about the guy in the Mercedes. He said the car was sleek with tinted glass, and shiny even in the dull, freezing drizzle. His description of the occupant was less about the guy's appearance and more about him being an oddball. He was 'bizarre,' the kid explained. Too old to be wearing a hoodie pulled up over his head. He smelled like booze, but seemed alert, watchful.

"He was scary," said the kid.

"Well, he pointed a gun at you, threatened you," said Ryan.

"Not 'cause of that. He was different. He spoke well, like a teacher or someone educated, even when he said he'd kill me, you know? He had crazy eyes; a mean face, and yet he was pleasant, like talking to your grandfather or something. I know that makes no sense."

They got back to the car and Sharp used his cell to call the station. He talked to Phelps, who put him through to the Sergeant. When he'd finished he checked his missed calls. Ingrid had called twice but left no message. He tried calling her but it rang through to the voice mail, his voice, telling callers to leave a message; Charles Mingus was playing in the background, Ingrid was rattling cups or glasses in the sink. When the voice mail tone chirped he hung up. The other day Sharp had given her a playful, flirtatious pat on the butt and she'd swatted his hand away.

"I'm busy right now," she had said.

She'd picked up her canvas and taken it to the spare bedroom.

"There's no space here. That's the trouble. We're always tripping over each other."

Sharp had shaken his head and moved to his favourite chair in the living room. He put his headphones on and turned up the amp to drown out Ingrid's diatribe. The whole country living thing had been her idea. Now that they'd arrived, right in the middle of that coveted peace and quiet, she was irritable, occasionally complaining she was lonely. She called him more frequently at the station to ask when he was coming home, even though his schedule was printed and pinned to the cork-board in the kitchen. She was venturing into the city more often. Sharp would drive her to the train station and she'd haul her cumbersome, leather portfolio onboard. When he offered to keep her company she accepted only occasionally. They would arrive at

Union Station and she would take a taxi to a gallery, alone. He usually wandered around and landed at a pub or lounge on his own, Brubeck or Getz pumping through his ear buds as he nursed a pint of ale and watched the people and traffic outside.

Chapter 6: The Pursued

He teetered on the edge of blackness as the Mercedes idled, and the hum of the car's engine pushed him toward sleep. He remembered a couple with a baby that used to live on his street. They would take the infant out for a ride in the car late at night whenever it was restless. The mother insisted a car ride put any child under in no time at all. He didn't like the baby. It was a square-headed, blue-eyed little freak that didn't smile at him, but stared as if angry, or insulted.

"Oh that's funny, he usually smiles at everyone," the mother once said.

He had met them at the mailbox at the top of the street, and he laughed off mum's comments, but remembered walking away chuckling and thinking, *He's on to me, the little bastard*. Or perhaps the infant was like him and had realized, in its little freakish mind, that it was staring intently at a brother, of sorts. It began in childhood, didn't it? That's what modern psychology tells us. One wrong move, or harsh word while that kid is on the potty, or wiping its own backside and you might have a sociopath, or even a deviant on your hands. He recalled, on the cusp of sleep, a scene from his own childhood. It was clear and penetrated his slide into oblivion, and he sat up, gripped the steering wheel and opened his eyes to the chilly murk beyond the windshield.

It was before his father died and it both thrilled and embarrassed him. He was young, perhaps eight or nine years old. It was summer and he was dead against enduring three weeks of summer camp. He thought that camps smelled horrible, a brutal musk of lake water, carbolic soap and unwashed feet. He hated group activities, despised canoes and those ridiculous orange life vests. How on earth were you supposed to enjoy the lake and the rhythm of the water with an enormous, canvas cervical collar strapped around your neck? Rage had overtaken him in tiny stabs when he thought about a fat, loud-mouthed camp counselor in a bright T-shirt and Bermuda shorts hollering orders and instructions. The food was barely edible. A load of starchy slop washed down with cans of budget brand cola, or medicinal tasting powdered fruit punch. And so he decided there would be an illness, a camp-ruining sickness to keep him at home that summer. He took a bottle of aspirin and washed it down with three parts orange juice and one part liquid bleach.

Later that afternoon, at the hospital, after they had pumped his stomach and sent a tube down his throat to probe his abdomen, he told the doctor a tall tale. His mother and father stood by with grave looks on their faces. He told the distracted doc about hitting his head in the garage earlier that day and feeling confused, and perhaps mistaking the aspirins for his chewable vitamins. The bleach he couldn't explain, other than he had a notion it might clean out the harmful effects of eating too many vitamins, or aspirin, or whatever those pills were. So, it was off for an MRI on his head while his mother bit her fingernails and his father found a payphone, called the camp and pulled him out for that summer.

He lay in the ward and rested. The hospital bed was old and its chrome rails were dented and scratched. He liked the look of the new, empty bed behind the privacy curtain to his left. He enjoyed ringing the assistance buzzer and running the nurses around for pudding cups and little mini juice cups with foil lids that you pulled off with one strong tug. He drank six in a row and crinkled the foil lids into a ball, and jammed the ball in the track under his hospital bed. He buzzed a nurse, the pretty one with bright pink lipstick, and told her that he needed to sit up but felt too weak to adjust the bed, and he'd rather have a beautiful nurse do it for him. She shook her head, "Oh, you're a charmer. Your mother's going to have watch you!"

She stabbed at the control and the bed began to tilt him upwards and then made a sound like an electric yawn, and stopped.

"Oh, now I wonder what's happened with this?" said the pretty nurse. She bent down to investigate and he put his hand on her back, over top of her bra clasp, which he could see through her white uniform.

"Don't be silly, now," she told him.

They switched him to the new bed and wheeled the damaged one away. He asked for more juice cups, but the doctor came in before the nurse returned with them. It was a different doctor: an obese, breathless man with a pitch black beard and an accent. He asked, "Well, how is your tummy and noggin'? You ready to go home?"

He didn't like the doctor and found his accent and choice of words especially off-putting.

"It's my *stomach* and my *head*. I'm not four years old."

He imagined the scene from the doctor's perspective:

The doctor lowers his clipboard and laughs. He draws out the laugh and waits for the boy to laugh, or at least crack a smile. He watches the sarcastic, peculiar boy in the hospital bed. The boy looks right through him. He is a deadpan, unusual little delinquent, as far as the doctor is concerned.

He rubbed his belly and was tempted to say something else rude to the fat doctor, but thought better of it.

"Thank you for helping me," he said.

"You're very welcome. You had a knock on the head, but you are not concussed. The machine that checked you this morning shows that you are fine, but just the same I have explained to your mother you are to have forty-eight hours bed rest and avoid working the mind too much, so no comic books and no TV, can you do that?"

"I will try my best. The TV part is fine and I don't enjoy comic books, but my mind is *always* working."

The doctor chuckled, and he gave the doctor a big, artificial smile.

"Well do your best, young man. Someone will be along shortly to assist you down to the lobby. Your mother is waiting there for you."

Again, he imagined what the doctor must have been thinking, and what the staff observed as the peculiar boy was discharged:

The fat doctor waddles to the nurse's station. The doc wants to read the charts kept by the pretty nurse with the pink lipstick. She saunters over to the doctor and the two greet each other.

"Did anyone suggest a psychological assessment for this one, the boy in 334?"

"Not that I'm aware of. Why?"

The doctor watches the boy in a wheelchair, being pushed along by an orderly. The boy gives the doctor an expressionless glance and then beams at the nurse. He reaches down and engages the brake on the wheelchair. The orderly stumbles slightly and winces as his forward motion abruptly stops.

"Hey, come on, pal," says the orderly.

The boy's searching little eyes are on the nurse. He hasn't even heard the orderly's voice. He can't even see the doctor, despite his considerable heft and jet black facial hair.

"Thank you, nurse. Thank you for the juice and the pudding cups."

The nurse takes the patient file from the doctor, closes it and and slips it under her arm.

"You're welcome. Be more careful in the future. Don't bump your head again!"

"Okay."

The orderly wheels the boy away. The nurse gives him a wave. The doctor looks at the file under her arm, and then at her slim waist, her hips and her panty-line that sits like an invitation beneath her crisp white uniform. He looks at the boy who is now waving to patients as he passes each room and nears the elevator bank. What a little fucker, *thinks the doctor. And then he checks his clipboard and wristwatch, exhales at the number of rounds left on his shift, and he moves on, huffing and puffing as he goes.*

It was always there, the urge to do *something* and then watch the ensuing trouble that *something* brought. He was out of hospital and at home with his mother. She seemed pleased to have him around. He helped her with household chores and one day they met his father at the office and he took them for hamburgers and milkshakes at a place with mini jukeboxes on the tables that played 1950s music, and had old-fashioned pinball games near the payphones. He took a handful of change from his father and went to the pinball machines. He dropped a quarter into one so that it would ring and beep, and play chiming music. He then dropped a quarter into the payphone and dialed a random number. A man answered and he said to the man, "I'd like to know if your wife sleeps in the nude."

The man said, "Come on over here and say that you little shit."

He replied, "I will come over at night and watch you sleep, and breathe. You won't even know I am there."

"Who is this? You're pretty brave on the phone you little shit!"

"I am brave at all times."

"You're a little brat, a delinquent."

"You're scared. I can tell."

The man hung up. He waited until he heard some clicking noises, and then the dial-tone.

When he got back to the table, his mother said, "Isn't this fun?"

"It's the greatest place ever!" he said.

His parents grinned and sucked their milkshakes until they made a gurgling, vacuuming noise.

He thought of the gurgling and saw his mother's face as she drank her shake, and he saw his father watching his mother. The look on his father's face was one of admiration. Admiration. It was nice to admire something, or someone. The gurgling stayed on his mind. There was a ravine not far from the house where he lived as a boy. A deep creek cut through and in the summer it ran fast, and *gurgled*, and its banks were teeming with life and covered in English ivy. He would go to the ravine with his net, a plastic bowl and a pocketful of trail mix. It all began innocently enough. He was out in the sunshine with the creek running and drugging the air with its humid odor. He was celebrating a summer without camp. He'd catch minnows in the bowl and then toss them on the crooked rocks that ran alongside the water. They'd jump and flip, and then slowly become still, as if they were unwinding. He discovered that he could catch small grass snakes, frogs, and even mice by trapping them under the bowl. He kept the dead animals in a pile under a tree. One morning he brought bobby pins and some clear thread he'd found in his mother's sewing kit. When he arrived at the ravine and crawled up the bank to his tree, he observed a possum sniffing around. He took the smooth, slightly gnarled branch he'd been using as a walking stick and rushed the possum. The animal moved downwards and slid off the embankment and landed clumsily on the rocks. He jumped down, landed with one foot on the creek rock and one foot in the gurgling water. He wound up and whacked the possum like he was chopping wood. He heard a high-pitched exhaling sound and the possum went still. He flipped it over and hit it again. He chose a bare and twisted tree near the water; its roots in the black earth on one side, and disappearing beneath the rock on the other. In his mind he named it The Tree of Doom. It took him some time, but he strung them all up: thirteen snakes, eleven frogs, eight mice, the possum, a dead bird he'd found and a dead cat he'd picked up on Hazel Street.

He'd found it by the curb, stretched out with dried blood on its head. He felt sorry for it and wanted to kill the driver that had run it over. Cats were part of a family. They weren't wild and therefore deserved some dignity. He thought it would be better off at The Tree of Doom than decomposing at the roadside. He stood back and admired his project. A horror movie Christmas tree. The work of a monster roaming the creek and countryside. He laughed out loud, and then screamed, "Yahoo."

Children fishing for minnows discovered The Tree of Doom. They ran home and alerted their parents, who called the police. The Tribune got wind of it and sent a reporter who took photos and wrote an article: *Macabre Discovery at Riley Creek*. It told about the tree, the carcasses and children stumbling upon the horrible scene. It interviewed a Constable Worsley, who expressed concern and hoped it was all the work of mischievous children, and not some deviant adult. They had opened an investigation and vowed to step up patrols in the area. After reading the article and staring at a large photo of The Tree of Doom, he went to his bedroom and flopped on his bed, and laughed and enjoyed a tingling feeling all over his body. It was so intense that he had to stretch, reach his arms high above his head and point his toes as far down as he possibly could in order to abate it, even though he really didn't want it to stop.

At the dinner table that night his father speared his salad and read the paper while his mother watched a casserole bubble through the oven window.

"Did you see that awful thing down at the creek?" asked his mother.

His father's mouth was full, so he pushed his lettuce over to one side and responded with a crunchy "Yep, teenagers I expect."

"It's scary, nothing like that happened here when I was a girl."

"Too many outsiders. All those new homes up on Hazel and Clark. City kids that have never seen nature before and they're probably smoking dope and drinking, getting all stupid."

His mother looked at him. He was staring at his father as he munched on salad. He hadn't touched his own.

"I think it's better that you stay away from there for a while, okay sweetie? You don't know who's lurking around down there."

"Okay, mum."

"Aren't you hungry?"

"I don't want any salad, thank you. Excuse me, Dad?"

"Yeah, kiddo?"

"Can I get a BB gun?"

His father put down the newspaper and sipped his lemonade, rolled his tongue around for a moment.

"Why do you want a BB gun?"

"To shoot cans and targets,"*and maybe the odd person*, he thought.

"Eat your salad and I'll think about it."

Chapter 7: Stan Hill

I'll tell anyone who'll listen—and they are dwindling these days—
that I was the one who stood up for Jarrod when he was a boy,
and right into his teenage years. Kids picked on him in elemen-
tary school. He took after my mum's side: a thin build that had a
certain fragility to it. He looked at the ground all the time, even
when he walked. Young boys see a kid like Jarrod and he might
as well have a target on him, or a punching bag around his neck.
Where we grew up boys were always breaking things, shoplifting
smokes and getting into fights. Everyone fought, but I got really
good, learned how to take a punch, feign, slip and counter and
eventually lay a thumping on a guy because of Jarrod, not because
I was interested in fighting, or because I had to stand up for
myself. I've been labeled a thug, I know that. Half of my pugilism
is a result of sticking up for my brother.

Jarrod got a part-time job as a stock-boy at the IGA when he
was sixteen. His first ever. We were at the dinner table one night
and my mother asked him what he was going to do with all the
money he was making. She hoped he was saving some of it. They
talked for a while and I tuned out until it became obvious that
Jarrod *hadn't* been paid. She asked him why and he said that Mr.
Gregory, the store manager, had called him a *little queer* and
refused to give him a paycheque.

Jarrod had been working at the store for a month and they
paid every two weeks, and yet there was no pay for my little
brother. My mother was beside herself and grabbed the phone
to call Gregory and read him the riot act. I took the phone from
her and told her to calm down. I asked Jarrod if his story was
straight up. I knew Gregory and there was no doubt he was a
dick, but something about the local grocery store manager
withholding some kid's $200 paycheque didn't make sense.

Jarrod swore up and down that Gregory had simply refused to pay him.

"You'll get your pay when I say so," Gregory had apparently said.

According to Jarrod, Gregory had also said that I was a *nobody*. That I strutted around town like some kingpin, but that I'd probably spend my life working at a car wash, or cleaning bus shelters. That did it. I put on my coat and boots and went to see Gregory before he went home to sit in front of his TV and drink himself into a stupor.

I got to the IGA as Little Ray Jenson was locking up. Little Ray was about fifty years old. He was Gregory's assistant manager. He wore a big, white beard and was so tiny he bought kid's clothes. He looked like a garden gnome. I told Little Ray that I needed to talk to Gregory right away. It was an emergency. He pointed to the back of the store, where the offices were located, behind the dairy section, through a doorway obscured by these hanging rubber strips. Gregory was at his desk surfing the net. He clicked to a screen-saver of a big, white yacht with its prow cutting through deep, blue ocean, but not before I caught a glimpse of a tangle of naked bodies on the screen. He looked up at me with his mouth half open.

"What are you doing here? How did you get in?"

"Little Ray let me in."

"You shouldn't call him that. His name is Ray. He doesn't like 'Little.'"

"I'm here for my brother's pay."

I put out my hand and Gregory smiled.

"I don't have any pay for him."

I kicked the side of his chair. Its rubber wheels squeaked on the linoleum floor and it slid about a foot into the desk. Gregory's head snapped forward and he hit his knee on the desk's edge.

"Hey, hey, Stan wait just a minute. Wait, wait!"

I had wound up to punch him in the head, but managed to halt the progress of what would have been a beauty, a possible jawbreaker.

"*Okay-kay-kay*, Stan, *come on* now," he said.

I waited there, not giving him much room. Little Ray showed up.

"Is everything okay, Norm?"

I told him things were fine, and to hit the road.

"It's alright, Ray," said Gregory.

"I can call the cops," he said to Gregory.

"*What* did he just tell you?" I said. I pointed towards the front of the store, and Little Ray ran along like a good little gnome.

"Can I get up? I want to show you something," said Gregory.

I moved back, ready to pop him if he got brave, or tried to bolt. Like I said, Norm Gregory is a dick. He argues with the customers because he thinks he's smarter than everyone. He's scruffy and unshaven. He always reeks of alcohol. He doesn't make eye contact when he speaks to you. But he *did* show me something. He handed me Jarrod's time card. It seemed that my little brother clocked in between five and six when he arrived for work, but never punched out. I thought at first that Gregory was trying to avoid paying Jarrod on a technicality; no time-punch to end your shift . . . no money. That wasn't the case. The problem was that Jarrod would clock in, work at a snail's pace for an hour, and then disappear. Like I said, he's good at disappearing, apparently. Gregory had Little Ray follow Jarrod one night. According to Little Ray, Jarrod went to Settler's Park and sat on a bench, smoking cigarettes. One time Timmy Clancy joined him and again, according to Little Ray, Clancy and my brother looked around like a couple of prairie dogs, and then put their arms around each other and hugged.

"Ray was going to talk to Jarrod, but I told him to stay out of it. I wanted to sit Jarrod down myself and talk to him. I just haven't gotten around to it," said Gregory.

"Why?"

"Well, for starters I knew he'd mention it at home, and make me sound like the bad guy and then you would come storming in here, and I *was right* about that!"

I didn't have much to say. I owed Gregory an apology, regardless of how big a dick he was. I had nearly pounded on him for nothing.

"You realize I'll have to fire him, right?" said Gregory.

"Yeah."

"I'm sorry, Stan. I know you think I'm a bad guy and you've hated me since I coached you in hockey and all the rest of it. But I can't pay your brother."

He looked at me and swallowed hard.

"I mean maybe I can give him a few bucks off the books, but he hasn't worked enough to earn an actual pay stub."

"Don't worry about it. Little Ray said they were hugging?"

Gregory scratched his head then looked at me reluctantly.

"Yeah."

"He saw it happen?"

"Yeah, that's what he told me."

I walked home and weighed my options. In the end I didn't want the drama and I didn't want to listen to my mother stick up for Jarrod. I went up to Jarrod's room. He was cross-legged on the floor with his headphones on. I snatched them off his head.

"Lie to me again and I'll break your neck. I'll fuck you up for good. I mean it."

I left the house and went out to Uncle Chow's Chinese Food, where they served me whiskey at $2 a shot and Chinese beer at a $1.25 a bottle. I remember thinking at the time: A Chinese restaurant with 1970s liquor prices; a grocery store run by a drunk and a real, living garden gnome; and boys on park benches hugging in the dusk. I couldn't wait to get out of this backward-ass little town.

Chapter 8: Warfield

Sheila had been in bed, wondering what she'd do if she bothered to get up. She thought of Candace, her mother, who would bounce out of bed every day at 6AM and expected Sheila and her father to do the same. Her mother made lists and attached them to the refrigerator with ridiculous animal-shaped magnets. The lists had chores that needed doing; the day's menu and approximate time the food—all delicious and homemade—would be on the table. Her mother couldn't stand still. She danced through the spotless and perfectly configured house on a mission. She was unstoppable. Sheila's father was the opposite. He was quiet and moved slowly, as if he intended to be late for wherever he needed to be that day.

As a child Sheila often sat at the top of the stairs when she should have been in bed. Her parents, more specifically Candace, liked to throw house parties. On many Friday nights their home was like a smoky, booze-filled speakeasy full of laughing and flirtatious neighbours. To Sheila there was a fascinating electric clamor in their home when half the neighbourhood was crammed inside, drinking and plunging wedges of rye bread into a bowl of spinach dip. One night, as Sheila spied on the adults, she noticed how nicely her mother was dressed, done up. She wore deep red lipstick and darted like a sparrow from guest to guest with a cigarette in one hand and a gin and tonic in the other. Sheila's father wore his standard house party attire: khaki trousers, a white dress shirt, and tan slippers. Sheila listened to him as he chatted to Bill, their neighbour from two doors down. Bill giggled drunkenly and remarked that it was a great party, as per usual, lively, plenty of conversation. Sheila's father took a swallow of whatever he was drinking and said, "If Candace shut her mouth for three seconds I'm sure you could hear a pin drop."

Bill exploded with his smoker's laugh. When he'd settled he slurred, "Hell of a woman though. You're a lucky man. Face like that, she could a been a model for God's sake!"

"She could have. She couldn't keep still for two seconds though. The fashion photographer quit. They brought in a sports photojournalist that usually covered the fucking hockey games and even he couldn't get a shot of her."

Again, more laughter, Bill obviously gassed and an entire pack of cigarettes into the evening. Sheila sat there in shock. She'd never heard her father swear before, and had never thought about what it must be like to be married to Candace Warfield, a black-dressed, red-lipped and beautiful ball of energy and curiosity, who fought hard to keep up with the Jones's. And that same evening, while perched on the stairs, the light around her vanished and she clearly saw their neighbour Bill, his beefy and happy face. So she went to it, allowed it to pull her in. And there he was, in a hospital bed, weighing about 125 pounds and coughing until he nearly jolted himself over the side of the gurney. She pushed that knowledge aside and ignored it whenever she saw Bill, or whenever his name came up. She thought hard about other things: bicycles, gym class, Jane Austin, and later on boys and track and field. She ignored it until Bill died of lung cancer when she was sixteen. She was brave at the funeral, but cried her eyes out in her bedroom that night. And yet she was blindsided by her own father's death five years ago. He was the calm, docile one, the one who seemed to take life as it came. But his brain surrendered to a massive stroke while he was sleeping. Her mother woke up one December Saturday morning, and he didn't.

When Sheila did finally roll out of bed she pulled on her running gear and went straight to the coffee-maker. She peeled a grapefruit while the coffee dripped into the pot, and she turned on the radio. The local news was a buzz about an evacuation in Courtland. A derailed train and the fear that some tanker cars might explode. She smiled and said, "BLEVE: Boiling Liquid Expanding Vapor Explosion."

She'd dated a firefighter once and remembered many of the terms, Fire Station Speak. She also remembered that he was a fake and a cheat. He had a wife, two kids, a dog and a big house with a Harley in its double garage over in Campbell. She remembered coming home after she'd found out. He had followed her and stood on her doorstep knocking and insisting that he could *explain everything,* while she stood in the bathroom staring at her red eyes and watching mascara run down her face. She wondered about herself. Was she mentally ill?

She saw things in the recesses of her conflicted mind, things she couldn't possible have known. And yet here was this guy, this fireman, with his motorcycle and his middle-of-the-night visits to her place, and his big plans for them to ride down to Vegas together. Meanwhile his wife was sleeping comfortably in their big, fancy house, oblivious to his Las Vegas plans and his nightly outings. She'd been duped. She had a a front row seat in the chamber of people's fate, but she couldn't see this asshole for who he was. She couldn't see three feet in front of her when it came to her own affairs.

Sheila stood at her kitchen window and ate her grapefruit in large chunks, juice dribbling into the sink. She'd nearly bought a town home in Courtland, brand new with plenty of marble and glossy, wood floors. In the end she'd asked herself why she, a perpetually single woman, needed three bedrooms, three bathrooms and a central vacuum system. She turned off the radio and flicked the switch on her police scanner. Sergeant Glendon was on the radio. Sheila liked his voice, so clear and precise. He was telling the dispatcher where he wanted to park the Command Centre, which was essentially an RV with the department's coat-of-arms emblazoned on its side. Rumor had it that Kyle McVeigh, the short, husky, newly appointed detective, had been taking his girlfriend into the RV until he was told to stop. She pictured McVeigh inside that thing, taking off his clothes—ugh!

She heard Sharp's voice come over the scanner. He was in pursuit of a vehicle that had refused to stop after they'd spotted the driver with an open bottle of liquor. Sharp remained calm, his voice as steady as ever. They were up near the boundary, near Pollard. Sheila washed her hands and wiped the grapefruit juice from her mouth. She did the same thing each time she saw or heard Sharp: she denied that she was attracted to him, that she was a conversation or two from being in love with him. He had been one of her training officers. He was a 1960s movie star type, like a Gregory Peck or Steve McQueen. The type her mother used to watch and swoon over when Sheila still lived at home. Sharp was cool, sexy in his evenness, and had answered Sheila's strings of questions with patience and in great detail. He was easy to be with. He was good with people, knew dozens of the citizens in his patrol area by name. He exuded confidence without the usual cockiness. Off duty, he was fascinating. He was quietly charming and knew about jazz music and loved to cook. He wore dress shirts with big cuff-links. He'd given her a ride home once when Sheila's car had been held up at the garage, waiting on a part for the transmission.

Sharp's car was an old Jaguar. It was immaculate inside and it smelled like leather and talcum powder. They had chatted easily and fluidly as they glided their way to Sheila's place, and when they'd arrived, she asked him in for a drink, but her voice and body language were obviously inviting him into her bed. She could have gouged her own eyeballs out for being so stupid.

Sharp had smiled and nodded, and then checked the dashboard's glowing clock. He had to get home. He and his wife were going to a concert. Sheila had felt like an idiot and considered crawling along the grass and up the front steps of her tiny house. She saw Sharp the next day, talking to his father, who was the divisional inspector—a stern and unapproachable man, and nothing like his son. Sheila had waited around to talk to Sharp, and sure enough he was calm and gracious, and made Sheila feel better about her impulsive invitation the night before. Sheila rode a community patrol car with Ralph Anderson that day. She couldn't stop thinking about Sharp and so she asked Anderson too many questions about him. Where he lived (out of town in a little cottage-like bungalow); if Anderson knew him well (yes, they'd gone to police college together, he was a good guy, that Sharp); what his wife was like (pretty, a bit flaky, an artist, a painter who had her paintings on display at galleries here and there).

"What's with you? You want into Sharp's pants or something?" Anderson had finally said.

Sheila had booked off sick the next day and taken her mother for coffee. She told her mum about her feelings for Sharp and her mother had been no help, telling her that we can't control or choose who we love. In the end Sheila resolved to avoid him, which was difficult. She even tried to convince herself that she disliked him, which didn't work. She coached herself not to think about him and to find a single man with some of the same qualities: calm and social, tall and slender, square-shouldered and handsome, beautiful eyes, strong hands, and scented with nice talcum powder or aftershave, or whatever it was that made him smell so good that she wanted to lick his neck.

She had tried to look at some of the single guys, ones that were actually available: Ryan, Phelps, Detective Gonzales over in the CIB Office. He'd been flirty when she did a week's training in CIB, but he was egotistical. Ryan was okay, a big lad with a slightly boyish face. Cute, not handsome, though. And clumsy, not a guy who could carry a conversation about anything outside of police-work or hockey.

Billy Goodrich was okay, but had a girlfriend. The decent ones usually did. The girlfriend's family had cash. Her father owned a helicopter, a *helicopter* for crying out loud. Billy was staying put. He joked that in five years he probably wouldn't have to work anymore. Those guys were always around for a beer and chicken wings down at Driscoll's and they liked that she could be *one of the boys*, but in the end they either had girlfriends, or they did nothing for her. So, she had accepted Barry Palmer's invitation to dinner. Palmer was much older. She knew that. A career constable, relegated to the Traffic Cars, he was closing in on sixty, but there was not a grey hair on his head and barely a wrinkle or mottle on his skin. Things went along well for about two months. And then one evening she saw his age in black and white. They were in Barry's kitchen making a salad. They had just ordered a pizza. Barry had told her he was planning an early retirement so that he could do something else. He was thinking about selling cars; a job at a high end dealership, as crazy as that sounded.

Conversation was going well and Barry lit some candles on the table. The pizza guy arrived and rang the doorbell.

"I'll get it," she said.

"There's cash in my wallet."

She picked up his wallet and tugged at a $20 bill tucked in there with several others. Out came his driver's license, with the obligatory mugshot photo on the left hand side. He looked so much younger. Better. His gun range membership card dropped out as well, complete with his date of birth. The images and information on the cards hung in her mind. He was old enough to be her father. She went to pay for the pizza. Her head went numb. She felt drugged and dizzy. She'd drank her beer too quickly. Her thoughts drifted towards the front door and then back to his wallet. She sat down for a moment. Everything that had been wrong with their short relationship flared before her like a series of bright, distracting strobes. She could hear Palmer talking to her, asking if she wanted a glass of water. She felt him touch her hand and then pull away.

He's hard to know. Of course he is, he's nearly as old as your father would have been. He keeps your relationship a secret. Big surprise, imagine the talk at the station, not just the teasing, but the concern among the brass. He doesn't talk of the future, until just now, when he blurted out that he'll be retiring soon. You're an idiot. That's because he doesn't see a future with you. The sex is fine for you, but obviously terrible for him. His face is expressionless and his body lacks motivation as he touches you, and as you touch him. He's probably bored; it's probably old news for him. He's not letting you in. Sometimes it's like he's just putting up with you. That's because he is! You idiot! He is putting up with you! You don't know this man and you never will . . .

She felt crazy. She rushed out of his house and past a confused delivery boy without looking back. He called after her, but she was already in her car and tearing out of the driveway. And she watched in her rearview mirror for him to come after her, which he didn't. His excuse, when they did finally speak three days later: *He had to pay the pizza boy.* They had talked on the phone since then, but hadn't made any plans. It was over, but neither of them would speak up and hammer that final nail in the coffin.

Sheila went for a run and decided on a longer route. Her stamina was limitless when she pondered her own loneliness and stupidity. She ran on autopilot, took the trail down to the overpass and stopped to look out towards Courtland, where you never would have guessed that half the area was being evacuated just in case a tanker exploded and rained down poison on the rows of brand new homes.

CHAPTER 9: SHARP

As they drive, Ryan talks about his plans. He tells Sharp, in confidence, that he'd like to get three or four years under his belt and then apply to a city department, maybe Toronto or Ottawa. Sharp half listens, not because he doesn't like Ryan, but because there are a few competing thoughts whirling about in his mind as they head back to their patrol area. *My final day can't come soon enough,* he thinks, while Ryan talks enthusiastically about the various opportunities a young cop could find on a larger force: Tactical Unit, Plain Clothes, Morality, maybe even Homicide. Ingrid has warned Sharp that he might miss the job more than he thinks. She claims that policing is part of his 'fabric,' which is wrong. He imagines who he might miss, who he might keep in touch with when he goes, and the list is surprisingly small. He feels bad about that. He doesn't hate them. He's developed some hate over the years, but it's for himself—self-loathing. The best job he ever had was working as a cook. Manny, the restaurant's head chef, liked Sharp, said he should enroll in a culinary program, get his journeyman's papers. Sharp loved the hustle and pressure of that busy kitchen. He liked the creative component of cooking, from the planning of the specials to the plating of the food and getting it out to the dining room.

He should have stayed there and become a chef, but there was Father Edward and his expectations. There was Brother Daniel and the ongoing sibling rivalry—never mind rivalry, full-out war on some days. Time and the job; Ingrid and her art; the rhythms, patterns, and simple rewards of life away from the police service have allowed Sharp a gradual, thorny epiphany. He despises himself for letting Father Edward drive him to that damn recruiting centre, years ago. He's tired; worn out from listening to women and children cry and men shout. He's had his fill of being second guessed and told to *fuck off*, and he's certainly through with wrestling people to the ground, having his face so close to them he can smell their cologne, or the food they've eaten that day, or their rancid body odor. So much is wrong, and he struggles with it. Is it him, or is it the department and its methods and protocols that drain him? He feels out of touch. He wants to do things his way.

He remembers an arrest that went sideways. The lead officer, a now retired guy named Jenkins, had gone about it all wrong. They had a warrant and were going to pick up a sexual assault suspect. Sergeant McCall, Jenkins and Phelps asked Sharp to come along. The suspect was a big man, six-five and nearly three hundred pounds. When Sharp and Phelps got to the house, a nice place, beside the park on Barrow Street, there were four cars and a total of eight cops, including Sharp and Phelps. Sharp wanted to say something, but thought it wasn't his place. CIB were there; two detectives had been investigating and conducting surveillance after three sexual assaults in under a month; mothers at the park with their young children. The culprit usually struck mid-morning, and seemed to know the most opportune time. He appeared when the woman was alone, grabbed her, assaulted her, usually by trying to rip away her bra, and then disappeared into the woods beyond the park. The detectives had been gathering evidence, and found that the suspect was right under their noses. He lived directly beside the park. Once he'd committed his crime, he walked a path through the woods and doubled back to his house. Sharp had read the sheet on this guy. He looked at his colleagues, gathering like a swarm. If it had been up to him, he would have made the arrest with one other officer and taken a different approach: polite, unmarked car, here's our warrant, please come with us, let's make this as uneventful as possible . . .

Instead, they put five cops at the front door, one with a shotgun, and three at the back door. The suspect lived with his mother. It was her house. They knocked loud enough to wake the dead and she just about fainted when she answered. The suspect showed up, quickly assessed the situation, interpreted it as a declaration of war. He rushed onto the doorstep swinging, and he could throw a punch, his arms as thick as the average man's legs. The ruckus brought the cops from the side door to the front porch. There was shouting and Sharp saw that one of the side door guys, PC Ingram, had his gun out. The suspect dragged four of them down the concrete stairs like a running back breaking tackles. Everyone collapsed in a heap, but the suspect wasn't finished. He booted the lead detective in the nuts. That got him a face full of pepper spray, which apparently had no affect other than to rile him even more. He somehow managed to get back on his feet, and there was Ingram pointing his Glock in the suspect's face. Sharp had seen enough. He also saw the headlines: UNARMED MAN SHOT BY POLICE. He rushed the suspect, grabbed the guy's wrist, dropped his torso down, swung his hips and legs up and got an arm-bar on the guy. The suspect growled and went to his knees. Sharp heard the guy's elbow pop and then a scream, and then a pile-on of blue uniforms; grunting and profanity, and threats of prison, and accusations of perversion. The suspect yelled that he had done nothing wrong; the cops had shown up at his house, scared his mother and made him feel threatened. He was wrong with his first comment, but absolutely right about the second. There were plenty of injuries: one broken arm, two broken noses, one chipped tooth, one sprained knee, two dislocated fingers and several cuts. It seemed hours before they had him cuffed and in the car. By this time half the neighbourhood, kids included, had poured from their homes to watch the show. When Sharp and Phelps cleared the call, there were sixteen cops roaming in and out of the house, up and down the side yard, and over at the park.

Later, there was beer and wings over at Driscoll's. Sharp went along to fit in, and because Jenkins said he was going to talk about the arrest. When Sharp got there Jenkins was playing an old Pac-man game and thumping his fist on the glass each time he lost. There was a group of eight cops sitting around a table, knocking down pints and shots and talking about the call. Who did what and who nearly had the guy, but then this happened, and did you see fucking Ingram with his piece drawn? That brought gales of laughter; they sounded like pirates after plundering a ship.

When they saw Sharp a cheer went up, and he smiled and obliged a few fist bumps and high-fives, but inside he felt disgust and disappointment with the entire mess. He stayed for one beer and then left. Phelps announcing to the table: "Hey, have you seen his wife? If I had that keeping the bed warm for me I'd head home too!"

The next day Sharp saw Father Edward, walking as proudly and stiffly as ever, sneering at the rank and file when he should have been stopping to say hello, asking how their families were doing. Sharp knew everyone's name. Not just his platoon, but the entire department. He knew for a fact that Father Edward, Inspector Sharp, didn't know everyone's name; the station duty operators, clerks and dispatchers were just faces and numbers. They were beneath him. The old man stopped Sharp and they ducked into the equipment room. Father Edward mentioned a dinner for Brother Daniel, who was turning 40. Sharp said he'd be there, and tried not to cringe, at least not visibly.

"I see you were at that call yesterday."

"It was a circus, no excuse for it."

"How so?" said Father Edward. He tilted his head upwards and Sharp could see a speck of blood on his white collar; a nick while shaving. He didn't bother to mention it. *Let it dry and turn brown.*

"Too many guys. We showed up asking for a battle."

Father Edward looked down his nose at Sharp, despite being of similar height.

"And you would have gone there on your own, I suppose. A six-foot-five linebacker of a sex offender with priors and you would have stopped by like it was a neighbourhood canvas."

"I would have had a partner along, but yeah, that's exactly what I would have done."

Father Edward smiled and looked beyond his son, an action designed to convey that Sharp's position was too stupid to deserve a response.

"Well, nice talking to you, *Inspector.*"

"Don't get *smart* with me," his father muttered.

The police department fades. Ryan has the heat turned up and Sharp is almost asleep, his mind now drifting to cloudy, but pleasant thoughts about running that B&B. They have gone and looked at three places. The one outside of Niagara-on-the-Lake is the front runner.

It's a large, brown brick Victorian home with four bedrooms and two baths, and good separation between the guest rooms and where he and Ingrid would live. He tells himself to sit up straight and call Ingrid, but a radio call comes over. Ryan keeps it up so loud it gives Sharp a start when the dispatcher broadcasts a family dispute in their patrol area.

Chapter 10: The Pursued

The car hummed and the heated seat was warm against his back, which had been sore the past week or two. He continued reminiscing. It was, by turns, pleasant and uncomfortable, a bit like wearing a straight-jacket made of silk and velvet, not that there was such a thing. He laughed at the thought, and at his boyhood memories. It was a long time before there was an assessment. Lord knew he did enough, pushed enough, to have one arranged. It wasn't as if he wanted one, not exactly, but he was aware that at some point there would be a nosy, do-good adult who would want to have a closer look at him. Examine his head. It was like a contest where he did things, many things: hammered nails into the sidewalls of the tires on Mr. Benning's Audi; dropped several lumps of dog waste into the mailbox and heard the mailman holler and slam it shut all the way from his bedroom window; caught 162 locusts and let them go in Mrs. Clegg's flower garden and then knocked on her side door and ran. He heard her screaming and laughed so hard he couldn't breathe when he got home and ran to his bedroom. He picked up the phone on a pole inside the Zellers department store, pushed the PA button and said things that weren't profane, but were certainly inappropriate Words like: *genitals*, *buttocks* and *circumcision*. He deepened his voice when he spoke into the mouthpiece and it sounded important, authoritative as it echoed throughout the store. And then he hung up the PA and ran for his life. He was glimpsed, but never caught.

Doctor Milling won the contest. She was a lady at the end of the street. He never liked her. She was English, proper and had sleepy eyes, and thought she knew everything, like most English people. After his father died she would come to the house for tea and his mother would call him downstairs, where he would refuse to sit, but preferred to stand while Doctor Milling asked the same bundle of questions she had asked the week before. She took all day with each question, and often had cookie crumbs stuck to her ugly lips.

"Now, how are you feeling? When I say feeling, I am not talking about whether you've caught cold or twisted an ankle playing outdoors. What I mean is what's inside, in the mind and in the belly, if the mind has anything playing upon it, or if the belly has nerves or flutters. If you have sadness that you can't control, or that you can't talk to your mum about."

He would stand with his hands still and at his sides, careful not to fidget.

"I'm fine, thank you."

That year he decided to go out for Halloween. His mother gently suggested that he might be getting too old; that this should be his final year for roaming the neighbourhood for candy.

"Next year you could dress up as a ghost or vampire, stay here and give the candy out to the children."

"That would be nice," he said.

He cut the sleeves off one of his dead father's old, blue blazers and pinned one of his grandfather's war medals on the left pocket. He found an old Bicorn hat in the basement and dusted it off. He went out alone, taking a flashlight his mother insisted upon. He used it only once, and that was to shine it in the eyes of an old woman out with her grandchildren. He didn't like old people and he especially didn't like them if they had an accent, which this old hag did. People who came from other countries, especially the English ones who talked and talked, needed to shut up, or lose their accents. His father had come from Scotland when he was a boy and he'd had no trace of an accent. He missed his father and missed the way he never said too much, but was always around and able to give advice and sit with you and watch TV. You just had to wait until he had finished reading the newspaper or filling out forms for work. Now he was gone and the house, especially the living room and chair he loved, seemed not only empty, but horrible. The space where his father used to sit at the kitchen table had a translucent rage around it.

When he arrived on Halloween night at Doctor Milling's house her husband answered the door. He was a very tall Englishman with a shocked look on his face. He waited for Mr. Milling's face to return to normal, but apparently he always looked shocked because it remained that way as he dropped two little packets of gummy bears into the Halloween bag. He supposed that if you wound up married to Doctor Milling you would have no choice but to have a shocked face. You probably went around listening to her longwinded questions and exact voice and wondered what on earth you had done to yourself. You probably thought about all your past girlfriends and then panicked over why you married Doctor Milling. The Millings did not have children and he supposed that was because Mr. Milling seldom stuck it inside of Doctor Milling. Who would want to? No sex. That was probably another reason for his shocked face. When his father was alive his parents did it quite often. He would crawl along the hallway on all fours and listen outside their door. His mother would sigh a lot and his dad would eventually make a growling noise which was quite funny. They made enough of a racket that he once farted loudly as they were sighing and growling and he then ran back to his bedroom laughing so hard that he nearly choked on his own saliva.

Mr. Milling called to his wife and the know-it-all doctor wandered out from the kitchen with a tea towel in her hands.

"Oh, hello, I didn't know you still went out trick-or-treating. Not that there is anything the matter with that. Do you have a friend with you? Who are you supposed to be? Napoleon?"

"*Fellatio* Nelson," he said.

Mr. Milling looked at his proper little wife. His shocked eyes became even wider.

Doctor Milling said, "I think you mean *Horatio*. That other word describes something that you have heard but it's likely you don't quite understand."

"No, I meant *Fellatio*."

"Well, you'll hear these words and it's best not to use them until you understand what they mean."

"I know what it means. It's what *you don't* do to him."

He pointed at Mr. Milling. Mr. Milling said, "Alright then, that's enough. Have as many sweets as you like, we're at the tail end of things anyway, isn't that right, dear?"

Mr. Milling moved like a giraffe and scooped up a handful of candy in his bony hand, dropped it in the bag.

"Does your mother know you're using those words and being rude to adults?" asked Doctor Milling. Mr. Milling mumbled something to her and touched her arm but she swatted his skeletal fingers away.

"My mother would appreciate it if you didn't visit our house anymore."

"Did she say that?"

"Yes, you talk too much and it takes you half an hour to ask a question. You overstay your welcome, and eat all of her cookies, *biscuits*, I should say," he said in his best English accent, "and your perfume smells like a mixture of flowers, mothballs and shit. It stays in our kitchen for an hour after you've left."

Doctor Milling was speechless.

"Take all the sweets you like, and off you go," said Mr. Milling.

He opened his bag around the small table that held the packages of candy. He then tipped the table and all of the packages fell into his bag. Mr. Milling and the doctor stood and watched. Doctor Milling appeared disgusted. Mr. Milling was now hyper-shock-faced and yet he was also grinning in a strange and tense way.

The assessment took place at Dr. Jones Smith's office. Dr. Smith was an associate of Dr. Milling. Dr. Smith asked the questions and he sat right across from the doctor. His mother sat off to one side on a couch tapping her foot up and down. He couldn't stop smiling at the fact that Dr. Smith had a high voice; an English accent, *of course*; and a small diamond nose-ring. It was also amusing that his parents had arranged for him to have two surnames. *Jones Smith. What an idiot*, he thought. He half-listened to Dr. Smith's questions and smiled, as he pictured what sort of life a person like Dr. Smith might have. There was a nice car, huge with big chrome wheels, outside the office, and he supposed it was the doctor's. *Driving the big car home to his apartment, sitting listening to opera, crying at sad movies, eating custard and drinking tea while sorting his collection of nose-rings and dried butterflies, and masturbating, definitely masturbating, probably while dressed up in something unusual, like a superhero costume.* That was the life he imagined for Jones Smith, Ph.D. Clinical Psychology and certified idiot.

The doctor seemed to interpret his smiles as coming from a boy with a happy, positive disposition. The doctor nodded with approval as he answered the questions calmly, but dishonestly. At one point, Dr. Smith asked him a question about his mother. He hadn't been listening. He missed most of it. His mother looked over at him with huge, sad eyes, and he answered, "I want to forgive everyone for my father's death, and I want to be there for my mum."

His mother burst into tears and Dr. Smith hurried over with a box of tissue in a plastic case that had little birds and flowers all over it. That wasn't surprising when you watched and considered Dr. Smith.

Pictures of pig's asses and snouts. That's what they should put on tissue box covers, he thought, as his mother snuffled and the doctor returned to his big, leather chair. The doctor said he was doing well, but then asked him about his concentration.

"Do you find your mind wanders off? It's alright to tell me if it does. We all have bouts of wandering mind. I know I do."

He told Dr. Smith that yes, his mind did wander and that it had gotten worse since his father's death.

"We will help you with that," said Dr. Smith. And then he leaned forward and said, "What about the things you said to Dr. Milling and the magazine your mum found under your bed? Do you think about the body, and sex a lot? It's natural, at your age, to have thoughts about those things."

He told the doctor that yes he thought about those things, but he was in no hurry to do them.

"Some of the boys at school talk about it all day. I'm an angel compared to them," he said.

Dr. Jones Smith seemed to enjoy this and tilted his head back and giggled. His mum did too. His mum looked wet-faced, but relieved. When they had finished, he offered Dr. Smith a handshake and said, "You have a cool name. It sounds important."

The doctor smiled and said, "I'm not important. I am just a person who enjoys helping other people."

And sitting alone in your apartment and crying, and wanking off in a superhero outfit, he thought as he and his mother put on their shoes and took their coats from the hangers.

He stifled a laugh and his mother playfully tugged on his hair and said, "What's so funny, buster?"

"You promised me a milkshake after we were finished."

"Indeed I did."

She shook the doctor's hand and they left. His mum seemed happier.

After the assessment, he switched schools. The new school was small and his class was in the basement. His desk had a barrier around it that the teacher would close when he was doing his lessons. The first day, before the teacher even talked, he approached her and said, "You're English."

She had been wiping down the chalkboard and she stopped, smiled and said, "Why yes, I am. How did you know?"

"Just a guess," he said. *Everyone around me is English, and a pain in the ass,* is what he'd thought.

She squinted at him and then put on some eyeglasses with mauve frames. They made her look young and pretty. She also had big tits.

"You're pretty and classy, like royalty, that's all," he added.

"Well you're the new boy, and aren't you a smoothie?" she said.

He hated the school. The only good thing about it was Miss Cookson's big breasts which bounced around, and on warm Spring days threatened to escape the lovely dresses she wore. He got caught drawing them once. Mr. Abraham walked past his desk, poked his head over the barrier and saw the paper. He reached over and took it, and studied it with his glasses at the end of his nose. He raised his eyebrows.

"Are you finished your history lesson?"

"Yes sir."

Mr. Abraham nodded and crumpled the tits drawing. He opened a history textbook to a page about Upper Canada and dropped it over the barrier.

"Read ahead."

"Yes sir."

"And stop drawing nonsense."

They're not nonsense, they're tits, he thought, but kept those thoughts to himself.

That Friday he arrived at school with three potatoes in his school bag. At lunch hour he went to the parking lot and jammed two potatoes into the exhaust of Mr. Abraham's car. He used the end of a dustpan broom to ram them right into the tailpipe. He gave the third potato to a boy named Jimmy Freely who constantly talked to himself and told lies. His most recent was that he had been on a mission to the South Pole where he and his brother had taken part in a military experiment. In fact, Jimmy had vacationed at his grandmother's country home in Vineland. When he gave Jimmy the potato, he told him to take a bite now and then, but keep the potato in his pocket, and not to tell anyone where he got it.

"How come?"

"It has special powers."

"Really?"

"*Really.* How do you think I get eighty-five percent on everything. I ate one of those potatoes. The only thing is, there was a boy in England who ate one and then told his father where he'd gotten it. The boy was killed the next day when a huge branch fell from a tree and decapitated him. He broke the rules and he paid the price. So, if you want it and you take it, you have to vow not to tell anyone where you got it."

Jimmy Freely bit into the potato, smiled and then wedged it into his pocket.

There was a tow truck in the parking lot later that day. It was hooking up Mr. Abraham's car. After recess, he walked past the office and saw Jimmy Freely sitting in a low chair across from Mrs. Mitchell, the principal. The chair was so low that Jimmy's chin was level with Mrs. Mitchell's desk, whereas Mrs. Mitchell sat up high, peering down at Jimmy. His mother picked him up at three o'clock. As he got into the car, she patted him on the shoulder and waved a large envelope.

"Your report card came today. I am so proud of you, B. And so are your teachers. You might be able to go back to your old school next year."

He wasn't really listening to her, and he hated when she called him "B"or "Buster." She had nicknames for everyone. He came to a realization as she chattered and drove out of the school parking lot. He closed his eyes.

"Are you tired, B? You could take a nap before supper."

Shut up, he thought. *You talk too much.*

Jimmy Freely sitting low and looking up at Mrs. Mitchell was burned into his mind. Mrs. Mitchell was an oddball. He had been watching her. She picked her nose and ate it once during a school play. And then she saw that he had been studying her in the dark auditorium, and she pretended she'd been scratching at the outside of her nose and then taking a quick bite on her fingernail. She looked at the fingernail as if it was painful and then put her hands in her lap. She then leveled her eyes on him, gave him a scolding look.

You're the one eating your own mucous you ugly bitch, he thought.

But still, she was the Principal. She ran the school.

He saw Dr. Jones Smith in his big chair, asking questions with three large, framed diplomas on the wall behind him. He had a diamond in his nose and talked like a girl, and was a complete idiot, but even still, he asked the questions and he made decisions about where children went to school and how much TV they could watch. If you had authority in life, if you worked your way to a position where you were in charge and could control people, you could do whatever you liked as long as you were careful and thought things out. He decided that day, as his mum hummed along to a song on the radio and they puttered home, that he would work hard and work ahead, and get back to his old school, and get out of it with honours, and go to college, *and* obtain authority in life. That way, instead of worrying about power, instead of getting just a taste of it that made him itch inside and tingle all over . . . he'd truly have it.

He'd burned through a quarter tank of gas. He put the Mercedes in drive and edged the front end out into the open. The lane way held only his tire tracks. The side road beyond was clear and looked like pewter now that the freezing rain had coated the snow. He drove the lane slowly and watched for the cavalry. He turned up the radio and his heart jumped at his good luck. They were playing some old blues and he turned the volume way up, hit the side road and tore away.

Chapter 11: Stan Hill

Jarrod's only friend, Timmy Clancy, was a strange dude. Seemingly mindless, he walked like he was floating along with absolutely nowhere to go. No particular expression on his pinched face. Nothing appeared to excite or interest the lad. Clancy was a high school dropout that lived with his mother in an apartment over the dry-cleaners where she worked. My father used to say that the cleaning chemicals had fried both their brains. And speaking of my father, I missed him. We kept in touch on the phone. Occasionally, I would call him up and tell him about my mother and Jarrod because he never asked. He would only say, "Work hard and stay out of their shit. Control the controllable."

I remember once when my father and me were in the garage. This was just before he packed up and left. That morning he had screamed at my mother, and Jarrod, and then stormed out to the garage, which was behind the house. He had his work bench in there, along with an old BMW 525 that he was fixing up. We all knew to give him his space, not to bother him if he went to the garage to decompress. I could get away with it though, and I wandered in that morning. He was stone-faced at first, so I just kept my mouth shut and watched him working a ratchet. He stopped, glanced at me, and then scanned the floor for something. I saw a greasy bolt near the front tire and picked it up and handed it to him.

"Thanks."

"You're welcome."

His arms were thick and strong and he wound the bolt back on in about six pulls. I always liked watching my father. He did things like he really meant to do them.

"You can grab a beer if you want. Grab me another one, too."

He lifted his chin toward the old fridge wedged in beside the work bench and the wall. I took out two cans, popped the tabs and handed him one. He stood and pressed his hand into the small of his back, leaned as far back as he could, and then sipped. He held up the can and looked right at me.

"You're alright."

We clinked cans and he put his down on top of the battery. He leaned under the hood and sighed.

"That kid, that brother of yours. He's another story."

He stopped and checked a hose clamp.

"Do you remember your Uncle James, big guy, always laughing and joking around? We visited him down in Clearwater once when you were little."

"Yeah, I remember him."

"Well, he's left the armored car place. He's setting up a security company down there and he wants my help."

"We're moving?" I asked. I was excited at the prospect.

My father took his beer and closed the hood. He didn't want to look at me, but he did.

"Your mother isn't the same person that I married. To be fair, I'm not the same person she married either. I'm going down south. We're going to see how it is, you know, being apart."

"I already know how it will be."

He looked at me and smirked, and then sipped his beer.

"What about me and Jarrod?"

He sat on the 525's hood and reached for his cigarettes.

"I've come at him from every angle. He doesn't change, he doesn't want to, and worst of all, she protects him."

He nodded past the bay door and towards the house.

"I've tried to understand those two. I don't get them and I'm not going to get an ulcer trying."

My father got up and went to the work bench. He dropped his empty can in the bin. He kept his back to me and sorted tools, tidied up his space with the cigarette in his mouth as he talked.

"You can come down, eventually, if that's what you want. I'll keep in touch."

I could hear the strain in his voice. The thought of not having him around was immediately painful. The thought of being down in Florida with him and Uncle James was immediately thrilling.

"What if you get down there and you get too busy?"

"That won't happen. It'll take time, but I'll get you down there if that's what you want."

I watched him exhale smoke towards the light bulb above the bench.

He still had his back to me. His shoulders were tense, like he'd shrugged them and forgotten to release the shrug. I would have gone to him and hugged him, but neither of us were the hugging type.

"Of course that's what I want."

I watched his shoulders drop. He crushed the cigarette in an old hubcap he used as an ashtray.

"Good."

I tossed my empty beer can into the bin, a perfect shot. I opened the door to leave.

"Don't let her find out you drank beer this early. Go brush your teeth or something."

"I will. When are you going?"

"Soon."

I followed Jarrod and Timmy Clancy about a month after I'd burst into The IGA. I wanted to know what kind of backward-ass shit they were getting into. It's easy to tail two dolts that shuffle along with their heads down and their hands jammed so deep in their pockets they could probably touch their kneecaps. It didn't give me the whole private-eye rush I'd been hoping for. It reminded me of the pointless and plotless TV shows my mother watched, where nothing really happened. My mother lived on reality shows once she got home from work. An entire show that followed three women around a kitchen while they baked a cake. Another one where they tracked two idiots bickering and complaining while they renovated a house. My buddy Scott is in college taking a film and media program. He says you can can make pretty good money in documentaries and reality TV. I wondered if I should get him to film Jarrod and Clancy, two aimless dick-heads. It would be as exciting as watching a bathtub full of water, but that doesn't seem to stop the cable channels.

My brother and Clancy liked to sit on the bench or the swings at the park. They liked to smoke cigarettes and slurp on giant drinks from the 7–11. I never saw them hug, or hold hands, but they walked shoulder to shoulder. There was something about the way they moved together that suggested they weren't just buddies. Which is fine, not my business, but Jarrod had always been cagey. My old man was a guy of few words, but he summed up my brother and mother that day in the garage. They were tough to figure out. You'd give yourself an ulcer trying to.

Chapter 12: Warfield

Sheila finished her run and arrived back at her place with only twenty minutes to spare. She tore off her sweaty clothes, let them fall to the bathroom floor, and waited for the water to warm as it sprayed from the shower-head. Three coins, a tiny pepper-spray canister and a single key fell from her jacket. The key was unfamiliar at first, but she cringed as she stepped into the shower. The key was for Barry Palmer's house. She'd taken it. Her plan *had* been to book a day off when Barry was working. She would go to his place, let herself in; prepare some Thai food out of a new cookbook she'd bought; put a bottle of Pinot Grigio on ice; candles on the table, and wait for him in her robe, wearing nothing underneath. She stood beneath the warm water and sighed. In retrospect he probably would have taken it all in and then yawned, or charged her with break and enter. She was glad her plan never did happen. She was glad it was finished with Barry. He was inattentive, frequently zoning out and saying, "Huh?" after she had said something. It was too much effort to repeat herself, so she'd tell him it didn't matter, and that made him shake his head and give her the silent treatment. What she *wanted* was to have someone, a man who wouldn't mind if she called him *hers*. Barry wasn't that guy. He was generous, lived well. His house was comfortable and she was envious of it. The bathroom was luxurious. There was room for the two of them in his shower and he would often invite himself in while she stood in an amazing cloud of hot mist. He was a perfectionist; protective of his stylish home. He was finishing his basement and said he'd surprise her when it was done. Sheila had asked if she could have a sneak peek. She'd even asked after they'd had sex, and Barry was lying on the bed, sleepy-eyed and in good spirits.

"That's like asking a sculptor to see his work before the last sprigging, or the novelist to see the book before he's penned the epilogue," he'd said.

She stepped out of her own drab shower and toweled off quickly. She rushed to her bedroom, chilled, and rummaged her drawers for her last pair of clean leggings. In the end he had too many moods and quirks. She would move on, but when she saw him at the station, she'd keep it civil, professional. And this would be the last time. No more involvement with the guys she worked with. Not even Sharp, in the unlikely event he became available. The thought of him free, with ring-less fingers, made her sigh.

Sheila lived in a narrow, brown brick row house at the east end of town. It was a working class stretch where people came and went early each morning and returned home after six each evening. They kept to themselves. Sheila had said hello to the couple next door once or twice. In the Spring she could hear the baseball game through their back windows. The couple would cheer now and then. She had once invited them for a drink and the woman looked at her with a dazed expression and said, "Yeah, maybe one of these days."

Yeah, well fuck you, Sheila had thought. She seldom saw the man who lived on the other side of her. He walked with his eyes half shut and seemed in a perpetual hurry. Sheila had seen him at the government offices downtown and assumed he worked there. She tried not to think about him for fear of darkness and a murky image tugging in her mind—something about him. He acted as if he'd just gotten away with something. Cop or not, she was right there beside him. She could hear his water running sometimes and once in a while she heard his elf-like laughter. They were separated by about eight inches of plaster, so she didn't want to know.

She had gotten to know Grace, an elderly lady directly across the street. Grace was one of the only neighbours to introduce herself when Sheila moved in, and when she eventually saw Sheila rushing off to work, in uniform, she became very friendly. She would bake muffins and leave them in the mailbox. Once, during a power outage that lasted eleven hours, Grace knocked on Sheila's door and offered a carafe of hot tea.

"I'm prepared. I have a gas burner in my kitchen."

About a month ago, Grace had undergone hip surgery and could no longer walk her dog, Leonard. Sheila arrived five minutes late, her hair still wet from the shower. She saw the peephole in Grace's front door darken for a moment, and then Grace answered and stepped back to invite Sheila inside. Her house was the exact same as Sheila's: low stucco ceilings, dark wood floor, and small windows that jammed when you opened them. And yet Grace's home seemed brighter, welcoming. Grace had taken the time to decorate. A radio played, and there was a little imitation fireplace flickering against the living room wall. Paintings of all sizes and quality hung on the walls, and the curtains and blinds were all open. When she had a day off, Sheila spent time with Grace. They had developed a routine, coffee and a bit of catching up before Sheila took Leonard out for his walk. When she brought the dog back, Grace would try to shove a rolled up $20 bill into Sheila's hand. She dreaded that. She didn't want Grace's money, but Grace was stubborn. They sat in the living room and sipped their coffee while Leonard waited in the hall, whining occasionally.

"I saw your boyfriend early yesterday. He was at your front door. I wasn't spying. You must think I sit and look out the window all day."

"No, I don't think that."

"I thought it was funny because he got out of his car and knocked on your door. I didn't know it was him at first. I'm used to him tooting the horn and seeing you hop in his car and zoom off."

"Well, he's not my boyfriend anymore."

Grace put her cup down and shifted uncomfortably in her chair. She rubbed her hip and shook her head in frustration.

"I'm sorry to hear that."

"Don't be. I'm used to it. I'm doomed to be single, I think."

"Nonsense, you're lovely. You're smart, you have a fascinating job, a nice disposition, and a pretty face."

"Attached to an angular, bony body."

"Slim. Most women would kill to be as slim as you."

"Grace, I'm not slim. I'm a human pipe-cleaner."

"He was too old for you anyway. By the time your children were ten years old, he would have been nearly seventy."

"We were nowhere near talking about those things."

"Well, there you have it. By the time you were ready, he might have been sixty-odd. And who's to say he could do his duty?"

"His duty?"

"Well, the sperm isn't exactly flowing like a river at that age." Sheila nearly inhaled her coffee.

She enjoyed walking Leonard. He tugged at the leash and actually pulled Sheila along. He would look back at her and show his teeth as if he were smiling. She had asked Grace what breed Leonard was and Grace said she had no clue.

"A mix of every mischievous breed known to man," she claimed.

Sheila thought he looked like a miniature German Shepherd, but with shorter, fox-like ears. They arrived at the park and she let Leonard wander along the trees and bushes at the park's edge. She thought about Barry. He'd noticed his house key was gone. That's what it was. He hadn't dropped by to make up, or officially break it off. Shallow jerk. What Grace had witnessed was Barry arriving to demand his key back. Sheila decided she would leave it in an envelope in his cubbyhole at the station.

They left the park after twenty minutes. The neighbourhood seemed dull. It always appeared to be in a light fog, or looked like it had just rained, whether it had or not. Sheila seldom invited people back to her place. She might if her home looked like Grace's. Compared to Grace's cozy little arrangement, her's didn't look like a home. It looked like someone had just moved in, and yet she had been renting it for nearly two years. Once, she had asked Billy Goodrich over for a beer after they'd worked a shift together. Billy had been in police college the year before she had. He was a life-of-the-party type, fun to drink with. His girlfriend was in Arizona that week. They had stopped at the liquor store to pick up a bottle of wine and a six-pack. When they got to Sheila's house, he said, "Oh yeah, these places. They remind me of like, fucking Siberia or something."

"Thanks," was all Sheila could offer as a comeback.

Chapter 13: Sharp

Ryan yawned as they arrived at the radio call and pulled into the circular drive of a sprawling home, a strange place with narrow, horizontal windows and an overdone water feature, complete with a decorative paddle wheel.

"Holy shit, it looks like a sci-fi river boat," said Ryan.

Sharp chuckled as they got out of the cruiser and went to the front door. The family answered, stood clustered together in the large, marble foyer like three well-groomed monkeys—their brown eyes blinking at the officers on their doorstep. There was dad, a short, stocky man, well-dressed; the type of guy who would normally come at you with his arm extended for a handshake and his business card ready. Sharp had seen his type more times than he cared to recall, especially in this patrol area. Three hundred grand a year, minimum, usually a family business. A harmless enough guy, but whatever you've done, he's done it twice, and whatever you own, you should have talked to 'his guy' first because ' his guy' could have gotten you a better deal. Mum was tall, white-blonde with jet black roots and far too attractive for him. She stood behind her husband smiling, but with concern otherwise etched around her pretty, blinking eyes. And daughter, fifteen or sixteen, stout and shiny-faced, more like her father. A large wad of gum rolled about in her lip-glossed mouth as she spoke.

"See, I told you they'd show up," she said to her mother. "This is like so lame."

She walked away and trotted up the stairs, apparently disinterested now that the cops had actually arrived.

The problem was their son, Andrew. Dad became agitated as he explained his son's growing attitude problem, mum kept placing a hand on his shoulder to calm him, and check his language. Andrew had started threatening dad when they argued.

"I'm not having it," said the dad. "He has it pretty good here and he gets a lot of freedom. We put down a few rules about curfews and chores around the house and he shuns them, and now he's gonna start raising his hand to me, swearing at me?"

"Has he hit you or shoved you, anything like that?" asked Ryan.

"Not yet. What are my rights? If I hit him——"

"I don't want you hitting him," said mum. She was adamant and took a step away from her husband.

"How old is Andrew, and is he here right now?"

"He's seventeen," she said.

"He's in the garage. That's where he runs when things don't go his way. He locks himself in there and throws a fit," said the dad.

"Not a fit, Doug, that's not fair," said the mum.

Sharp knocked on the garage door and he and Ryan stood off to one side. Andrew did not answer, but instead hit the button for the main door, its electric motor and chain moaning and lifting it slowly. Sharp and Ryan went around to meet Andrew, a big kid for seventeen, pushing six and a half feet and still bony, plenty of beefing-up yet to occur. Sharp introduced himself and Ryan and asked Andrew why his father called the police. Andrew was nervous. Sharp watched his body language and eyes as he spoke haltingly, upset enough that tears weren't out of the question, but the boy kept it together and ran through a list of grievances:

He was not going to law school and working at the firm, where dad was a senior partner. *Children* had nine o'clock curfews, not seventeen-year-old guys. He didn't want to play baseball any more. He hated team sports. His old man said he had to do something and his old man had been quite the ball player in his day. All Andrew wanted to do was go away to school and live on campus. He couldn't wait for next year.

"I am getting out of here!" said Andrew. He punched the wall as he vowed to escape the confines of his luxury home. Sharp noted some blood on his knuckles, along with dried blood, tiny smears of it here and there on the clean drywall.

"Let me see those hands," said Sharp.

Andrew held out his hands.

"You know, when you get older, like me, those hands are going to be stiff, arthritic."

Andrew looked at his knuckles and then jammed his hands in his pockets.

"Wait here," said Sharp.

Sharp went to the cruiser and opened the trunk. He unzipped his gym bag. He kept a few things stuffed in there along with his work-out gear: a spare knife, some rope, a compass, a waterproof container full of matches, some protein bars. Plenty of their territory was rural, and Sharp spent his share of time on dark country roads. He took his focus mitts and sparring gloves out of the bag and returned to the garage.

"Here, do me a favour and put these on. Help him with the straps there, Ryan."

He had Andrew throw some punches at the mitts. The kid was long-armed and lanky and seemed to like hitting the mitts.

"This is a lot easier on your hands," said Sharp.

After a couple of minutes Sharp lowered the mitts and took them off. Andrew tore the Velcro straps from the gloves and Ryan took them.

"You could put a heavy bag in here, or a double end ball," said Sharp. "I can give you the number to a great gym, they have a lot going on there—boxing, Muay Thai, Jiu-jitsu. You should go and check it out. You could take some lessons and if you like striking you could get your dad out here to hold the mitts for you, maybe the two of you could jump some rope."

"He wouldn't do that."

"Why don't you ask him?"

Andrew shrugged. Sharp placed his hand on the boy's arm.

"He runs the house. I hate to break it to you, but you're going to have to follow rules wherever you go, whatever you do. Some of them won't be negotiable, that's just a fact of life, but some you can change if you sit down and communicate."

"I can't communicate with him. He doesn't listen."

"He says you run in here whenever you guys butt heads. Is that true?"

Again a shrug of the shoulders.

"Ryan, could you tap on the door and get Doug out here?"

Sharp took out a business card and wrote down the gym's website on the back.

Doug arrived and Andrew became despondent. Sharp had them stand close to each other.

"That's your father. He works hard and he's built something here. He does it with you, your mother and sister in mind. If his rules don't make sense, be a man and respectfully ask him for some time to sit and hear your case. Don't come out here and punch the walls."

Sharp directed his attention to Doug.

"He's not a little boy. Look at the size of him. He's taller than I am. He's as tall as Ryan here. Sir, I'm not a social worker and I am not trying to interfere in your family business but I've been responding to these types of calls for a few years now. He wants a voice at the adult table and he'll get it one day, at college or at work, wherever. If he's never had a voice at that table with you, he won't know you anymore, and you won't know him."

Doug raised his eyebrows and looked at his son.

"I suppose," he said.

"There is no supposition. You have to communicate, allow him a seat at that table, and you, Andrew, have to approach him with the respect he deserves. He's been around a little longer than you."

"Are you going to make us shake hands?" asked Andrew.

"I can't make you do anything. But, if I come back here and someone's been punched in the face, I can make an arrest. You seem like a nice family. No one wants that."

Sharp had Ryan park the cruiser around the corner to make their notes. It was something Granddad Victor always suggested. Once the call is done, leave, don't hang around. Make your notes elsewhere. Lingering reduces your impact. Ryan chuckled and turned his map light on.

"You're that guy on TV in the afternoon, the bald dude giving advice to all those fucking rejects."

Sharp didn't look at Ryan. He kept writing, but said, "Not quite."

"Yeah, you're cooler than him, by just a small margin."

"Well, thanks, Ryan, you prick."

"You know what though? They always seem to listen."

"I don't talk down to them."

"The thing is, I'm not sure telling that kid to take MMA is gonna get the Nobel Peace Prize. He'll be able to kick his old man's ass."

"He won't. Besides, if he joins that club he'll see he's not tough. Those places have a way of humbling you and training you at the same time."

"I should come out," said Ryan.

"Yeah, you should, I'd love to knock around a young string-bean like you."

Ryan laughed.

"Where to?" he said.

"Let's go to the north end and cruise around."

"The place with the homemade croissants?"

"We could do that," said Sharp.

They pulled away from the curb and Sharp thought about taking his own advice and sitting down with Father Edward. He'd tried that before. It had ended with his old man calling him a hippie. Ridiculous. Sharp mined his gut for any desire to try again, but found himself thinking of being far away from uniforms and the distinct smell of the station; the subtle vinyl-coffee-stale smoke reek of the cruiser; the ferocious attitude of his brother and the disapproving glare of his father.

He picked up his cell, happy to see it at 3/4 power, and dialed Ingrid.

Still no answer.

Chapter 14: The Pursued

He settled the car down and programmed the cruise control. The highway was a narrow, two-lane ribbon that disappeared, dug into the horizon no matter how far he drove. He felt relief whenever the monotonous drive was punctuated by a farmhouse, a barn, or an oncoming car. He'd reached an end. Things had been ending, like the acts of a disturbing play, since he was a boy. It felt final and cruel now, as he cruised with his hand resting atop the leather steering wheel. His mother had passed on last year. She hadn't wanted a funeral. She left her house and its contents to him. He'd stopped by once and couldn't bring himself to do anything more than wander through the home and close the bedroom doors, empty the fridge. He transferred her money into his account. He had more money now than he could use. He could by a car like the one he had stolen, but what fun would that be? He could calm down and do his job, climb the ladder, but that was getting long in the tooth. His feelings about his job were so mixed, so complicated, that he strained to see the highway and the washed-out horizon he was chasing. He could do his job with his eyes closed. He was always good at anything he attempted in life and he sometimes set out to be good overall. But it didn't come naturally. The available space in his mind and heart for consecutive days of being upstanding and constructive was limited, and the real him choked those things out.

"Choked, of course," he said, and laughed.

The car shuddered and the back end lost traction for a split second. He thought of all the things he could get, if he wanted them: a promotion, a new house, line of credit, wife, two kids, two cars, trips to the cottage, beer fridge in the garage. He'd watched his colleagues around him and the lives they led, the things they had, the things they counted as important and he couldn't help but feel they'd all missed out. Absurd. That's what life was. Absurd

and filled with worms and parasites that perpetuated the absurd-
ity. He slowed the Mercedes and pulled a sloppy, skidding U-turn.
He took it up to 180 as he roared back in the direction he'd come
from. He winced at the truth, which had been poking at him
since the childhood reminiscing he'd done back at the feed mill.
He'd *been* forgetting things. He'd *missed* cashing his paycheque
three times over the past few months. He'd been misplacing
things, messing things up. He'd left his car door open, the engine
running, when he'd run into the liquor store for some Crown
Royal. The gas company returned his cheque for his last payment.
He'd neglected to fill in the amount. He'd found a plastic jug of
laundry detergent in the fridge—no one but him could have
placed it there. Most of all, he was forgetting his whereabouts;
what he had done the week, or month before. That couldn't happen, not with the life he'd been leading.

He went to the doctor after awaking one morning feeling
hung-over. He hadn't had a drop of liquor the night before. There
was a tingling in his tongue and lips, of all places. He hated his
doctor. Hated them all for that matter. A pompous, arrogant and
self-aggrandizing profession. The doctor referred him to a neuro-
surgeon and told him not to worry or overreact. It could simply
be stress, or lack of sleep. He asked about the sleeping pills; was he
taking them and had he suffered any side-effects? He seldom took
them, but lied to the doctor—told him what he wanted to hear.
The doc said he'd be in touch.

He'd forgotten all about it, told himself not to panic, but kept
doing these foolish things, committing these lapses. It had even
started happening at work. He'd been asked for some papers. The
request had been left in his inbox. He'd searched everywhere, but
couldn't find them. One morning, Skinny MacKinnon came up
to him and said, "Is this yours?"

He handed over the papers.

"Yes, where did you find these?"

"Near the sink, in the washroom over at the coffee shop,"
skinny MacKinnon nodded backwards, as if the coffee shop were
right behind them. He had an accusing look in his eyes.

"Thanks. I'd better be more careful."

"Tell me about it. If *I* did that one of you old-timers would have me castrated."

Skinny walked away.

Not a bad idea, he thought as MacKinnon pushed open an office door and disappeared from sight.

Three months after his doctor's appointment he received a call to come to the hospital. So he went and sat stock still while they conducted an MRI—the third one of his life. He'd had one as a boy, and then another during college when he'd hit his head during Judo after completely botching a break fall. Two days later the specialist called him to come and discuss the results of the MRI. The specialist was a neurosurgeon, and had the face and build of a twelve-year-old boy, along with a stupidly deep voice, so baritone it was a wonder that patients actually heard the first few words he'd said. They'd be busy thinking: *Good God what a mismatched and idiotic voice you have.* He began smiling as the specialist talked and switched on a lighted portion of the wall to reveal images of a brain. He pictured a league of people out on the street, walking around town with advanced tumors and brain cancer because all they'd heard was a ridiculously deep voice, and not the actual diagnosis. He laughed at the thought.

"Is everything alright?"rumbled the specialist.

"Yes, thank you. A nervous chuckle, I suppose."

"Okay, well, step closer if you don't mind."

He rose from his plastic chair and walked to the back-lighted wall. The specialist used a black pointer to identify a group of dark dots and streaks on the brain, just over the ear.

"Scarring, lesions. They are not primary, or vascular, which is good news. They will warrant some more investigation, and monitoring, but I'm thinking immune deficiency, or cell death and malfunction. There's typically not a single cause . . ."

He noticed the specialist's neck. It was thin. He could strangle the specialist with ease—a wispy neck like that. Not that he would strangle the specialist right here in his office, but he could if he wanted. He looked at the image of the brain—his brain.

It didn't look real. The so-called lesions would not have been noticeable if the baritone neurosurgeon hadn't traced them with his pointer. He buttoned his sports jacket, turned towards the door and walked out.

"Excuse me? Where are you going?" said the specialist. His big voice filled the room and small reception area like it was the voice of God.

"It might as well be," he said, chuckling.

He reached the lobby and hit the button for the elevator. The receptionist scrambled out of the reception area and rushed towards him.

"Sir, the doctor hasn't finished talking to you."

He ignored her. The elevator arrived and he remembered when he was a boy that one of the English people in his youth— there were too many to remember which one—called the eleva-tor a *lift*.

"It also lowers, moron," he said.

He got on the elevator and pushed MAIN and then the CLOSE DOOR button while the receptionist and twelve-year-old neuro-surgeon stood and watched him as if he were a carnival act.

"Have a nice life," he said.

The doors closed and the *lift* lowered him.

He passed back through Pollard, onto the larger highway sys-tem and pushed into suburbia. He passed a police cruiser that whipped by him, headed in the other direction and he watched his rearview for its roof bar to light and flash, but nothing hap-pened. He went into a donut shop and bought a coffee. The whiskey had given him a headache. The fuel gauge was just above the halfway mark and he cruised past a huge gas station and car wash, deciding that he wouldn't need to fill the tank.

"I'm done," he said.

He sipped his coffee and said, "Now, honey, that's good coffee."

He thought of the three women he'd had in his life. Three. Not many for a man his age. And all of them boring, and com-plicated, and needy. He thought of lesions on a brain, not his brain, necessarily, but on a brain in general. His disinterest in the lesions was powerful.

He didn't want to know anymore about them and he wasn't going to spend days, weeks, and certainly not months surrounded by know-it-all doctors talking to him, and about him, like he was nothing more than a malfunctioning lawnmower engine. Fucking pompous, self-important, sterile, blithe, egotistical, overpaid, morons. They thought they had power and he supposed—had to admit—they did. It must be a rush to tell someone they're dying and then wander off to the parking lot, hop in your Porsche and whiz over to the club for your noon squash game, with not so much as a pang of pity or empathy for the poor fuck you left behind in your cramped office, with its uncomfortable seats, dog-eared magazines, cloudy aquarium and fat, robotic staff. And why were all doctor's office assistants fat women wearing those clinical smocks? Why did they wear medical garb? All they did was file paper, make appointments and harass the poor patients. They didn't do medical work. They just put you on hold for minutes at a time. If it were up to him he would limit the number of fat assistants in each medical office. One fatty per office and *that one* would wear civilian clothing and keep her fat thoughts to her fat self. And no lunch at your desk either. Feed like a hog down in the cafeteria so the patients don't have to smell your tuna fish sandwiches mixing with your awful perfume. And any doctor found being rude or insensitive to a patient would be injected with germs, perhaps a flesh-eating bacteria, and the patient he'd offended would have the opportunity to sit, or better yet, stand with that doctor and break the news:

"Well, you have flesh-eating disease and it's going to consume your limbs first and then your torso, until its ravaged your vital organs. Now, the limbs we can amputate as the disease begins to consume them, that's not a problem, but the vitals, well, that's another story *good God* is that really the time? I have a four o'clock tee-off and I haven't even changed clothes yet. Where does the time go? We will need to run some more tests. We should be able to get those for you in, oh, I don't know, six months . . ."

"They don't save anyone," he said. "They just drag out the inevitable."

He laughed, nefariously. Perhaps the lesions had always been there. *Perhaps* they helped to explain who he was. They hadn't shown up before though. That was the thing.

"Fucking nonsense," he said.

He leaned on the horn for no reason and the truck in front of him signaled and moved to the right lane. He had a flash of a thought: put the window down and shoot the truck driver. He shook the thought from his head and reminded himself that he killed for a reason.

It was never random, although it might seem random to the dull and moronic, to those with no imagination. He took the Mercedes up to 120 in a 60 zone. He was asking for it now. He knew it.

"I take lives! And I take your fancy cars as well!"

He entered an on-ramp too quickly and nearly spun out. Once on the highway he grabbed the left lane and shot the car up to 180. There were so many thoughts jamming and crowding into his mind that he pictured the Oshiya, in Japan, shoving people onto already packed commuter trains so that the doors could close and haul them off to work their boring, depressing jobs, or take them back to their tiny, humid apartments that didn't have beds. They slept on floor mats and ate from big rice-cookers that sat in closet-sized kitchens, and they thought they had it made. What a fucking life. What a fucking world. He wondered if Japan had someone, an equivalent to himself, wandering or driving the streets and completely fooling everyone in the process. He supposed there must be at least one like him in each country, and he laughed and felt energized by the idea.

CHAPTER 15: STAN HILL

I had nearly given up on following Jarrod and Clancy, and then one day I saw them meet a guy named Marc Grasp at the abandoned railway station. The train hadn't stopped in our town for a few years, and the station was boarded up, covered in graffiti. There was a rusting, chain-link fence that separated the old platform from the tracks. Weeds had found their way through the cracks and fissures of the platforms and pavement, and the glass that had once provided shelter from wind and rain was long gone, broken by vandals and swept away by town work crews.

My brother and Clancy followed Marc to a leaning, windowless kiosk that was once the ticket office. The three of them sat on a busted-up bench. I stood behind a large, wooden sign that advised anyone who could read its fading letters that the land was available for redevelopment. And anyone with half a brain knew the only thing that would develop here were more weeds, broken bottles and trash. No one was going to buy this land.

I was a fair distance away from the three amigos, but no so far that I couldn't figure out what was going on. Jarrod handed Marc some cash. Marc counted it and tucked it in his pocket and from that same pocket produced a baggy that he jammed into Jarrod's hand. Marc then smiled at Clancy and young Timmy smiled back. Marc handed Clancy a baggy as well and then stood up, opened his coat, unzipped his pants and tilted his head, indicating the old ticket office. Clancy and Marc both wandered behind it—out of sight, thank God. Jarrod stayed on the bench and played look-out, glancing around once or twice, but then he fumbled around with rolling papers, set a paper on his lap and began rolling a blunt.

This would ordinarily be none of my business, except that I kicked in $300 a month to buy groceries and pay bills. My mother's job didn't quite cover everything and my old man was sending what he could. I didn't want my little brother using what little money we had to buy weed, but I didn't want him paying for it the way Clancy was.

I waited for the party to break up. I listened to the breeze drift through the old train station. I stood among the litter and crumbling pavement and inhaled the stink of rust and wood rot. I stepped out from behind the sign as Marc walked a path that had been worn through the dry grass and weeds. He was surprised to see me. His eyes went round and he shuddered, and then stopped, and looked back towards where he'd come from.

"Hey, Stan."

"Never mind *hey Stan*. What are you doing with those two dickheads?"

Marc zipped his coat all the way up and tilted his head as if he didn't understand the question. I took a step towards him. He put his hand up like he wanted to high-five.

"Hey, Stan, I don't want any trouble. It's just a little shwag, you know?"

"How old are you, Marc?"

The question caught him off-guard and he looked down the front of his leather coat as if it might provide him the answer.

"I'm thirty-two."

"Exactly. You're thirty-two and selling to them, and getting serviced by Clancy."

Marc gave me a strange, almost coy smile that I didn't like one bit. I pointed to his pocket.

"That's *my* money."

Marc placed his hand on his jacket zipper and looked at his boots.

"If I see or hear that you've stepped within ten feet of Jarrod again, I'll fuck you up."

"Like I said, Stan, I don't want *any* trouble."

I put my hand out.

"Come on, Stan, that means I'm out fifty bucks and then I owe to the guy who supplies me."

I kept my hand out.

"You should have thought about that before you took cash and a blow job from two minors."

"It's not what you think. It's just a little business," said Marc. His voice trembled and there was sweat around his hairline.

"Really? If it's just a little business, all legit, why are you doing it in a fucking ghost town?"

Marc dug into his pocket and took out the bills, handed them to me.

"Garrett supplies me. He won't be happy about this. You don't want to get on *his* bad side."

I took a step towards Marc. He backed up and stumbled, nearly fell down.

"I know Garrett. You can tell him to drop by my place any time."

"Okay, but what am I supposed to do when he freaks out on me?"

"Have Clancy give him a BJ," I said. I turned and walked back towards my car.

Jarrod wore his hair long, down near his shoulders, which came in handy. I found him in the living room, stretched out on the couch like he'd put in a hard day's work. I dug my hand into his hair, twisted it and pulled him to his feet. He wound up to bitch slap me and I gave him a gentle head butt on the bridge of his nose. He began to scream for mummy and sure enough she came roaring into the room and skidded across the floor in her stocking feet. She demanded that I let Jarrod go, and so I did, very suddenly, and he dropped to the floor like a lazy sack full of lies and bones. I calmed my mother down and told her I'd seen the buy and gotten the cash back from Marc Grasp. My mother knew Marc and his family. They'd run a puppy mill for a couple of years until the government shut it down. My mother was an animal-lover: wildlife protection T-shirts, endangered species coffee mugs and coin-rollers she filled and gave to the SPCA. She was pretty hardcore. She didn't approve of the Grasps and she gave Jarrod shit for even associating with Marc. I have to admit that I stood back and enjoyed that. I winked at Jarrod and he yelled and threw a pillow at me, so I kicked him and then told my mother act two of the story, the part where Jarrod's douche bag best friend paid for his ganja in trade.

My mother took a step back and crossed her arms over her chest, an excellent sign. I left them to discuss the day's events and went to Uncle Chow's for a beer and an egg roll.

That night I was packing my lunch for work on Monday. My mother walked into the kitchen and sat at the table.

"Did you want some tea?" I asked.

"That would be nice."

I put the kettle on and then wrapped up my sandwiches.

"I could have made those for you."

"That's alright."

"What do you think happened today? Do you really think that Timmy Clancy and Marc did what you said?"

"Yeah, I can almost guarantee it."

She furrowed her brow and began to fidget with the salt and pepper shakers.

"I don't want Jarrod associating with Marc."

"He's buying drugs from him, I don't think they're exactly friends."

She sighed.

"Jarrod needs to smarten the hell up. You should send him away to that school," I said.

"You're hard on him. He hasn't handled things as well as you have, what with your father and all."

"*Don't* stand up for him. He's hanging with the town misfit and he's turning into one right before our eyes."

Her tone sharpened and she stood up.

"He's your *brother*. You should help him. I don't know why you hate him so much. That's your father's influence. Your father is a very cold person, him and this nonsense about only caring about what you can control."

I poured boiling water into her cup and dropped a teabag in, and then a spoon.

"Your tea is on the counter," I said.

And then I went upstairs to bed.

Chapter 16: Warfield

She walked quickly, more of a march. Leonard was panting when he got home. She gave him a rub on the head, knocked on the door. Grace invited her in for one more coffee, but Sheila declined.

"I have a lot to do," she said.

Back at her place, she sat on the couch with the TV off and the drapes drawn tight. She sighed when she pictured Grace in a chair at her front window, watching the neighbourhood like a sentinel. Sheila did not want to end up on her own. She supposed that she should go out and do something, buy some ornaments and some new curtains or blinds that didn't look like giant bandages. Some paintings, or art would be nice. She reached for some home decor magazines beneath the coffee table, wiped the dust from them and began flipping the pages. Her mind darkened and the room went with it. She closed her eyes and saw movement, magnetic and nauseating, a quick shot of motion sickness. And then it came, and went within seconds. She remembered, as a child, her father had a cheap old camera that used disposable flashbulbs. If you looked at them too closely the flash remained, lingered in front of your eyes for a second or two, and then dissipated in a series of black and yellow dots.

"Oh God," she said.

She saw Sharp and did not want to. She opened her eyes and looked around her living room. It was as spare and colourless as ever. She could hear rain, or maybe sleet ticking against the window. Her surroundings were the epitome of calm and quiet and yet she'd just seen Matt Sharp's face twisted in fear and disbelief. She saw his lips part slightly and he exhaled and released a sigh of resignation. She saw speed, felt it as well, her own mind thrust forward and then it spun for a sickening moment. She had gripped the armrests of her chair so tight her fingernails pierced it. She jumped from the chair, hit the scanner's ON button and picked up the phone. It rang seven times before Ralph Anderson answered. She liked Anderson, but didn't need his sarcasm and strange humor right now.

"It's Sheila."

"Oh, hey Warfield. You know they're gonna be calling you in? They're thinking of bringing in extra help, a couple of tanker cars—"

"Yeah, I heard. Hey, is that chase still on?"

"Chase?"

"Sharp and Ryan were in a chase."

"Oh, that, no it's done. They lost him. Bastard left the highway and ripped away on one of the side roads. Stolen car."

Sheila rested her forehead on the kitchen counter and enjoyed the relief. The scanner sparked to life. The dispatcher came on and read back a CPIC check.

"You have a scanner?" asked Anderson.

"Yeah."

"And you're *listening* to it now, *and* calling me?" He snorted and laughed, and then added, "Warfield, you need to get out more."

"Maybe I'll see you soon," she said.

"I have a hunch they'll put the call out."

She signed off and watched water drip from the old faucet. It made a dull tapping sound as it hit the enamel sink. She took out a bag of lettuce she kept in the fridge and pulled out some vegetables, set them on the counter. She took out the cutting board and a knife, and then looked at the kitchen table—which was actually a fold-out card table—and saw herself sitting there, eating a salad on her own.

She went into town and found a parking spot just down from a store called Home Sweet Home. The weather had become increasingly miserable, so she zipped up her coat and pulled up her collar to keep out the freezing drizzle. The store was larger inside than she would have imagined. They had the things she was looking for. She left with an empty purse and two paintings, place mats, a new shower curtain and a vase that had been $125, but was reduced to $75, if she paid cash.

Sheila arrived home and placed the new items throughout her narrow home, knowing she had very little decorating flare. She opened the tool box and discovered she had no picture hooks, so she hammered two finishing nails into the plaster, hung the paintings, and hoped they would hold. She made her salad and ate it on the couch, admiring a home that was finally coming to life. She thought about paint, something nice, a pastel. She wrote it down on her reminder list, which was held on the fridge by a magnet. Her mother had given her the magnet. It was black and white, and cat-shaped. She held it in her hands, rubbed her thumb along its rubbery surface.

They'd had a nice home, a decent family life, before her father died. Her father's calm and seemingly carefree attitude had kept her mother's well-meaning mania in check. Now, her mother was unbearable at times. A nice person, a great person, but so hurried and meddlesome that Sheila felt she needed a nap after spending an hour or two with her. And the thoughts, the information that came to Sheila had always sat like a monolith between them. Occasionally, her mother attempted to chip away at it.

"What is it that you see? How did you know about that airplane when you were a child? How did you know about Uncle Chris?"

"I didn't know about Uncle Chris."

"Oh, Sheila come on, you started crying as soon as Dad picked up the phone and said hello to Aunt Cheryl."

"She called at midnight. No one calls at midnight unless it's something urgent."

Her mother would sit back and narrow her eyes.

"Why won't you talk to me about it? I know what a premonition is."

"Mum, I have good intuition. It's not like I'm a psychic!"

"Did you know about Dad? Sense it or *intuit* it?"

"No!"

"Alright, spare me the attitude. If I had a gift like that I would use it, that's all I'm saying."

"I don't have a *gift,* Mum."

And that was the problem, she thought, as she finished lunch and took her dishes to the kitchen sink. Her mother could, and would turn it into a circus. Neighbour after neighbour, scads of sixty-year-old women—*zoomers,* her mother called them—filing into her mother's cozy living room to hold Sheila's hand and have their fortunes told.

And her mother would blurt it from the rooftops: *My daughter the psychic cop!* It wasn't like that. It didn't work that way. Sheila dipped her face towards the sink and splashed it with cold water. She did her best to ignore it when it came to her job. It would drive her crazy otherwise. There were exceptions. Life was full of those. She'd been worried just now when she'd seen Sharp in distress. Apparently a false alarm. There was the incident last year with Billy Goodrich.

They were on a community patrol car. It had been quiet and Billy Goodrich was reading from a book claiming to have the best one-liners and wise-cracks ever written. Sheila was driving and they were both laughing, both in good spirits. The dispatcher broke the silence with a priority transmission. A bank had been robbed in Dufferin, a town one patrol area from where she and Goodrich were posted. Billy tossed the book near his feet, turned up the radio and flipped open his notebook.

". . . *suspect is armed with an automatic handgun. He is described as male, white, 5 feet 8 inches, medium build, 35 years; brown, shoulder-length curly hair, unkempt; rough shaven; wearing a red windbreaker, blue jeans and beige work-boots. Be advised we have two possible suspect vehicles: a white, late model Toyota or Mazda sedan, and a blue, full-sized panel van, possibly with a ladder fastened to the roof. Both vehicles were seen leaving the area at high rates of speed . . .*"

"I'll take the van," said Billy, "if the perp was wearing work-boots."

Sheila agreed. She had already turned around and headed toward Dufferin. Other units joined in and the dispatcher began assigning quadrants. She instructed Sheila and Billy to remain close to the highway that might take the suspect vehicle east-bound into their patrol area. They drove onto the highway, and, seeing nothing of interest, they exited and took the service road back to the edge of their patrol area. Sheila bit down on her lower lip as Billy talked, his deep voice just a vibration inside the cruiser, his words becoming a jumble. Her mind darkened. She checked the sky for thunderclouds, knowing full well the cloud cover, the darkening, was occurring inside of her. She stared hard at the road, but finally had to pull over.

The cruiser's tires and rims scraped the curb as they stopped. Billy Goodrich was talking until she ground the rims and tires, and then he began laughing. She wanted to scream for him to shut up. She closed her eyes and allowed herself to drop into the gloaming.

She saw a man, in a public washroom, at the mirror, shaving. He pulled at his hair and it came away, all of it, revealing a bald scalp, shiny, well-coloured and smooth. There was a black leather tote bag beside him and he reached into it, pulled free a garment of some type, a shirt perhaps. She could hear Muzak and Billy Goodrich's voice. He sounded like tuba. He gave her a thump on the arm.

"Don't, asshole," she said.

"War, you're sitting there pale as a ghost, rocking back and forth. You're not gonna puke, I hope."

"No, I'm fine."

Billy Goodrich also found this funny, and through his laughter, said, "You don't seem fine! You look puke-city."

"God, Billy, stop yelling, I'm right beside you, not standing across a field."

"Who's yelling? What's with you?"

"It's that time of the month if you absolutely have to know. I cramped up."

She hadn't, of course. She had used this excuse before, on occasion. Guys had little to say in response. They usually became all brotherly, or concerned.

"Sorry, War, how am I suppose to know that? Did you want me to drive? You okay?"

Sheila rubbed her belly for effect and then nodded. "Yeah, maybe you should drive."

"I'll keep my voice down. Do you need to book off sick?"

"No, it'll pass. I'll be fine."

They switched places and Billy sat staring at her as if she were a stray animal.

"Ready?"

"Yes, Billy, I'm ready."

"Man, am I ever glad I have a dick."

"I was wondering how long before you said something like that," she said.

She shook her head in mock disgust, and Billy smiled, and dropped the cruiser into Drive.

"Do me a favour and head over to the mall," she said.

He sped up and took the left lane. "Drug store, right?"

"No, you jerk. A guy just robbed a bank. He's going to want as much anonymity as possible. The mall has a huge parking lot, plenty of people. We can check the lot for a blue van, or white Toyota."

Billy gave her a sideways glance.

"You know you're pretty hot when you take control like that."

"Oh God, Billy, shut up!"

He laughed and sped towards the mall.

They arrived and found a blue van near the grocery store at the south end of the mall. There was no ladder on its roof, but Billy got out and checked the hood.

"Warm," he said. He wandered around the vehicle and tried the side and rear doors. They were locked.

Sheila led the way and they used the mall entrance closest to the grocery store.

"He's not in there." She pointed at the grocery store. "He wanted to bury his van where it was busiest, but he won't go into a grocery store. Nowhere to hide," she said.

"Good call," said Billy.

His head rotated left and right as he walked up one side of the mall, his shoulder close to the storefronts, while she did the same on the other side. They would give each other an occasional look of assurance. Near the centre of the mall, beside the fancy popcorn place and coffee shop, a man emerged from a narrow corridor that hosted only a hair salon, dry cleaners and the public washrooms. He looked at Sheila and his lips twitched; he pulled his shoulders back, a subtle movement, but still there. He was walking swiftly, carrying a large black leather bag. He increased his speed slightly, almost expertly, and checked his wristwatch as casually as he could. She stopped and turned while Billy Goodrich went ahead, cautious as a cat. She watched the man walk away from her: male, white, 5 foot 6 maybe; cleanshaven, bald, blue jeans and a navy sport coat with gold buttons. He was gaining on her and would soon be gone. He did not look back. Billy had stopped and was now watching her.

"War?"

Sheila walked quickly and then broke into a run. She pushed her sidearm forward to unlock it from her holster. Finally he looked back.

She expected him to run, but he slowed and joined other shoppers in rubber-necking, trying to figure out why there were two cops running through the mall, one them yelling, "War!" a nickname she would definitely have to change. The bald man had one hand in his pocket. The other gripped his briefcase. He gave her a *What is your problem?* look as she approached him, drew her gun and told him to drop the bag and get on the ground. Billy arrived and stood on the other side. He had the man at gunpoint as well, all the while looking at Sheila as if she were insane. Billy yelled, "Do as she says. *Right* now."

Phelps and Daniels had arrived, along with the Road Sergeant and two Provincial cars. They took the perp into custody without incident. He smiled as they cuffed him and said, "I swear that after today that was gonna be my last one."

Goodrich reminded him of his rights. He sneered and then gave Sheila a crooked smile. He was glassy-eyed and he studied her for a moment, and then let out a quiet grunt.

Back at the station they finished searching the bag. It held deodorant, a hairpiece, shaving cream, $6K in cash and a Walther 9mm. The funny thing was they found no ammunition, neither in the gun nor on the suspect. Phelps and Daniels found the perp's old clothing at the mall, stuffed deep in the men's room waste-paper bin. There was a disposable razor in there, too. They also found stubble in the sink.

Billy Goodrich sipped at a coffee from the vending machine. He had been quiet, almost forlorn, since arriving back at the station. He was filling out some paperwork for Gustersen, who was doing prisoner intake. He dropped his pen and got out of his chair, closed the door. He sat on the edge of the desk, his flashlight twisting on his belt and within inches of Sheila's fingers.

"How did you know?"

Sheila kept writing in her notebook as she replied, "There's only a salon down that lane, a fancy women's place that does nails too. There's a dry-cleaners and he didn't have any dry cleaning. Other than that, there's only the washrooms."

"Maybe he was a dweeb dropping his dry-cleaning off?"

"He was freshly shaven, too fresh. I knew he'd just come out of the washroom."

Billy slid off the desk and popped some gum into his mouth. He studied her like she was the morning crossword.

"What?"

"You're holding back on me, War."

"God, Billy, I can't explain it. It was the way he looked at me. He looked as guilty as a dog who'd just shit on the carpet. He was walking too fast, trying to look casual and doing a bad job of it. We already had the van in the lot, and he gripped that bulky bag like it had a bomb inside."

Billy stretched and groaned.

"Uh huh," he said.

"What's your problem?"

"No problem, just a little professional jealousy. I would have walked right by that dweeb. Wouldn't have given him a second thought."

"I had a different vantage point," she said.

He cracked the gum in his mouth and offered her a high-five as he left. She took it and he walloped her hand.

"Back in a minute," he said.

Chapter 17: The Pursued

He ambled along now, gave the car a break. The temp gauge needle was a touch over the midway point and he knew he'd been pushing the motor. He drove on the outskirts and thought about his next move. It was conceivable that he could take the car back, wait until 3AM and just park it a few houses down from where he'd taken it. But he had nowhere to go if he did drop the car off. That ending feeling was dogging him. He passed a bus stop and glanced at the handful of people waiting. They had lined up neatly and orderly, like well-tended sheep, in single file. He used to meet his father after work in the summer. His father was in sales and stayed close to the office in July and August. He prepared for his heavy travel schedule in the fall and winter and would leave the family car in the garage, and come home on the either the 4:20 or 4:55 bus. The bus stop was on the north side of Clemmens, a busy four lane street. The only street of that size in the town where they lived.

He was allowed to walk on his own to meet his father provided he stayed on the south side of Clemmens and waited for the bus to drop his father off. There was a church and cemetery on the south side and there was a bench near the cemetery's wrought iron gates. He would sit on the bench, wait for the bus, and sometimes pick flakes of black paint from the gate. He ate some of them once and felt ill and dizzy that evening, and wondered if he ate two or three times the amount, if he might die and be buried in that cemetery. He wanted to ask his father about the likelihood of this, but thought better of it. Summer was half over. It was hot and humid. The ground shimmered in the heat if you stared down Clemmens. The cars smelled stronger. Their oil and gasoline hung in your nostrils and the sound of engines and brakes was close and warm, right around your ears. The 4:20 bus came bouncing along and let off three people, but his father wasn't among them. He waited and picked at the peeling paint. A car stopped at a red light just to his left. Its engine growled and the back end was jacked up. It was bright blue. The deadly sun glared off the windshield, so he couldn't see the driver. When the light turned green, the car revved and roared. The rear tires screeched and it whipped by him. There was music thumping from it and he got a glimpse of the passenger's long hair as the wind blew it around and the car screamed past the cemetery.

The 4:55 bus arrived two minutes late and its air brakes hissed and the door whined as it opened. He couldn't see if his father had exited the bus until it drove away in a haze of diesel smoke. Finally, there was his father, standing in his white golf shirt and plaid trousers, his big briefcase dangling from his arm. He squinted and smiled, and reached for his sunglasses hooked on the opening of his golf shirt, right above the second button. There was a roar, an engine screaming and straining. There was a long horn, someone pressing down on the steering wheel and holding the blast so that it absorbed the very air he was breathing on Clemmens Avenue. And then there was a loud metallic thud and screeching, and grinding. The jacked up blue car he'd seen moments ago mounted the curb and boulevard on the north side of Clemmens. It moved like a metal projectile shot from a catapult. There was an explosion of glass and metal; the bus shelter erupted in a plume of glittering debris that came down like hail and made a strange, tinkling sound as it hit the asphalt. A woman screamed and cars slowed down and stopped very suddenly. Someone yelled, "Call 9–1–1."

The bus shelter was gone and so was his father. The blue car had plowed across the roadside and over the concrete pad that held the shelter so quickly, it was like the bus stop had never existed. It was like his father had never gotten off the bus. And why would he have? There was no bus stop there. Sirens began to wail from a distance. The jacked up blue car sat askew on a section of grass boulevard just down from where the bus shelter used to be. It had also knocked over a lamppost. He watched someone climb out of it. He has never been certain, but he recalls that the passenger was smiling when he first got out of the car. He staggered slightly as well. He had long hair down to his shoulders; he was shirtless and had a concave chest and skinny limbs. He went around to the the driver's side of the blue car. The driver was trying to start the car but it was choking and sputtering. A short bull of a man hopped out of a little truck and walked towards the blue car. The man wore a tank top and was covered in tattoos. He pointed at the blue car's passenger and the skinny passenger seemed frightened and stepped back from the driver's side of the car. The short bull of a man yanked open the door and pointed his thumb backwards and yelled something at the driver. The driver got out. He was young and wore a baseball cap on the back of his head. He did not appear frightened or concerned when the bull pointed at the embankment. He walked like he hadn't a care in the world and sat on the grass, rubbing his arm as if it was sore. The skinny passenger followed, but walked a large semi-circle around the bull, as if wary of what the tattooed bull might do.

The police arrived, three cars within seconds of each other. And then an ambulance and a fire truck. An older lady pointed at him. She used her hand to shield her eyes from the sun and the other to waggle her finger at him. A police officer crossed Clemmens and approached him. They had blocked the road and there was no traffic. The police officer was a woman and she wore a different type of hat. The badge seemed too big for it. She had a nice smile and there was sweat over her lip and around her nose.

"Are you okay? Did you see what happened?"

He nodded and she looked back to where the ambulance and fire truck were parked.

"You saw the whole thing?"

"Yes."

"Would you come with me please?"

She led him to her car and let him sit up front. The engine was running and it was cool inside and smelled of her soap or deodorant. The radio chattered and there was an electronic box below the radio that beeped now and then. The police officer took off her hat and opened a notebook. The area around her car seemed strangely quiet. The ambulance had gone, and he wondered about his father, even though the truth was gnawing at him from somewhere deep in his chest. He thought that perhaps his father had seen the jacked up blue car zooming along and had ran. He was very perceptive, his father was. He talked to the police officer and didn't mention why he was standing on the south side of Clemmens until she had introduced herself, taken down his name and asked a few questions. And then, with low, quivering voice, she said, "The man who got off the bus was your *father?*"

"Yes."

She looked out of her window and then placed her hand at the back of his neck. She had glossy fingernails and she squeezed, pressed them into the skin and it felt amazing. She swallowed two or three times in quick succession and lowered her window.

"Sergeant! Sarge?" she said.

She kept her hand on his neck and looked over at him. She was trying to look calm, but he could see fear in her face. The Sergeant was a tired looking man who kept removing his hat and running his hand over his cropped hair. She released his neck and got out of the car. The Sergeant got in. He listened to the Sergeant who talked, of all things, about bravery for a good minute. He knew, at his core, that his father was dead. He'd known it as soon as the blue car had obliterated the bus stop and shelter. He watched the female police officer as she stood outside and wrote in her notebook. She seemed upset and kept moving her shoulders as if she was trying to gather herself.

They drove him to the hospital, and as they arrived he saw another police car pull up. His mother rushed out of that one, and when she saw him she whimpered, and ran to him.

"You're okay, you're okay, it's going to be okay," she said.

The doctor had another take on things. He walked into the waiting area and pointed to a nurse like she was a dog. The nurse hurried them all into an empty room and sealed him, his mother and the doctor inside. A clock ticked on the wall. He remembered it had a brass face and *Donated in Loving Memory of Eddie B.* engraved on it. The doctor kept his distance.

He told them, with the tone and inflection of a man calling bingo numbers, that his father had been dead on arrival. He had suffered massive head trauma and, if it was some consolation, hadn't felt much pain. The car's impact would have been too swift and forceful. He then adjusted some pens in his cloak pocket and said the police wanted to speak to his mother. He left the room and two police officers entered. They were older men, and one was very gentlemanly, a nice person with a soothing voice who asked his partner to get some coffee and soft drinks.

The boys in the jacked up blue car were aged eighteen and twenty. One was unemployed and the other had recently dropped out of school. They were both *known to the police*. The passenger, the twenty-year-old, had been too drunk to drive, so he had asked the eighteen-year-old to drive. The eighteen-year-old's license was under suspension. They were both now under arrest and in trouble, plenty of it, according to the police officer.

"How do they have the money for a car?" his mother asked.

"The car belonged to the oldest one's brother," said the police officer. They would go to jail. The police assured them of this. But, he would see the older one when he was a teen, three or four years after his father's death. The older one would be out and about, working on a road crew, painting white lines up and down the highway, and so on. It amazed him whenever he would catch a glimpse of the older one, either in town or on the road crew, that this person, this moron, this complete and utter piece of shit, was living and breathing, drinking cold water from a plastic flask as the town truck delivered him from job to job. While his father was dead. Decomposed and vanished into the earth by now. He wished he was older, and stronger, so he could kill the one on the road crew. His father had loved a cold glass of ice water. They would stand at the kitchen counter and gulp down a glass so frigid it would sting at your temples and made your neck quiver.

"Ah, it's the best drink when it comes right down to it," his father would say. He would slam down his glass and laugh because he always finished first.

The younger one, the other piece of shit, moved away, and his mother had heard, through the grapevine, that he was back in prison. He'd been caught in a stolen car with a trunk-load of stolen goods, still driving with a suspended license.

Whenever he thought of this he was filled with something like passion. He was euphoric and he once told his mother that this was the best news he'd heard in his entire life.

"Well, B, we have to forgive though. We have to empty the anger from our hearts and move on. God will look after the rest."

She had gone back to church. She carried a small bible in her purse and was often involved in church activities and community outreach. He went with her sometimes, and he liked many of the people. He admired and loved her for going, for picking up the pieces, but knew he had a different mission, a very different calling.

"A special ministry," he said aloud, and laughed.

He drove the Mercedes slowly, a Sunday driver out for a jaunt. He loved and hated thinking back. His father's death was always referred to as *the accident*, and while he never disputed anyone who called it *the accident*, he screamed inside that it wasn't. And he became superb, an expert at keeping it inside, stowed away in his depths, where it simmered, while on the surface he was well-spoken, intelligent, determined.

When he was seventeen he went to a Sunday service with his mother. The Pastor talked about Job from the Old Testament, and how sometimes it appears the very worst that the world can give just rains down on you, and that God seems to be in the background, ignoring your struggles. The Pastor then, rather clumsily, talked about perseverance of faith and about a lady, a member of the church, who had beaten cancer for the third time. He talked about her grit and her attitude and strength in the face of the disease, and congratulated her, told the congregation that through it all she had only missed two services and one bible study. He asked the lady to stand. She did so reluctantly and everyone clapped. Her daughter was there and buried her head in her hands, and sobbed with joy. Even the Pastor's voice wavered with emotion as he said that the church family would never stop praying for her continued health, and giving thanks for God's healing touch.

And then the Pastor began talking about a fine young man. A person that brightens the room with his smile and who has shown strength and maturity beyond his years. A person who has supported his mother by towing the line and being a constant, strong presence in her life. He realized, as the Pastor went on, that *he* was the young man. It was too late to get up and creep down the aisle, and run out the back doors.

His mother was already clutching his hand and weeping. The Pastor was already grinning and stealing glances at him as he spoke, causing many in the congregation to look at him and his mother. The Pastor finally spoke his name and was happy, almost boisterous when he said, "Would you please stand up so we can all get a look at you!"

He stood. The applause was thundering. Ladies were teary-eyed and men gave him loose but serious nods of the head as if to say, *Atta boy!* He found that he too was crying. Tears of joy, he supposed, but his elation was not over pride, or having been moved by their admiration, or touched by the *spirit*. It was over having fooled them all. He could fool anyone. He sat down and the Pastor wrapped up by saying, "And if I can ever assist you, young man, a reference, a piece of advice, you just say the word. With God you can do anything."

I might just take you up on that, he thought. The congregation continued to nod and smile approvingly.

"Praise God!" said someone. The clapping dwindled, and he nodded and smiled back, while thinking: *God is a* drunk *in a blue muscle car . . .*

CHAPTER 18: STAN HILL

Garrett the bush-league drug lord did show up at our house a few days after I had intervened at the old train station. I heard the beat of his car stereo from the kitchen and went to the living room, where I watched him from the behind the curtains. He was alone. He climbed out of his car—an old, corroded Merkur—and peeled off a pair of driving gloves, tossed them back into his shit box while he looked around, cased the place. That got my temperature up pretty fast and I could feel it was time to smash something. Garrett wore mirrored sunglasses and a pea coat; baseball cap backwards on his empty head. He also chewed on a wad of gum and blew a bubble with it as he stood by his car looking at our house. That did it. I wanted to hurt him. I waited until he started up the walkway and then went out the side door, quietly unlatched the gate and came around to the front walkway. Garrett was already lifting his leg to climb the front step. I chuckled and moved up behind him. He turned, surprised to see me. I kept walking, pressing him and he backhanded me across the face. He was pretty quick and I could taste blood immediately, I'll give him that much.

Street-fighting is blunt and dirty art. If you can't take a shot, you shouldn't be doing it and you'll learn that pretty fast. But, if you have a decent chin and you can ignore the split-second rolling in of the fog, that whir and disorientation between your ears when you get rocked, and you can keep moving forward, and counter-punch no matter what, well then *you're* golden. You'll win way more than you'll lose. I clocked Garrett so hard his skull bounced of the storm door, and I danced leftwards to let him fall off my front step and onto the concrete. He was out cold and I stood and waited for him to come back to the light. I picked up his baseball cap and put it on my head, the right way around, and then I took his car keys out of his pocket.

It took him a minute, but he came to and propped himself up on one elbow and rubbed his face. He was still trying to figure out what happened.

"Did you have a nice sleep?"

He looked at me, squinted to get me in focus and then shook his head.

"You're a dead man," he said.

"Am I? You're supplying weed to that bonehead Marc Grasp, who's selling it to kids and getting a BJ in return."

Garrett didn't know what to make of this. He shut his eyes tight, re-opened them and slowly got to his feet. I stood and got ready for round two, although I doubted he had it in him.

"You don't rob cash from my associate," he said.

"*Associate,* that's excellent, Garrett. You mean Grasp. Who doesn't even know what *associate* means. You know, Garrett, you ought to hope that no one had the presence of mind to use their phone and film the *romance* between your *associate* and Timmy Clancy. The cops would go on a field trip with that. They might even look you and Grasp up on some sort of indecency charges. You *never* know."

Garrett felt for his car keys. As he dug through his pockets, he said, "Yeah, well you're forgetting your brother was there too."

I dangled his keys on my finger.

"I need those," he said.

"Come and get them," I said.

"You're fucking certified, Hill. *Psycho.*"

He remained where he was. His face and body language said he was done. If he'd had a white flag he would have waved it. I tossed him his keys and said, "If I see you or Grasp near Jarrod, or my house again, I'll fuck you up and put you in a box when I'm done. And as far as my brother goes, he'll wind up the same way if he's not careful."

Garrett picked his keys up from the walkway and massaged his jaw.

"I'll also go to the cops with that little bit of film footage," I said.

Garrett looked at me and narrowed his eyes.

"They'll join the dots right back to you, genius, and Grasp will just throw you under the bus."

"I'm gonna kill Grasp," he said.

"Yeah, good idea, smartest thing you've said so far."

He stood there and took a deep breath and patted the top of his head.

"Can I get my lid back?"

I took his hat off my head and tossed it to him. He put it on, turned and walked away.

"You've got it on backwards," I called to him.

He kept walking and flipped me the bird as he reached his car. I laughed and watched him drive off. I don't like people bothering me, showing up or calling on me unexpected. And I don't even *have* a cell phone, and if I did I would be the guy with no clue how to use the video function, but I was glad that Garrett believed I could.

I didn't sleep well that night. Garrett was a loser, but he fancied himself a criminal. I tossed and turned around murky dreams of him and three or four guys jumping me, taking the boots to me, or worse still, harming my mother.

After work the next day I went to Wild Wheels. Garrett's brother Damien owned the place and Garrett hung out there. I shook my head as I pulled up. *I live in the only town on earth where the local drug dealer spends his days pumping air into bicycle tires.* There were no words to describe how badly I wanted out of this hayseed dump. The stereo was on so loud it rattled the water bottle display on the front counter. Garrett was in the back, sitting on a plastic chair watching Damien tune-up a bicycle that probably cost a thousand bucks. He had it up on a stand so he could spin the pedals with one hand and spray some penetrating oil onto the chain with the other. Garrett stared at his brother intently; his facial expression was that of an ape, amazed at the ingenuity of his human counterpart.

I rang the bell on the counter and walked around it, and towards them both. Garrett stood up right away and looked to his brother—who was actually a pretty decent dude. His older brother stepped away from the bicycle and turned down the music. They both stared at me, but neither one spoke.

Finally, Damien very firmly said, "No customers back here. Sorry, staff only."

I stopped out of fighting or punching range and held out $50 to Garrett.

"What's this?" said Garrett.

"What does it look like?"

He stepped closer, keeping a close eye on me, as if I might detonate.

"If I wanted to hurt you you'd be unconscious by now, Garrett. Just take the fucking money."

"Just take it, bro, and then I want you to bounce, Stan. I don't want you in my shop," said Damien.

That disappointed me. I'd thought that Damien and me had a clean slate.

"You're jacked-up 24/7, fucking 'roid-raging, or something," he added.

"I'm not on 'roids," I said.

"Well then you're crazy, so drop the cash and leave, *please*."

Garrett took the money and counted it twice.

"It's two twenties and a ten, genius, it's not that difficult," I said.

I walked away and shut the lights off as I rounded the counter, leaving them in near darkness. Garrett called after me. His voice and choice of words just begging me to go back and crack his skull.

"I'm glad you came to your senses. I didn't want to see you get hurt!"

I inhaled and shut my eyes against the red blur edging its way across my field of vision. I stood by my Jetta with clenched fists and my eyes shut so tight my sinuses tickled. If I had gone back in there I might have demolished the entire shop, and beaten Damien and his primate brother with a tire pump or something.

"Hi, Stan!"

I opened my eyes to see a young kid on a bicycle stopped near the back bumper of my car. He was a nice kid, about fourteen years old. I'd coached him in rugby a couple of years ago, but I couldn't remember his name. He had always been a smiley kid and he was smiling at me now, which disarmed me and actually sent a wave of sadness straight up my spine.

"Hey buddy."

"Are you ever gonna coach again?"

"Yeah, I'm not sure about that."

"Coach Daniels needs an assistant," said the kid.

"I'm sort of doing my thing these days, looking to move down to Florida with my dad."

"Cool, will you coach down there?"

"Maybe. I have to get down there first."

The kid looked around and then eyed the front door of Wild Wheels.

"I need a repair kit for my tires," he said.

"What does that cost?"

"I think $10, but I'm not sure."

I took out my wallet and gave the kid a ten.

"Oh it's okay, Stan, my mum gave me the money."

"Go on, take it, since I'm not coaching rugby anymore."

He wheeled closer and took the ten.

"Thanks a lot, Stan."

I sat in my car and watched the kid lock his bike in the rack outside the shop and walk in. I could hear the music was back on. I liked the kid. I remembered he was good-natured—not the best player, but he'd played hard and listened to my advice. I started my car and pulled out, aimed it towards the factory and drove. Meeting up with that kid had calmed me. I thought about Jarrod and how we had never had any kind of rapport. I realized as I headed back to work that I was done with Jarrod. I had spent years trying to figure him out, and standing up for him. I was going to call it quits and leave him to become whatever he became. You control the controllable.

I thought of my dad and his life down south. The air near my father's condo in Florida is an amazing alchemy of scents. I like to sit on his balcony and inhale the surf, sand and the sweetness of sunblock and body lotion. The sun there burrows into you, warms you to the bone. The beer is cheap and my old man keeps it in a cooler, on his balcony, twelve cans each morning buried in ice. We pick at them all day and each one is so cold and perfect, especially the one we drink after we get back from the gym. We shotgun that one down as soon as we burst in the door. There's a sports bar and seafood restaurant across from my old man's place and on weekends we go to both of them. The servers smile and the kitchen help hoot, holler and laugh. One of the cooks at the sports bar sings along to the music and the waitresses yell for him to keep it down back there, and he laughs and sends out free baskets of garlic bread. Monday morning arrives and my dad is out of bed without an alarm. He's showered, fresh and making toast and coffee while I'm dragging my ass out of bed and then fumbling with my shave cream and razor. By Thursday I'm also up and ready to go at dawn. My father's enthusiasm for his business is infectious. We cruise to his office in an old Beemer he picked up cheap when he moved back. You can buy a pretty sweet car down there for next to nothing. No rust, no salt stains on the carpets, the cars down there all look brand new. Jimbo—which is what everyone calls my Uncle James—is a riot. People are drawn to him. He's my father's younger brother and he's big like my dad, except he doesn't care much for running or the weight room so he's heavy, and covered in tattoos. He's looking after the security guards while my father looks after the alarm installation part of the operation. Between the two of them they make a good team. Jimbo made it clear he also wanted me down there with them.

"Another year, maybe two, we get some critical mass," he would say, then grab his belly and give it a shake, "and we bring you down here. By then you'll know enough about the biz."

The year I turned nineteen I spent most of the winter down there. I celebrated my birthday with my father, Jimbo and some girls we met at the sports bar. And speaking of that, it's a nice change to be around women who actually talk to you. They have a confidence about them. Maybe it's because their hair is soft and smells like shampoo, and their shoulders and legs are bronze and smooth as glass. They're not stuck-up and they don't sit together in bars like a pack of sickly hens and cluck, and give you the stink-eye. They get up and walk around and mingle, sit at your table and tell you to keep the drinks coming. And nine times out of ten, they'll give you their number. Six times out of ten they'll come home with you. The odds on everything are better in my father's life.

That winter I got a good look at what my life would be like. I actually stayed with him a while. It wasn't a holiday where I just got my case unpacked and it seemed that I was stuffing clothes back into it and heading to the airport. I got into a rhythm, tasted the place, digested it, had it in my veins. It was a drag to come home. I was so bummed on the flight back I avoided eye contact with other males for fear I would wind up beating the shit out of one of them. I drank too much and fell asleep. When we landed I looked out of the little plastic window and saw piles of melting snow along the taxi-ways, and vehicle exhaust from snowplows and baggage trucks hitting the frigid air in dirty grey plumes. I sat back and said, "Shit."

The lady beside me hadn't said a word to me the whole trip, other than *hello* when she first sat down. She was older, maybe in her mid-sixties. She looked at me and said, "Funny, I was just thinking the same thing."

The air is dank in this town. It carries the faint resin odor of the factory and when that isn't creeping up your nostrils the place smells musty, like an old hoarder's basement. The beer does not taste the same and God bless the folks at Uncle Chow's, but getting back to town and walking in there is like walking into a Chinese morgue that just happens to serve garlic spare ribs and chicken-fried-rice. I've decided I won't go there anymore for fear I'll chug four or five cheap beers, wolf down a plate of noodles, and then slit my own throat.

Jarrod hadn't changed much in the time I was down south. He still lay on the couch much of the time. He'd rummage through the kitchen cupboards, unable to find what he was looking for. He'd wind up standing near the stove with this pained look on his face. If my mother was nearby he'd say, "No chips?"

She would sigh and say, "No, Jarrod, I buy two bags each week and when they're gone, they're gone."

One morning he staggered into the kitchen while I was chopping up some fruit and fixing some toast. He took the coffee pot, poured himself a mug and dribbled a trail of coffee across the counter-top. He slumped into his seat and slurped at his coffee like he was eating hot soup.

I'm good at avoiding eye contact with people and in doing so I probably reduce my number of physical altercations by around 70%. That morning I glanced over at him, and once I began looking, I couldn't stop. He was shirtless and unshaven. His hair hung in his face like the ropes of an old mop. When he sensed that I was watching him he shot me a narrow-eyed look and a brazen nod. That was it. I dropped my forearm and swept the knife, cutting board and the beginnings of a fruit salad off the counter. Jarrod had to duck chunks of flying pineapple and melon. I grabbed him and yanked him to his feet. He tried flailing his arms but I caught one and put a good squeeze on his radial nerve and that calmed him pretty quick. I shoved him over to the sink and pushed his head in there, turned on the water, snatched up the dish soap and splattered a good spoonful in his disgusting hair. I kneed him in the hamstring and he grunted and gasped while I worked the dish soap into his head. He called for my mother, but she had gone to work early. I laughed and wedged his skull under the tap. He tried to elbow me and I made him pay by hooking him in the liver. He let out a high-pitched squeal and went limp, muttering a string of profanity while I finished the job. When I had most of the soap rinsed out I rushed him to the living room and shoved him full-tilt onto the couch, which tipped over. I tossed him a tea towel.

"There, you little pussy, that would cost you fifteen bucks at Sal's Barbershop," I said.

He was doing this angry crying thing he did, trying to sound tough and resolved but weeping and spraying snot out of his nostrils while he threatened and yelled. I could swear he was a bastard at times like that. Wherever he came from, it wasn't the same gene pool as mine.

"I'm calling the cops," he said.

I put my knee on the tipped couch and got right in his face.

"You do that. And once they're gone I'll fuck you up beyond belief."

The next day after work, with the reek of hot metal and melamine in my clothes, and the sun and sounds of Clearwater in my mind, I arrived home to find the cops at our house. It was an annoying little gathering: my mother and Jarrod side-by-side on the love seat, she with a fake smile to hide the concern on her face, and he looking particularly smarmy. The cops were sitting together on the couch. One was a tall lanky dude with tight, curly hair named Palmer.

He talked in these ridiculous point form utterances. I would assume that people saw him as brief, succinct, yet eloquent, but I saw him as a dick. He and I had crossed paths before. The other cop was a woman, new, also tall, but with a wholesome, farm-girl face. She would have been hot if her body wasn't so stork-like. Palmer talked while the stork scribbled notes. He asked me to sit for a moment and so I pulled up a chair. He gave me the nice talk first, how he'd advised Jarrod of his rights; outlined the Criminal Code definition of assault. The stork joined the chat and advised of the array of social services available. Constable Palmer started back up: Domestic situations could be tough, challenging, but there was help. And then he drew his shoulders back and lowered his voice, gave me the speech and about the use of force. I kept my mouth shut and did my best to look chastened. There would be no charges this time around, he advised. Both cops stood up and their belts, holsters and keys groaned and jingled. Palmer reminded me that he'd used his discretion, and let me off easy. He glanced to Jarrod, who played along with a solemn nod.

When the cops had gone, my mother excused herself to start dinner. Jarrod left the couch with renewed energy. The most spring I'd ever seen in his sloth-like step.

"If you touch me again they'll come back and charge you, and guess what? You won't get to Florida if you have a criminal record. You won't get your papers."

He grinned and I averted my eyes; couldn't look at him. The idea that he and two cops had turned things upside-down had me boiling inside. I left quietly, hopped in my car and went for a drive. A fast one, a real rip through town, without a thought or care about being pulled over. I was sick and tired of it all.

Chapter 19: Warfield

Her phone rang in the mid-afternoon. It was Anderson. The station sounded busy; the phones were going off and she could hear someone shouting instructions in the background.

"Can you come in? It'll be O/T, only time and a half, but you probably already know that, listening to a scanner and all," he said.

"I shut it off, actually. But, yes I can come in."

"See Glendon at the command centre, just in behind—"

"I know where it is. I'm leaving now. Also, Ralph?"

"Oh, first name, she *must* want something!"

"The scanner, I bought it secondhand, I don't sit around, I would appreciate it—"

"I won't say shit to anyone, they already think you're loco."

"*Thanks,*" was all she could say.

"Except for me, War, I don't think you are. I'm on your side, especially if you're buying at Driscoll's on Friday."

"I'll buy you a boilermaker."

"Done. Go check in with Glendon, the old fart's juggling manpower right now."

Glendon was in a foul mood. He talked about the damaged rail cars as if someone had planned the whole mess just to keep him at work. She hitched a ride with him and two others. He dropped them off at different points around the perimeter. She wound up relieving a guy from the other platoon. He went by 'Buck.' She couldn't remember his real name. His cruiser was parked across Reynolds, blocking the north access to the new townhomes. The roof bar was old and didn't strobe. The lights made a clicking noise as they turned and flashed. She shut them off, put on the hazards and the spots, and stood outside, her butt resting on the cruiser's hood. There was no one around and the wind blew damp and cold. She could feel her face chapping, and she'd grown tired of standing. A pack of boys came by on scooters and skateboards. They were young, scruffy and all in need of a bath. The ringleader stepped forward and asked if it was true the neighbourhood was going to blow up.

"Probably not. We have to take precautions."

They seemed disappointed and left, the wheels of their contraptions squeaking or scraping the tarmac.

She got back in the cruiser and rummaged through the glove box. She opened the log and the second name she saw was *Barry Palmer*. He had just scribbled his name and *OK* in that day's entry. You were supposed to record the mileage, log the gas, mark an X in the Circle-Check box. Someone had changed *Circle Check* to *Circle Jerk*. Probably Barry. He liked breaking the rules, but denied it every step of the way. Sheila had seen how the Inspector and Superintendent looked at him, with concern and amusement all at once. They would likely be glad when he took that early retirement. A lot of them would. He pushed people's buttons. He was the type of guy that you loved to have on your side. If you didn't know him, he gave you as cold a shoulder as humanly possible, and if he disliked you, he was a menace. She had once told him he was a troublemaker. They were working together. They were also involved at that time. She had tried to avoid spending a ten-hour shift with him and get on another car, but they were all doubled up and the roster was booked. Sergeant Gable had looked at Sheila with his reptilian eyes.

"The paperwork's done. I'm not dragging guys off cars and getting into musical chairs. Why, you have a problem with Palmer?"

"No, sir."

"Then why are you still here?"

She walked toward the door as he muttered at her back.

"Unbelievable," he said, and then, "Fuckin' broads. I can stay home and get this shit."

She was fuming when she left the station. She let the door slam, knowing it would bother Gable, and didn't bother to look back. She stood in an alcove near the compound and let her temper settle before riding with Palmer. The first half of the shift was busy. They arrested a young offender for a break and enter. They did six traffic stops, the last one blew over and they booked him for impaired driving and went back to the station to confirm the roadside results and process him.

Palmer was interesting to watch. He was very friendly to the average Joe; helpful and good at conversation. He had been rough and stern with the young offender. He did small things, like grip the kid's forearm really tight. He was strong, Palmer was. He had a huge set of hands and wiry body. When he walked the kid to the station's side door, he kept stepping on the back of the kid's boots and tripping him, and then slowing and waiting while the kid regained his balance. He rolled his eyes as if the delays and clumsiness were the kid's fault. He gave the impaired driver a hard shove into the back of the cruiser. The guy was upset and choked back tears.

He told them he was sorry. He said his job required him to drive. He seemed like a decent guy and Sheila felt bad for him. She was going to explain that he might not blow over the limit once they hooked him up to the breathalyzer at the station. He claimed to have had only two glasses of wine and speculated that he'd failed the roadside test because he'd drank them on an empty stomach. Palmer spoke up before she did.

"Tell it to the judge. And shut the fuck up. I'm trying to listen to the radio."

He turned the radio up loud and drove, positioned at the wheel with a grin on his face.

Later on, around ten, it began to rain and the radio calls slowed. They were in a parking lot eating noodles out of take-out containers.

"You like to stir things up," she said.

He ignored her at first. He swallowed, took a sip of his green tea, and said, "That's because these are so tasty. I like plenty of hot sauce in there."

She waved her plastic chopsticks at him.

"That's not what I meant. Don't be awkward."

"Oh, are we about to have a domestic?" he said. He let out an evil snicker, took a napkin and wiped his mouth.

"I mean you like to antagonize, just a little."

"How so?"

"If you see a woman in a Porsche you drive right by, but you go out of your way to nail a guy in a Mustang or 'Vette."

He ate some more, put his head back and grinned while chewing. He had a nice profile. Regal.

"Two reasons: first, they're most likely to be causing trouble, or breaking the HTA. Second: I do it for you. A lovely woman like you might want to ditch an old man like me for a younger model."

"I wish you wouldn't say things like that."

"It's true. You'll grow tired of me eventually, or the other way around."

She ate her noodles. He could build you up and cut you down in a single sentence. First, he was self-deprecating, calling himself old, admitting that she was *lovely*, implying she was perhaps out of his league, and then telling her he might be the one to break it off.

"You know I'm teasing," he said.

"Yes." She stopped eating and covered her food.

"Sheila, we work on a department with three hundred and fifty sworn members. Everyone more or less knows everyone. If this is going to get complicated, dramatic . . ."

"It isn't."

"We're at *work* right now."

She turned on the map light and gave him a look.

"I *was* talking about work."

"No, you were talking about *me*. My sparkling personality. Let's keep it about work when we're at work."

"Whatever you say."

"One of the things I like about you is that you aren't clingy. You keep things casual, conversation included."

"I'm allowed to have an opinion. You pick on people."

"Who do I pick on? I'm supposed to be friendly with that little urchin we arrested? Breaking into a church and pissing in the hallway, right underneath a security camera? Make nice with the drunk in the Mustang? I pick on them if they've done something wrong. That's my job."

She shook her head. She didn't know where to start with him when it came to work. He was clever and knew how to play the system—he'd been at it for over twenty years.

"You pick on Stan Hill."

He stopped eating and sighed.

"Sheila, don't fall for his shit and listen to his blarney, please. He's got most of that town fooled; the hard-working boy toiling at the factory in a backward town. When the whistle blows he speeds to the library in that ridiculous car of his, walks in and feasts on great literary works he doesn't understand. And then it's off to the rugby pitch, or it *was* until he punched some kid's father in the face. And now his brother, ragga-muffin of the year, has vanished. Two others as well, all younger lads. And now we're giving Hill a second look. He's sly, he's violent, he looks down on everyone around him. He hated that brother of his. I think *who he is* begs for a closer look. So don't talk to me about Hill."

Sheila disagreed, but didn't want to argue. She believed Palmer was manipulating things. She was disappointed in herself as well. It was apparent that she wasn't good at separating work from her life outside of it.

Barry was easy, interestingly eccentric away from the job. He was just plain mean sometimes when he was on the job. They went back on patrol and she couldn't concentrate. She felt as if the conversation they'd had was a fight, and that it *was* personal.

She wanted to make up. She wanted to touch him, or lean over and kiss him. She closed her eyes and bit her lip, sat there like a lump. That's what her mother sometimes called her.

"Sheila, are you going to sit like a lump all day? Get out there and do something."

She caught Palmer looking at her.

"What?"

"You don't know what to make of me," he said.

She nodded.

"Watch the road. Just forget it," she said.

"Forgotten," he said.

He shook his head and pointed to a pick-up truck, a red dually with smoked glass and massive chrome rims. It ripped around Barkley Street on a red; didn't even slow down. Palmer chuckled.

"Now *that's* going to be an expensive right hand turn," he said.

She watched him maneuver the car and catch up to the pick-up truck. *A mean person,* she thought, and felt terrible for thinking such a thing. She was sleeping with him, after all.

Glendon's voice came over the radio and tugged her from her recollection. He advised that the Ministry of Environment had downgraded the threat. Some of the Fire Department apparatus was packing up. He told the officers on the perimeters that people might start showing up, wanting to get back to their homes. They were to keep the perimeters in place for another hour or two, just to be sure. Sheila spent the next hour turning residents back. Most were visibly tired and irritated, but said they understood, and turned around, headed back into town, or back to the community centre. Two guys showed up in a huge, black Caddy SUV. They were well-dressed and looked like TV show hit-men. They shut down the engine, got out of their mammoth vehicle and approached her. She didn't like their body language. The tallest one did the talking.

"So, what's the delay?"

"They need a bit more time to ensure the safety of the area, sir."

"Radio said the tankers were okay. No more threat."

"I understand that, but they have to double-check and get it right before they let everyone back in."

"So, the DJ on the radio knows it's safe, but you jokers don't?"

"We're following what the Ministry tells us. They're the experts and they say another hour, give or take."

"Yeah, this is all great, safety and blocking roads, but I've got a flight to catch tomorrow morning and I need to get into my house and pack."

"Another hour or so, sir."

He looked back at his friend, who wore mirrored sunglasses and was smiling like the whole thing was a joke. The tall man stood his ground and twirled his key ring on his index finger. There was a key and a small square remote. It had an emblem on one side and tiny rubber buttons on the other. The man stopped twirling it and, without looking, pointed it at the huge vehicle. The lights on the Caddy flashed. He made a sucking sound with his mouth and offered Sheila a final glance of disgust.

"Let's go," he said to his sidekick.

Sheila couldn't catch her breath. She saw the tiny remote in front of her face, still spinning around the man's finger, and then spinning without his finger, suspended on its own, defying gravity. She rushed to the cruiser and got in, locked the door just in time. Light disappeared. She went blind. She knew her sight would return, but it was still terrifying each time it happened. It hadn't been this bad, complete blindness, for a long time. She opened her eyes wide, stretched her lids with her fingers. There was only centrifugal blackness, and miles of it. She felt for the lever for the windshield wipers, turned them on just to hear the swishing sound they made. She was exhausted and could think only of her bed, crawling beneath the down-filled comforter at the end of her shift. The light would not return and the man's key remote was gone and yet still spun. She knew it was there in the darkness. She saw Barry Palmer, and she felt absolutely no affection for him. He was in his house, sitting alone by the fireplace, a small box on his knee. In the box a half dozen car remotes and keys. Square ones, oval ones, some with silver trim, expensive looking. He liked cars. He had mentioned he wanted to quit the force and sell them. He owned one car to the best of her knowledge. What was it? She'd driven in it. She'd paid no attention to the make. A Chevy maybe?

He had a double-garage, but just the one car, she was certain of it. Although she had seen a pick-up truck in there once when she'd first started going over there, hadn't she? His face was different, as he sat there, fireside, and examined the car keys. He wore an expression she'd never seen before. Okay, she didn't know him exceptionally well, but she'd seen him happy, concerned, angry, tired, excited and in ecstasy—if you could call his muted reactions during sex ecstatic. There was something juvenile about his facial expression.

The look in his eyes was that of an overindulged boy who'd just gotten away with yet another transgression.

The light seeped back. Outside it was as dull and dreary a day as she had ever seen, but she was glad for it. Sheila fought back tears. She looked around, for fear that some resident, or worse, one of her colleagues had just arrived and was watching her: the vacant, teary-eyed cop with a white-knuckled grip on the steering wheel of a parked cruiser.

"I am so tired of this," she said.

There was something else. She saw it as if viewing it from the end of a long, narrow tunnel. It pulled at her like sutures tug the skin around a laceration. She managed to shut it out. She longed to talk to someone, to attempt to explain what went on inside her head.

Without thinking, fighting as hard as she could to empty her complicated mind, she took out her cellphone, scrolled her embarrassingly short contact list and found Grace's number. Grace sounded cheerful when she answered. Leonard barked once in the background.

"You sound terrible. Did you catch a cold walking Len earlier?"

"No, I'm okay. They called me into work—the train derailment."

"You be careful. There's explosives on that thing."

"It's okay now, they are winding things up. The area is safe. Listen, Grace, when you saw Barry, my ex-boyfriend today, do you remember what car he was driving?"

"It was a nice car, a four-door, I think, but still racy looking."

"Do you remember what colour it was?"

"Silver," she said, without hesitation. "Shiny as a new tin can. It had smoky glass, too."

"And how was he dressed?"

"He looked sloppy, quite frankly. He was dressed young with a hood up over his head until he got to your front step and took it down."

"And you're sure it was him. Barry?"

"It was him. I watched him walk back and get in the car."

"Thanks, Grace. Thank you."

She pushed the cellphone's button hard and tossed it on the passenger seat. She dropped the cruiser into reverse and nearly slid off the road. She rammed it into Drive and the tires spun on the slick pavement as she sped off.

CHAPTER 20: THE PURSUED

He sat, as incredible as it was, just across and two parking spaces over from a police cruiser. Inside the black and white SUV, a young provincial copper in his own world, head down, writing diligently in his notebook, looking up periodically to scan his surroundings, but never really paying attention. He sipped his coffee, now stone-cold, and then threw the dregs onto the passenger seat. He felt a tantrum brewing. He started the car and drove out slowly, fighting the temptation to stop right in front of the police cruiser and do a brake-burn, smoke the cop out and *then* take off.

He wouldn't take anyone else, at least not like he'd taken the three. But he was thinking of one last thing; something he hadn't planned for, but the more he played it in his mind, the more it felt like unfinished business. His mind was a kinetic tangle; perfect plans forming, only to be replaced by memories, or fragments that he supposed were memories.

The first victim was supposedly a karate expert with belts and medals in two different styles. He had been standing in between the corn dog and hot pretzel concessions, checking his watch and looking around like the world, or the whole fair, owed him something. He wore a shirt with the Kanji symbol for karate stenciled on the chest.

He spat on the ground and although the ground was dirt and the young man stood beneath a portable, canvas big-top, he took offense to the young man's spitting and watched him, shadowed him for a little while. He moved like he was up to something, this young punk. This piece of shit. The kid entered the beer tent, sidled up to the long, temporary bar and bought a pint in a plastic cup. There was something about him, the way he swaggered. He put his keys and wallet on the bar, and propped his foot up on the rail, drank his beer like a cowboy in a low budget Western movie. So he sidled up to the bar as well and ordered a ginger ale. On this night he was wearing a black shell jacket with MEDIC printed along each sleeve in bright yellow letters. He had, in fact, worked for the ambulance service for a while, but found it gory, and the profession itself was populated by individuals who couldn't get into med school, and yet talked and carried on as if they were doctors, mobile surgeons just itching to break out any and all equipment they could possibly use on the unsuspecting moron on the stretcher. Any excuse to charge up the defibrillator, or tear open a foil pack of epinephrine. The short-lived job had had its moments though. Once, after completing a patient transfer to an out-of-town hospital, he donned a white cloak he'd snatched from the staff area and wandered into a corner room—701, he remembered the number. He acted like he was on his rounds and picked up the clipboard attached to a plastic line on the end of the gurney. In the gurney, a boy of about seventeen, messy-haired, very thin, barely filling his baby blue gown.

"How are you feeling?

The boy had been watching a small TV set that hung from a robotic arm near his bed. He blinked and rubbed his eyes. He talked slowly and deliberately.

"I think the anesthetic is wearing off, a little anyway. Is Dr. Gray not around?"

"He's taken some holiday time. I'll be looking after you for a while."

"Oh."

"I'm Dr. Mith, that's m-i-t-h rather than m-y-t-h, like the fable or story."

"Oh, good to meet you."

He glanced at the boy's chart and saw he'd had emergency abdominal surgery, a laparotomy. He also noted a box at the end of the chart that stated the boy was a *heavy alcohol and recreational drug user.* He put the clipboard down and stepped closer to the bed.

"Going cold turkey, I suppose."

"Huh?"

"You must be out of your fucking mind for a joint or a drink, or even a cigarette."

The boy looked at him and then at the TV, and then at his gown, which he adjusted to cover more of his bony legs.

"You're a doctor?"

"No, I'm a moron off the street who wandered in and found this outfit. I just *told* you I was a doctor."

"Okay, cool."

"So, am I right?"

"You have no idea," said the boy.

"Do you want a cigarette?"

The boy stared at him as if he were a madman.

"Fucking right."

He took out his pack, and his little plastic lighter and placed them on the food tray beside the bed.

"Help yourself."

"Uh, should I get wheeled outside?"

"No, this is a private room. I'll just open the window and close the door. You can use the cup as an ashtray. I'll get one of those bitches to get you a fresh one."

The boy smiled and took the pack in slow motion, pulled out a smoke and lit it.

"I have to run along, I'll come back for those. Smoke as many as you like."

"You're sure this is cool?"

"Absolutely. It's just a few cigarettes."

"Hey Dr. Gray can *stay* on holiday if you're the man in charge!"

"Yes, I am the man."

He opened the door to slip out to the corridor, but before he left he turned to the boy and said, "Between you and me, that Dr. Gray is a real asshole."

The boy laughed and smoke billowed from his nostrils.

"Yeah, totally," he said.

The beer-drinking punk at Skyward kept his eyes straight ahead and sipped his foamy pint.

"You practice karate, I see."

The punk swallowed and looked at him curiously.

"How do you know I don't just wear the T-shirt, like someone didn't give it to me?"

He placed his arm on the bar, rolled up the sleeve of his shell jacket to reveal his Judo tattoo.

"You move like a fighter. I'm a second degree black belt in Judo."

"Cool, yeah, it's all good. I`m like Goju-ryu and then some Shorin and some Kobudo stuff. I've been to a boatload of tournaments."

"Excellent, Kobudo. Weapons."

"For real. You did weapons? I didn't think a Judoka did weapons."

"No, I just like them, that's all."

"Cool."

"I wish I could drink one of those right about now, but I refuse to drink and drive," he said, looking at the punk's sweaty plastic cup.

"Yeah, I have to say it's going down well."

"Well, when I get home there's an entire fridge full waiting for me."

"Cool."

"Well, I should go, I'm building a Dojo right now. It's a lot of work."

"Really?"

He drank his ginger ale down and walked away. "Enjoy the fair," he said.

He'd taken the punk's car key and pocketed it in one smooth motion. He went to the parking lot, got in his own car and kept the beer tent in sight.

It was nearly 6 o'clock when the punk walked out of the beer tent and down a long aisle of parked cars. He put his own car in drive and drove slowly, the gravel crunching beneath the tires. The punk stopped at a Chevy pick-up truck and he watched the kid search his pockets for his keys, and then glance back in the general direction of the beer tent. He kept his distance and watched the punk eventually turn his pockets inside out. He was a lean, strong kid, a fighter, no doubt.

The kid tried the door of his pick-up truck, and then shook his head and leaned against the truck with body language that suggested frustration.

He took his foot off the brake and coasted over to the punk slowly. He lowered his window.

"Everything alright?"

"Yeah, I just had two pints, most of it was foam anyway."

"I'm not asking because of that. You look distressed."

The punk tapped on the window of his truck and closed his eyes for a moment.

"Lost my keys. I guess I'll go and hunt for them."

"I'll go with you. Hop in, I'll drive you back up there."

"Cool, thanks."

They did not find the keys of course. He left the punk talking to the bartender and pretended he knew the lady who ran the Lost & Found. He came back from his staged visit and reported no keys. No luck. The punk asked to use the phone to call a tow truck. He nodded and drew the punk away from the crowd of half-drunk men around the bar.

"I have a Slim Jim. I can run home and get it. It'll be Darcy's Towing and they'll charge you $60 to open your truck. Do you think you left your keys in there?"

"I might have. There's junk in there, so it's hard to tell. Could have dropped them on the seat."

"Why don't you come with me? I'm just around the corner. We can grab a real beer, get the Slim Jim and be back here in a half hour. Plus, I'm building that Dojo in my basement. I wouldn't mind getting an opinion on it. From someone who knows what they're talking about."

"Dude, that would be cool if it's not putting you out."

"Not at all."

The punk glanced around as they drove. The house was *a little* further than *just around the corner.*

"We're nearly there. I'll just come right out and ask you this: You don't teach, do you? I'll be damned if I can find a decent

Karate instructor. I'd like to do private and semi-private lessons. Grappling arts two days a week and striking arts for two days. I have a friend who can teach some wrestling. He was a good wrestler in his day."

"Yeah, dude, you know, I'm just here from up north for a bit. Supposed to meet up with a buddy, but he went and got himself married and she's studying, so he's helping her and trying to get out to see me. It's a train-wreck."

"Sounds like it."

He pulled into the driveway and hit the remote for the garage door. Once inside he hit the remote a second time and the door rolled down. They entered his house from inside the garage.

"This will take just a minute. My tools are downstairs, so we'll grab what we need and you can take a quick look at the Dojo, well, the beginnings of it."

He could see a confusion in the punk's eyes. He could sniff out confusion a mile away. The kid looked around and scratched at his neck. He walked slowly, cautiously.

"You're walking as if my floor is going to crumble beneath your feet."

The punk smiled and looked back down the hallway towards the door to the garage.

"Did you want a quick beer?"

"No, I'm good."

He opened the basement door and started down. He waved for the punk to follow him.

"Come on down, or wait there, it's up to you."

He reached the bottom of the stairs and hit the wall switches. The pot-lights came on row by row to reveal a comfortable room with a large sectional leather couch, a gas fireplace and huge wall-mounted TV. The TV came on, as did the short amber flames in the fireplace. He turned and watched the punk descend the last few stairs.

"I never asked your name."

The punk's face had changed. His jaw was set. His eyes were now two, apprehensive slits that sat just below his square forehead. The punk used his fingers to brush a strand of hair from his face.

Everything seemed to be happening slowly, far too slowly. He opened the door to the laundry room and walked in. The punk followed.

"It's Dale. So, are you like a medic at the fair, or what?"

"No, I used to be. Someone gave me this jacket."

"So are you security?"

He took his keys from his pocket and unlocked a narrow, metal door that opened inwards.

"My future Dojo," he said.

The punk stood in place, near the washing machine.

"Let me just switch on the light and you can give me your expert opinion."

He moved away from the door and made a gesture, the palm of his hand lifting toward the low ceiling.

"I made this myself. Dug it out and dry-walled it, put in the floor, which I'll cover with an athletic surface that I've just ordered. I will be putting in a back entrance. I wouldn't expect students to walk through my laundry room."

"Do you live alone?" asked Dale.

"I'm married. My wife is at work. She's a nurse. Also a black belt."

"Cool, so can we get the tool and get back to my truck?"

"Of course. You *don't* want to see the dojo?"

He heard Dale come up behind him and he stepped aside, and then slipped behind Dale. He watched over Dale's shoulder and enjoyed seeing what the punk saw, only the punk was seeing it for the first time: the room sat a good eight feet below floor level. There were no stairs. The walls were a clinical white and perfectly smooth. The floor wasn't a floor at all; it consisted of combed earth which made the room smell like a garden. He shoved Dale hard in the back. Dale flew forward and hit the dirt hard.

"What the fuck, dude?!"

He drew his Sig and fired three shots: two into Dale's chest and another into his head. The boy appeared to want to say something, object, or perhaps make a threat, but he flopped to the dirt instead.

It was a year before he took the second one. He surprised himself when he did. When he thought of Dale, he often thought: *Well, I'll never do that again.* In the intervening time he kept himself busy with smaller things, causing as much trouble as he could while attracting as little attention as possible. He even dated a woman, Claire, who worked at the community centre, but she asked too many questions and wanted to quickly insert herself into his life.

"When all I wanted was to insert myself in her," he said, and laughed.

He made a left turn and headed back towards the rural roads.

The second one was a lost soul, a loser with multiple ear piercings and a gold stud in his pug nose as well. He especially hated those. The boy was carrying a ripped satchel, wandering the dark parking lot at Skyward, checking car doors and peering inside.

"Why do I bother coming here?" he'd asked himself as he drove his own car up behind the kid and stopped. The kid turned and froze. He got out of the car and approached the kid. He was wearing his casual events jacket, a thin navy blue nylon thing that was neither warm nor waterproof. It had no shoulder badges, only P O L I C E written in white, reflective letters on the left side of the chest, and across the back.

Although it was hate at first sight, he was friendly to the kid.

"You lost? You okay?"

The kid walked toward him. He kept an eye on the boy's hands and body language.

"Hi. I wasn't looking to swipe a car. Honest."

"What are you doing then?"

"Are you security?"

He turned his flashlight on his jacket's reflective letters. The kid narrowed his eyes, and then said, "Oh, *shit*. I'm just looking for something to eat, for real."

"Something to eat?"

"Yeah, this morning I found a bagel with peanut butter on the seat of a van over there."

"And you ate it?"

"Well, yeah."

He laughed, and asked, "How do you know who prepared it? You have to be careful in this area. It might have been made by some farmer with cow shit all over his hands."

The kid studied his face for a moment and determined it was alright to laugh along.

"Are you from around here?"

"Not exactly. I'm two towns over, but I'm not getting along with my parents, so I'm following my thumb for a while."

"It's a tricky thing, parents and their children."

"Yeah, I know, right?"

He watched the kid and kept smiling, and thought: *Yeah, I know, right*. What on earth does that even mean?

"Why don't you hop in the car. I'll buy you a burger and drop you at the bus station afterwards."

The kid looked at the car and then at him. There was distrust beneath the boy's smile.

"The thing is, they don't want loitering here, especially at night. So, if you don't want the ride out of here, I'll have to write you up for trespassing."

"I'm not under arrest?"

"No, I just said I'd buy you some food and point you home, or further down the highway, whatever you like."

"Well, then I guess I'll take the ride."

"Alright then."

They drove out of Skyward. There were plenty of people around despite the dark. There was a fireworks display scheduled. He turned to the kid and said, "Oh no, that's my ex-girlfriend, duck for a second would you? She'll see there's someone else in the car and think it's a woman."

The kid ducked. He chuckled at the kid's passivity as they ripped away from the fair.

"Just stay down until she's right out of sight. It took me a month to break it off with her. Do yourself a favour and never date a nosy woman."

"Yeah, I know, right?"

The kid's name was Will, and once he got over the fact that he was with a cop but the cop wasn't using his 'police car' he became chatty and appreciative. He watched the kid load French fries into his face and nearly changed his mind. Perhaps he'd give Will some bus fare and send him off to find himself. But his pang of altruism quickly faded as Will dipped French fries into a pool of ketchup that he'd created on the outside of the fast food bag. He pictured Will, walking aimlessly, taking food and shelter wherever he could find it, and then perhaps taking a ride from another punk, and cooking up some scheme; a theft or robbery, something the two of them thought was clever, except that it would be anything but clever, and someone would be left seriously injured, or dead in the end. And Will would eventually stand, weeping, while his family sat in the courtroom and wiped tears as well. He would have a lawyer singing his praises: *a good boy, just a little troubled, but he's over that now. Never meant any harm. Led on by the treachery of others.* The courts and prisons were full of nice boys suffering from lapsed judgment, or nasty friends. Poor kids. Pieces of shit.

Will had a banged up laptop in his satchel. The battery was low and the charger wasn't working. They went back to the house on the pretense there was an extra AC adapter there, same brand, just sitting around gathering dust.

"You might as well take it. That way you can keep in touch with your parents. They must be worried about you."

"You're not gonna report me as missing, or take me back to them?"

"How old are you?"

"Nineteen next month."

"Well then unless you've broken the law I can't take you any-where. In fact, I can pull off here and you can hop out and be on your way, but you won't have the power cord and I just might have a spare bus pass in my desk at home."

Will smiled as if he wanted to ask: *Why are you being so nice to me?* But he didn't. He sipped at his drink, biting on the end of the straw and looking out the window as they drove.

Will set his laptop on the kitchen table. He had little interest in his surroundings; a trusting soul.

"I'll go and get the power cord. In the meantime you should let your parents know you're okay. Tell them, what was it you

said? 'You're following your thumb for a while.' You should have
enough power left to do that."

"Okay," said Will.

"Help yourself to a drink from the fridge. There's beer. I'll
go and find that cord."

The gunshots to Dale's head and chest the prior year had
made a bloody mess. He'd had to remove, replace and re-tape the
drywall. And then there was new primer and paint, and he cursed
himself for opening fire on the punk and creating hours of work.
But he'd brought a 15 amp circuit to the room where before there
had been no power. And he'd installed a proper vent. He'd listened to his favourite blues CD while he worked. When he'd finished the wiring he placed a fan in the room and set it on low
speed to move the air.

He returned to the kitchen with a ligature he'd fashioned out
of plastic-coated cable and two plastic shovel handles tied securely
at either end. He did not want any more blood, and so he rushed
Will from behind and had his neck wrapped up before the boy
even reacted.

He dragged Will to the basement room, turned the crank to
drop the new steel staircase and carried him down. He spread
Will's fingers and pried off his tarnished skull ring. He tugged
loose the earrings and nose stud, along with a bent house key
from the boy's pocket, and dropped them in a brass bowl in the
corner of the room. The various rings and studs tinkled as they
fell onto one of Dale's rings, wallet chain and empty money clip.

He built a fire later on and sat nursing a large glass of Merlot
while Will's wallet shriveled in the flames and his laptop warped,
melted, popped, and filled the room with an unpleasant, chemical
odor for a few minutes. He sipped his wine and tried to catch his
breath. He was nervous this time around, and he rose and wandered his cozy, tidy home, checking the blinds and curtains and
ensuring that the doors were locked. He returned to his chair and
turned on the TV.

I won't do that again, he thought, and he inhaled and held
his breath to fight back tears. They ran down his cheeks in spite
of his efforts, but he did not sob, or sigh, or do that ridiculous

hiccup, hitching thing people do when they were overcome with sadness. He wasn't entirely certain why he was crying, other than he'd pictured Will's parents in a hospital room with an opaque curtain drawn around them. There was a doctor in there with them too. He was young and sported a fashionable haircut and he conducted himself as if his profession had taught him to heal and find comfort for the ill and diseased, but to look down on them as well. The doc was tired and rubbed his sore eyes as he told Will's folks their son was dead. He stood and waited for them to react, and when Will's mother lost her legs, nearly fainted, and Will's father held her up, the doctor left the room.

Chapter 21: Stan Hill

Jarrod has a way of balancing expertly between surly and sorrowful. When he left a room, he managed to change the atmosphere. He left in his wake a vapor of sadness and disdain. And when he vanished, disappeared in early November, he left behind consternation and sadness for my mother, and a dull worry and relief for me. My worry was for my mum. My relief was for getting a break from his shoe-gazing, the-world-is-against-me attitude. I think my mother immediately saw my relief, and she misread it. She picked up the phone one night, after she'd had some wine and shed some tears, and called distant relatives, and then called my father to yell at him about selfishness and responsibility. And then she made one last call, sipped her wine, popped her Darvocet, ran her mouth and started a shit-storm that threatened to trap me in this backward-ass town. She *called* the *cops*. She told them, fueled by cheap Chardonnay and pain medication, that her oldest son Stanley *might know* more than he's letting on. *Thanks*, Mum. Excellent move and totally ignorant to the fact that I have a short-list of people I would love to see vanish, and Jarrod *isn't* on it. He doesn't even rate!

The cops had been to our house a couple times after Jarrod disappeared. We were late calling them, and I wore that one. My mother didn't talk to me for days when the police arrived and asked why we had waited three days to call them. I told them that Jarrod was aimless, and hopeless at keeping in touch. He'd take off for a day and then sleep over at Clancy's place and I'd have to drive over and confirm his whereabouts, and give him shit for worrying my mother. He'd had a so-called job that he ditched to go wandering around town without letting anyone know. He wasn't the most reliable lad. Palmer and the Stork sat me down and asked if I could shed any light on things: where he might have gone, and why? I told them what I could, which wasn't a lot. At one point, Constable Palmer tapped his pen impatiently on his little notebook and said, "This is your little brother. Your poor mother is worried. You don't seem concerned."

This cop, this Palmer, sends the gauge on the dickhead meter higher each time I see him. He feigns that he's just doing his job, serving and protecting. But he enjoys inconveniencing people. I can see it in his eyes.

He once pulled my buddy Graham over. Graham drives a pretty sweet A-4 that he fixed up. Palmer's usually out in the boondocks lurking on some country road with a radar gun. Graham told me that Palmer was an epic ass-wipe that day. Graham said that he told Palmer he didn't think he'd been doing 30 clicks over the limit. Palmer started slapping the radar gun like it was someone's face and then he'd push some buttons and show the reading to Graham, and each time it would be higher.

"How would you like me to write this for 75 over and take away your license, you moron?" he'd told Graham.

Palmer was staring at me, awaiting my answer. I had been daydreaming about what a dolt he was. So I answered him: "Why don't you fuck off, dude, *seriously*. You don't know anything about me or my family."

Palmer grinned and stood abruptly, and left the room. The Stork looked at me curiously and politely told me if I thought of anything else to give them a call.

My first meeting with Detective Kyle McVeigh took place on my driveway. He'd driven up behind me as I pulled in from work. He was a short man, but walked like a tall man. I think the cops made a mistake when they eliminated height requirements, and it's Joe Public that pays for it. There are a lot of cops out there with Napoleonic Syndrome now. McVeigh was a small dude who wasn't good at small talk, which was fine because neither was I. So we got along for the first twenty seconds. He wanted to know of my whereabouts, a step-by-step account of how I spent my time the day before and the day after Jarrod hit the road. He was quick to point out that I had also been at Skyward the same day as Jarrod. McVeigh also had it on good authority that I'd been with someone and that we'd been filming at Skyward. That was true. Me and my buddy Scott had been there. Scott was back in town on a break from college. He had some camera equipment. I had gone with him for a laugh. I had put on an oversized plaid shirt and some denim overalls. I wore a straw hat and Scott's sister had given me freckles by dotting brown eye-liner all over my face. She also gave me this set of fake buck teeth that looked pretty convincing. All three of us were on the floor laughing once she had finished the makeover.

Scott and me drove to Skyward and I walked around the fair asking people questions, laying on an over-the-top hick accent and telling people my name was Willie Tuck Maynard III, and *wasn't Skyward the greatest dang fair for miles around?* Scott filmed me and he was jacked with the footage. The people I approached seemed to really like talking to me—now there's a *big* surprise. I had no idea what Scott would do with an hour of me goofing on the locals—without them even realizing it. As it turned out, Scott did nothing with it. It was practice for him, and a chance for us to get out together. The cops had an idea of what to do with it though. Detective McVeigh wanted the camera and the footage. I told him to go and see Scott. He was the producer and director. I was just a lowly thespian.

"That means *actor,* by the way," I told Detective McVeigh.

"I'm aware of what it means," he said.

"Sure you were," I said.

He left and gave me the stink eye the entire time he backed his fading Taurus out of the drive. I was hoping he'd back into Mrs. Darling's fence across the street. She was almost eighty and had gone from absent-minded, that gentle senility that old ladies have, to batshit crazy. She had these cheapo security cameras on her veranda. If McVeigh had dinged that fence she would have been out of the house like a flash and swung a broom at McVeigh. I would give 2–1 odds that an idiot like McVeigh winds up shooting her and then he's on the national news, which would have been awesome. Unfortunately, he saw the fence while also staring me down, and he dropped it into drive, and away he went. I called

Scott and we figured he'd let McVeigh have the camera. There was nothing incriminating on it. And if he was looking for footage of Jarrod he was shit out of luck because we never saw him that day. Me and Scott decided to make McVeigh's access to that camera as awkward as possible. Scott told me he was a busy man, hard for a person to track down, especially if that person was a cop. We had a good chuckle about that.

I worked as many hours as I could and when I wasn't at the plant I stayed out of trouble and read a collection of Chekov I'd found at the used book shop—a hardcover, thick as a brick with gilded letters, for $4. You can't beat that.

A guy like McVeigh finds you like a virus though. He's one dimensional. He's walks like he's jacked from weightlifting, but the funny thing is he's not ripped. I doubt he even pushes any iron. He wears his hair in an undercut, trying to hide the fact he's a cop, which is fine, but then he should lose the flavour-saver mustache, the blue blazer stained with doughnut sugar, and stop wearing khaki pants with spit-polished hobnail boots. I suggested this to him once and he looked down the front of his blazer, rubbed his thumb on a faded, white stain on his jacket's lapel and then said, "Why don't you mind your own business?"

He's a shiny-faced dude and probably has to watch his weight. There is a definite Humpty Dumpty gene lying dormant in McVeigh's five-foot-six body. He and I now hate the sight of each other. He told me that I think I'm smarter than everyone, which is true, at least in this inbred little corner of the world. But our inability to get along is also because he's stupid. And I told him this right to his face one afternoon when he showed up at the plant to ask me some questions on my lunch hour.

"Oh, I'm a lot smarter than you'll ever be," he said.

"No you're not."

"Yes I am."

"Really? Which way does the Niagara River flow?

"South."

"Wrong. North."

He shook his head and drummed his fingers on the steering wheel of his Taurus.

"Who was Thomas Paine?" I asked.

"Who?"

"Thomas Paine."

"I don't know."

"He was one the founding fathers of the United States. One of the first political activists. He wrote a book, more of a pamphlet, called *Common Sense* that influenced—"

"Yeah, yeah, alright, so you kept your high school history books."

"What does *vapid* mean?"

He squinted and waved a hand out the window, towards the sky. "To do with *this*, air and atmosphere and so forth."

"Wrong. It means *stupid*."

His jaw went tight and he put on his sunglasses.

"Okay," he said. "Who was Sir Robert Peel?"

"A British Prime Minister that founded the first organized police force."

"*Fuck* you, Hill. Just because you have a bunch of facts stored in your head doesn't make you smart."

"Yeah it does."

"I don't have time for this," said Detective McVeigh.

He rolled up his window and drove off. And then his brake lights flared and his back-up lights came on. I stood outside the plant, near the picnic tables and waited for him.

"If you're so good with *facts* maybe you'd better get them straight about your missing brother."

He drove off before I could answer. McVeigh likely finished at the bottom of his class in school, but he is single-minded. A dog with a bone. I knew he wasn't going to back off. I called my father and updated him. My old man said to be careful about antagonizing McVeigh. It might be fun to do it, but don't get on his bad side. It was a little late for that. He also told me they would have enough business to justify bringing me down there in about six months, so hang tight and never mind the pissing off the cops. Control the controllable.

I saw McVeigh's car around our part of town more often than I would have liked. A week after our little game of curbside

Jeopardy, McVeigh was at my door, flanked by a big cop named Cornish, a local who had joined the department and had played rugby in high school. Cornish and I knew each other; had briefly played on the same team. McVeigh gave me a nasty smile, as if to convey that Cornish was on *his* side now.

"We'd like you to come down to the division and answer some questions," said McVeigh through his smirk.

"About what?"

"Don't mess with us, Hill."

"Am I under arrest?"

"No, but I thought you had nothing to hide. I thought you were ultra-intelligent. That's what you were telling me the other day."

"I never said I was *ultra*-intelligent. I said that you were stupid."

McVeigh looked to Cornish with a sort of *you see what I've been putting up with?* face. Cornish nodded and looked at me as if I were a misbehaving child.

"Alright, let's go," I said. "I'm blowing out of here for Florida in a few months, so we might as well get this over with."

I rode in the back seat and watched Cornish through the steel mesh. He was getting fat. His neck was fleshy and he'd acquired a double chin since I'd last seen him.

"Hey Cornish, you playing any rugby these days?"

He put his enormous skull back near the mesh to answer. He still had a cauliflower ear on his left side.

"Nah, I got no time. What about you?"

"I wish. I haven't played or coached in a while. How about the gym? You pushing any iron?"

McVeigh cocked his head toward Cornish and rudely interrupted our little chat. "Don't talk to him. He's not interested in rugby or the gym, he's going to make some smart-ass joke."

Cornish took his head away from the security screen and McVeigh gave me a stupid smile in the rearview. I ignored him.

"Hey Cornish, is your father still working at the refinery?"

"Yeah, but he can retire in two years. Hey, I heard your old man has is own company or something?"

"Yeah, down in Clearwater. I'm going down there to work for him once he snags some more contracts."

"Beauty," said Cornish.

McVeigh smiled as we pulled into the police station. "We'll see about that. We need to *clear* some things up before you head to *Clear*water."

I hated McVeigh with all of my heart at this point.

"That's clever. Did you learn that on Hawaii Five-O?"

"I don't watch TV," he said.

"Hey, look at that *vapid* sky," I said.

I pointed out the window and they both actually looked. I laughed pretty hard at that. McVeigh went all crazy-eyed. Cornish was oblivious.

We drove into the sally-port and McVeigh rammed the car into Park.

"We'll see how *funny* you are inside," he said.

They had the whole thing set up and waiting for me, and I have to admit that while I had nothing to hide, I was nervous seeing the bare concrete-block room painted in a hospital green; the plain, thick-legged table with the tape machine on it; the three plastic chairs and the heavy door with the obligatory security glass window. McVeigh obviously had no leads—nothing that would guide him to what really happened. He was dealing with thin air. He wasn't looking anywhere else. He had set his sights on me. This became obvious as I wandered in to that damp, concrete room.

The interview went pretty much as I expected at first. McVeigh took off his doughnut jacket and hung it on the back of a chair. He directed me to sit across from him, and Cornish closed the door and stood like a sentry. McVeigh rolled the tape and had me state my full name. He then asked me where I had been on the day Jarrod disappeared. I told him I'd had the day off, and that I was going to stay at home and rest, but that my buddy Scott was in town and had called and asked me to ride along to Skyward with him.

"So you were at Skyward Fair that day, the seventh?"

"Yes."

"Did you see your brother that day, at Skyward fair?"

"No I did not."

"You were there how long?"

"About two, maybe two and a half hours."

"Two and a half hours at a non-peak time, walking around with a video camera and you never saw him?"

"No, and I wasn't handling the camera. It belongs to Scott."

"Fine. And what were you doing there that day?"

"I was helping him film something, sort of a joke documentary. You'd have to ask *him* about it."

"We will. We have. But you were in disguise. Is that correct?"

"I don't know if I would call it a disguise."

McVeigh opened up a folder and took out a photo. It was a screen grab of me from Scott's video. There I was, all dressed up like a hick: lopsided hat, buck-toothed, smiling at the camera.

"I am showing you a photograph. Is that you?"

"Yes."

"Taken at the fair on the seventh of November?"

"Yes."

"Is that representative of how you typically dress?"

"No."

"Would you say you are in disguise, then?"

I'd had enough of McVeigh. The urge to punch him was so strong that I'd placed my hands under my knees. I decided that I would stop answering him, but his face, the look of satisfaction and victory all over it, was enough to make a monk want to shout.

"You were walking around Skyward making fun of the patrons and in disguise. That's essentially what you were doing that day. Is that correct?"

"Is there a law against that?"

"Just answer the question, please."

I sat back and crossed my arms over my chest.

"What time did you leave the fair?"

I smiled at him, but didn't speak.

"While you were there that day, did you argue with security when they asked you to leave?"

Still, I did not answer.

McVeigh pushed the STOP button and stood, walked the cramped room. He was pissed. Cornish stood guard, but looked uncertain. McVeigh stood on his toes and looked over at the tape machine, making sure it was off. He walked and ran his finger along a groove in the wall.

"I'm just gonna come out and tell you, Hill, that you'd better answer my fucking questions because you know what? Things don't look good for you right now."

He pivoted on one foot and swung around to face me.

"It was your own mother who called us."

"My mother is stressed. She's upset. She dotes on Jarrod—"

"She *dotes* and you *hate,* from what I can tell."

"I don't hate him. He's my kid brother. He's lazy. He gets—"

"*You told* Garrett Petit that if he didn't watch his step you would put him in a box and do the same to your brother. This was after you knocked out Garrett on your front steps."

"We'd had a fight. He came around looking for trouble, acting all mafia. You say shit when you fight. You've never been in a fight?"

"That's true, you say things, heat-of-the-moment things during a fight, but you seem to have an issue even when you're not fighting. A habit of telling people how badly you're going to hurt them, *fuck them up,* and you also seem keen on the idea of putting them in a box, or making them disappear."

"That's bullshit."

"Is it? Timothy Clancy told us that Jarrod was very scared of you. Apparently, you had told Jarrod you would maim or kill him on several occasions, including one, recently, where Jarrod took three cans of beer from the fridge in your garage. When you caught him you grabbed him by the scruff and laid out a plan to drown him in the river and fix things so he'd never be found."

"Clancy is a flake and that's hearsay. You're relying on what that flake says. You didn't hear it from Jarrod."

"Maybe, but Clancy has detailed accounts of your brother's fear of you. Clear and convincing recollections."

McVeigh leaned on the wall beside Cornish, and looked to the ceiling as he spoke.

"So, I've got several people who confirm you regularly threaten with bodily harm, or death. You've hit several people and *somehow* avoided an assault charge. Your mother reluctantly tells us you are angry, hot-tempered, and that you were at odds with Jarrod. I have you walking around at the fair in disguise the day Jarrod goes missing, and you don't seem all that upset, or anxious about any of it."

McVeigh came over and sat down, beside me this time.

"So, if you look at things from my perspective, you can see how it might be best if you took this seriously."

"You're not relying on the most upstanding citizens. Garrett and Clancy are idiots. I have a job, pay taxes, contribute something towards the economy. I can read *and* write."

"What about Norm Gregory over at the IGA? He can hardly walk. His legs are so bad he drives back and forth from the store on one of those rechargeable scooters. You went storming into his office and threatened him too, didn't you?'

"Yeah, that's right, but I was *standing up* for Jarrod, by the way. There was a misunderstanding."

"And you dealt with it by nearly knocking Norm Gregory out of his chair? He's an old, disabled man, waiting on a disability pension."

"Gregory isn't disabled or old. The only disability he has is too many beers and frozen pizzas."

Cornish chuckled at this and McVeigh stood up and gave him a look. "What are you doing?"

Cornish shuffled his feet. "Nothing."

"So shut up, or stand outside then," said McVeigh.

I began laughing and McVeigh turned on me, placed his hands either side of the table and leaned in and blasted me.

"This really is a *joke* to you, huh?"

I didn't answer him.

"You have an anger management problem. You have a superiority complex."

"That's not a difficult thing to develop around here."

"Yeah? Such a terrible place this place, huh? A quiet town with a nice main street, lots of green space, an arena, a library, five different churches, a synagogue, a low crime rate. That's why you go around telling people you're going to *fuck them up*, I guess?"

"You make it sound like I travel the countryside threatening people on a daily basis."

"Just about everyone I talked to is scared of you. You told Del Brooks you'd kill him."

"I never said I'd *kill* him."

"Really? Why is it that everyone I talk to associates you with threats and violence and yet you sit here playing the nice guy? You *never* told Brooks you'd kill him?"

"I think Sasquatch will beat me to it," I said. I chuckled. I knew it wasn't a bright thing to say, but I couldn't help myself.

McVeigh scratched his head and sighed, and then left the room, slammed the door.

For the record, Del Brooks is a headcase. Not the dangerous type, but the monotonous, pain-in-the-ass type. Del used to work at the plant, but retired a couple of years ago. We were glad to get rid of him. He did nothing and filed a grievance about every little problem in order to maintain his do-nothing status. When Del retired they got him a cake and we all signed a card and brought him into the lunchroom. He ate three huge slices of the cake and went home with a sick stomach that afternoon—that's the level of intellect you're dealing with. These days he sits in Donovan's Tavern at the end of the main drag. He's always there, at the bar, making a pest of himself and retelling the same moronic story about the night that *changed* his life. We've all heard it at least twice and if you're a regular at Donovan's you've heard it thirty times. Just after Del retired he was in the local newspaper. He'd been driving along one of the concessions at dusk when, according to him, something stepped into the path of his truck. Del slammed on the brakes and this thing, this creature, stood in the road and stared him down. And guess what? This was no black bear or buck. This was a *Bigfoot*. Del honked the horn and yanked open the glove box for his camera—which he just happened to have loaded and ready. By this time, the Bigfoot had been frightened by the blast of Del's horn and high-tailed it into the woods lining the concession, but not before Del snapped a picture. The photo itself is basically a murky blur, framed by the passenger side window of Del's pick-up truck. If you stare hard enough you can make out the roadside, and in the gloom there is a shape near the trees. It doesn't look like a creature. Some people thought it was a bear. To me it always looked like a dark gap in the trees and bush. Del insisted it was Bigfoot and the Tribune did a full page article that featured Del's blurry photo and another of Del standing on the roadside in daylight, looking all determined and pointing to the approximate spot where the Bigfoot thrashed back into the woods that night. I am not convinced there is an undiscovered species of primate living in North America, camping out deep in the forest and wandering into towns after dark to forage around the dumpster at Burger King, or stand in the middle of the road flipping the bird to cars or trucks. But *if* there is such a creature, it lives in the Pacific Northwest; not here in the brush and woods backing onto a manufacturing plant. So Del Brooks did not see Bigfoot. Del Brooks saw a dark gap in the trees, and has too much time on his hands, and a brain the size of a walnut.

Detective McVeigh re-entered the room. He tossed me a bottle of water. I stood up to leave the interview.

"Where are you going?"

"I'm leaving. I'm not under arrest, am I?"

"But you're smart, remember? Way smarter than me. If you were smart you'd stay here and finish this."

I sat back down.

"Where were we? You threatened Del Brooks. Let's talk about that a little," said McVeigh.

I had gone into Donovan's for a beer. I rarely go in there, but I'd had a shit day at work, it was raining and cold, and I was thinking of Florida. I saw Del at the bar turning a half-empty pint glass in his hand. I intentionally sat at the other end and ordered a beer and a shot of rye to warm me up.

"How are you, Stan?"

I gave Del a nod and sipped my beer, and watched a tennis match on the TV above the bar. Within a minute Del had wandered over and taken the stool beside me. I ignored him. He tried to talk shop.

"I heard Terrence left. Are they gonna replace him?"

I shook my head and watched the TV, wishing the volume was louder.

"Bad day? I guess every day is a bad one over there. I don't miss it I'll tell you."

I shook my head and downed my shot.

"Chris, get Stan here another, on me," said Del.

"I'm okay, I don't need another."

Chris the bartender brought over the bottle and free-poured me another shot, right up to the brim. Del Brooks gave us both a satisfied look. He winked and tilted his head to the filled shot glass, pointing out the generous pour, that he had some weight at Donovan's. I took the shot glass without spilling it and drank it down.

"Thanks," I said.

Del finished his beer and had Chris draw him another. Two guys from the post office came in and took a table near the dartboards. Apart from them we were the only people in the place. Del sipped his beer and let out an exhausted sigh, and then: "Yup, that was a night I'll tell you. A night I'll not soon forget."

I kept my eyes on the TV.

"You look at life differently once you've had an experience like that," said Del.

Still I kept my mouth shut and watched the players fire the ball back and forth in a volley that didn't miss a beat. I wondered why I'd never tried tennis. Maybe I'd take it up once I got down to Clearwater: find a girl and that's what we'd do on weekends, play some tennis, among other things . . .

"You know what I'm talking about right, Stan?"

I sipped my beer and watched a player hesitate on her backhand. She let the ball whiz past her. It went out of bounds, and she went down on one knee and pumped her fist. The crowd yelped with surprise as she gambled and watched the neon ball touch the court just an inch outside the line.

"You never believed me. It's okay. It doesn't offend me. I *know* what I saw. The town knows what I saw."

"Bigfoot doesn't exist."

"He does though. I saw him."

"*Him?*"

I took out my wallet and left some cash for the beer.

"You have to go deep in the woods. That's what I've been doing. I'll prove it. I'm ready this time. I have provisions," said Del. He rapped his knuckles on the bar.

I poked Del on the shoulder. I'll admit I got in his face.

"There's *no* such thing. And if you talk this shit around me again *I'll take* you deep into the woods and you *won't fucking* come out. Got it?"

Del stared at me, obviously insulted. Chris the bartender came over and took the cash off the bar.

"Take it easy now, Stan? I mean, no one knows for sure, right? Who's to say that it doesn't exist?"

"Cool your jets, Stan," said one of the post office guys.

McVeigh was right. I had left a trail of threats, ugly ones, all over town. I didn't belong here, in this room, with this detective and his sidekick Cornish—a guy who in high school was a complete dolt and copied other people's tests so frequently they shut him in the principal's office during exam time. McVeigh sat staring at me with a satisfied look on his shiny face. Cornish glanced my way and the look he gave me said I was screwed.

Chapter 22: The Pursued

He drove the speed limit now. It was late afternoon and the sun had begun to pierce the cloud which had sat above him like wet concrete for much of the day. The gas gauge was below a half tank. He pulled off the road and drove a rutted laneway; a feeling of familiarity, quickly replaced with a stampeding happiness, as he rounded a potholed bend to discover an abandoned home surrounded by huge, dormant trees. The place was drab and vacant and yet his elation caused him to shut his eyes and drag his faulty memory. He lowered the window, shut the engine down, listened to it tick and hiss as it cooled. He lit a cigarette and blew the smoke towards the derelict home.

He watched the house for signs of life, wishing that its paint was not peeling, its roof gutters were not overgrown with weeds and vine, and that its front windows were not shattered. It had been a radio call, some years back. A child choking. Urgency in even the dispatcher's voice as she announced the call and confirmed that fire and ambulance were responding. He'd been down the road on Concession 14, no more than three miles away. He'd pulled over two plaid-shirted, mouth-breathing apes in a primer-covered Saab. They'd done nothing wrong, but he looked their car over and asked the driver to pop the trunk latch. One of the apes had argued, called out that he knew his rights as the trunk clicked and he opened it up, and rooted through the contents: hockey equipment that reeked of body odor, an empty pizza box, corroded jumper cables. He took his mag-light and popped a hole in the taillight; the plastic had snapped easily. He'd gotten back into the cruiser to write them up for a busted taillight—the best he could do to ruin their knuckle-dragging day.

The call had come over while he was filling out the top portion of the summons. A toddler choking. The address had five digits, so it was rural, and he looked northward out the passenger side window of the cruiser. His gut coiled and his heart leaped when he realized the choking child was just up the road. He tore out of the concession, leaving the apes round-eyed and confused in their car. He did 190 up the rural road and expertly pressed the brakes as he reached the vicinity, squinting for the address. A young boy stood near a mailbox up ahead, violently waving his arms. His name was Ted. He turned out to be the choking toddler's brother. He was out of the cruiser and up the front steps in several, long, athletic strides. The mother was red-faced and distraught, and stabbed her finger towards a little child on the couch. She shouted that he'd swallowed a ball, a toy ball. The child wore only a pair of boxers, little airplanes and helicopters printed on them. His pudgy legs were stiff, his toes curled downwards. His face was twisted, his eyes alive with fear and shock. His skin was ashen, and his mouth was open. He picked up the child, its bony chest against his trembling palm. He tensed his forearm and used his free hand to strike the child on the back, dead between his little shoulder blades. He did this twice and worried that if he struck any harder he'd break bones. The little boy would have a bruised back as it was. He thumped a third time and a white object—a miniature ping-pong ball—shot from the little boy's mouth, bounced off the floor and up onto the cushion of a nearby chair. He sat the child on the edge of the couch and held the toddler steady while the little fellow took huge greedy breaths and began to cry.

"Don't cry. You're a brave boy. Fill those lungs with air."

He moved to one side in order for the child's mother to take over. There was noise and the clomping of boots in the front hall. The brother guided in two firemen. The first approached the couch with an orange Flynn pack in hand. He spoke without taking his eyes off the boy.

"He's breathing now."

"Ping-pong thing, a toy. I knocked it out a few seconds ago."

The fireman nodded and opened up the resuscitator, began rooting through oxygen masks, each one in a little plastic bag.

He went to the dining room table to sit for a moment and get the family name and some basic information from Ted, who seemed keen and excited by the commotion, now that his little brother was gulping air and the colour was returning to his face. The ambulance crew arrived next, along with the toddler's father.

The father was well-dressed, a tall, important looking man in a black suit. His brow was knitted and sweat-covered. He looked at his wife and little son and wiped his ridged forehead, and asked, "What happened?"

His wife explained, assisted by the her oldest son Ted when she stopped to sniffle, or her words failed her. Her husband glanced around the room, noted the little ping-pong ball on the chair. He walked to an area near the TV and gently kicked some toys off to one side. Among the toys was a plastic rifle with a mesh bag containing white plastic balls attached below its barrel. The father said, "Teddy! Take this and put it in your room." He pointed to his youngest boy and said, "He shouldn't be anywhere near it!"

The fire department packed up and left. The ambulance crew checked the boy, peered down his throat with a little medical flashlight. One of the paramedics took the child's blood pressure.

"You should be keeping a closer eye on him," the man said to his wife.

She did not answer, and did not look at him.

The ambulance crew left. He walked them out. He knew one of the paramedics, Blake, from a charity bike ride he joined every summer. Blake offered a fist bump and said, "Nice work."

"It beats standing with the radar gun down on number 6," he said.

Blake laughed and they went to their vehicle. Doors thunked shut, the emergency lights stopped blinking, and they drove away.

He went back to the living room. The boys were sitting cross-legged on the floor. The little one had a chirping voice and was asking for a grilled cheese sandwich. *Perhaps I should have left the ball in your throat,* he thought. He smiled and gave his head a quick shake. The husband had taken off his suit jacket and hung it over the dining room chair. He'd loosened his tie and was talking to his wife. His tone of voice wasn't angry or accusing, but it seemed impatient. He told his wife that it was her idea to try and manage the household, watch the boys and look after her work-at-home job. She sat and listened, fresh tears on her face as her husband took her to task.

Young Ted kept staring at his Sam Brown belt, holster and handcuff pack. He was a boy of about nine or ten. A decent kid, you could tell. A helpful soul. He winked at Ted and then turned his attention to the father.

"Excuse me, can I have a word before I leave?"

The father turned to him. The mother stopped mid-sentence and stared at him.

"With you," he said. He pointed at the father.

They walked outside to the cruiser. He'd left the driver's side door open and he pushed it closed. The father said, "Listen, I know he shouldn't have had access to those balls. They're a choking hazard. There's a warning label right on that thing. I've told my wife that she needs to step up her game, but you know how it is with boys. Anyway, I can assure you—"

He put his hand up to silence the man, and stepped closer to him. They were within an inch of each other in height and so he looked right into the man's eyes.

"You have a nice family. Your life nearly changed today, but it didn't. It ended well. Why don't you stop acting like a *cunt* and go in there and give your boys a hug, and *thank* your wife for all she does?"

"What did you say?"

"Your *heard* me."

"Yeah, but just a—"

"*Don't* you *fuck* with me."

The man blinked a few times. It was as if someone had flicked a switch and shut him off. He nodded and looked back at his house, and then put his hands in his pockets and walked up the steps and back inside.

He opened his eyes and the contrast between the house in his memory and the derelict structure before him filled him with sadness. His emotions were ebbing and flowing so violently that he gripped the steering wheel and thumped his forehead against it. He backed the Mercedes down the laneway and wondered where the family had gone, where they lived now. He found himself breathless and gripped by a panic attack as he shifted to Drive and waited for whatever happened next.

Chapter 23: Stan Hill

Detective McVeigh had asked me something, but I'd missed the question. The lights in the room were bothering my eyes. I could feel my patience falling away.

"Hill, are you going to answer the questions or not?" He pointed to the tape machine.

"Yeah, I'll answer them."

He had been pacing and now he sat, opened up his notebook and pushed a red button on the player. We picked up where we'd left off. I answered his questions and kept my answers to *yes* or *no* as much as I could. Towards the end of the interview, McVeigh said, "Do you have a cell phone?"

"No."

"If I were to run a check, I would find that you do not have a cell, or similar handheld device?"

"That's correct."

"You were at Porter's Auto and Detailing in November. You had your car's interior steam-cleaned."

"Sure, I do that twice a year. If I don't it smells like the factory in there."

"Do you remember the date? The last time you were there?"

"No."

"I'll refresh your memory. It was November ninth. Two days after you'd visited the Skyward Fair."

I had to think about that. He was right. I looked at him and he stared me down. I eventually blinked and listened to the sound of the tape machine running, a quiet hiss and whine as the tape spun.

"Scott and me were in the car. We had some fast food, he slopped some coffee on the floor. I keep my cars clean."

"Just a coincidence then."

"Yes."

He stopped the tape machine. He unfastened his cuffs and rolled up his sleeves. While he did this he said, "I'm going to hit that button once more. If you have anything else to say, I *suggest* you say it, whether it's about you, or Scott, or where you went and what you did that day. Now's the time."

He did not look at me. He hit the button and rolled his sleeves back down. I put my mouth a little closer to the mic and said, "I didn't get along with my brother. Truth be told I don't respect him, but I did not kill him, nor was I involved in his disappearance. You are going around town dredging up stuff that has nothing—"

McVeigh shut the machine off and yanked the mic away at the same time.

"You're an idiot, Hill," he said.

"Can I go now?"

"We're done for now. You can go."

I got up to leave. McVeigh tapped on the door so that Cornish would move his big carcass out of the way. As I walked into the hallway, McVeigh said, "You '*didn't*' get along. You '*don't*' respect him. Past tense. Interesting."

I was fighting myself. I wanted to clock him one. I was certain he'd broken some regulations by turning the tape machine on and off to suit himself. He was manipulative and just plain twisted, even for a cop.

"Figure of speech. He's not *here,* so I used past tense. I said '*didn't*' because he's *missing.* You want an opinion? You want to know what I think? You've never asked me what I actually think. You're too fucking busy trying to engineer this thing so that it looks like I abducted him."

McVeigh exhaled, his cheeks puffed out like a trumpet player's.

"Okay, Hill, what do you think? This ought to be stunning."

"My mother gave him money a few weeks back. Did she tell you that? She gave him some cash from her savings because she believes my old man hasn't given him a fair shake. He's invited me to go down south and work for him, but he wants nothing to do with Jarrod. Jarrod's a drop-out. He can't hold a job. He lies through his teeth about everything. He does drugs, takes my mother's pain-killers if she doesn't lock them up. Clancy, your favourite source of information, is Jarrod's boyfriend, in case you haven't figured that out. And they're not going to *come out* in this town. So keep an eye on your number one informant because I'll bet you a box of doughnuts that Clancy disappears soon himself. He'll join my little brother—wherever he is—and they'll shack up and smoke and drink their way through that money. When the *cash is gone* they'll be back, back to walking the streets aimlessly and doing small-time drug deals at the old train station. And you know what? When that happens I'll write an open letter to the Tribune about our little interview here, and about how you used your authority to try and skew things. You're a *fucking* idiot."

I could tell by the look on Cornish's face that he'd bought what I'd just said—hook, line and sinker.

McVeigh looked smug. He moved his lips around like he was lost for words, which he probably was.

"Don't talk to me like that. And they won't publish your letter. They won't print a disgruntling letter from you. We're just doing our job."

I laughed.

"I think you mean *disparaging*. And I wouldn't bet against the morons at the Trib. They gave Del Brooks page two, the full fucking page, because he claimed he saw a giant ape on the road."

McVeigh stood there, lips pursed. Cornish was smiling and shaking his head.

"Have a nice day," I said.

McVeigh was not a guy who let you have the last word. I was halfway along the empty corridor when he said, "Coached any rugby lately?"

"No, why?"

He smiled and shrugged his shoulders. "Little boys, well, younger boys, right? That's who you coached."

I didn't like the look on his face and I was an inch away from charging him, dropping a rib-cracking tackle on his ass.

"Well?" he said.

"It ranged, ten to sixteen, seventeen years old."

"You enjoyed it though."

"Sure, I love the sport."

"Yeah, I'll bet."

"What's your fucking problem, dude, seriously?"

"What's yours? No one's really sure, but I'm aiming to find out."

I walked the dank corridor quickly and got myself outside. I looked around for my car and then gave my head a shake, and started my walk home.

The next morning I went outside in a rush and late for work. The cops were coming up the walkway as I was heading down it. There were three police cars. A tow truck was backing up to take my car. McVeigh held up some papers. I saw the Provincial coat of arms at the top of the page.

"We are taking your car for expert exam," said McVeigh.

He looked so happy, such an epic, self-righteous grin that I knew two things: first of all, I could just about see and feel the pleasure of my right hook connecting, flush, with his face, and if I didn't turn and walk back to the house, I'd wind up rocking him. Second, this was personal for him. It might have started as police work, but now he was just plain after me. I was the older, abrasive brother who'd eliminated his weak little sibling, maybe even had a practice run and abducted two other young men from the local fair. I wondered what Palmer had told him, or if my mother had followed up with more phone calls. The whole thing had started off as a game, the dimwit detective in pursuit of the local thug. The trouble is the thug finished high school and made honours in English and History. The thug reads two books a week and reads the newspaper, cover to cover, each day. And the thug has no time for his dickhead little brother, or the rusting and dowdy town he lives in, that's all true, but *he didn't* kill anyone. The thug figured he'd have some fun with the detective, let him come, full bore, only to discover he had jack-shit for a case. But, as my hand trembled to find my house key and he followed me up the front steps, squawking at me, I realized things were turning. There was a momentum shift that I could taste. I felt as if I might actually get framed. I was going to call my father and get his opinion on what I should do, but he'd just tell me to stay the course and watch my temper. And I didn't want him asking me the question: *Did* you kill him? I didn't want to hear that from my old man. We seldom talked about Jarrod, or what was going on back here, so I decided to control the controllable and let McVeigh do what he needed to do with the car.

"Where are you going? I'm talking to you," said McVeigh.

"I'm going inside my house and calling a buddy to give me a ride to work."

"We can drive you to work."

"No thanks. The more time I spend with you bastards the more complicated my life seems to get."

Chapter 24: The Pursued

If there were people he hated it was the Hill family. The mother was semi-reclusive, a dullard. Spaced out on cheap wine and pain-killers. The father, Vincent, was the opposite: a cool, suave American with shoulder-length blond hair and an arrogant face. He went to the tanning beds at the salon in town. His skin was a copper colour, even in February. Mercifully, he'd buggered off back to Florida to open a business. It was a funny arrangement: him down south and sending up money to support the home-stead. He probably had a matching, copper-coloured slut down there, someone who went to parties and loved the beach. Whatever the case he hoped Vince Hill stayed down there. They could have him. The youngest boy, Jarrod, was stupid like his mum. He was an acne-covered bag of chips on two legs. The boy wandered the town and its outskirts aimlessly and had fallen in with a little loser name Clancy. So now, the two boys shuffled along, their pants buckled well below their scrawny hips and their logo T-shirts three sizes too big flapping like flags in the wind, the two of them eating junk food from a paper bag. When ambling along a dirt road on the outskirts, they looked like something from another planet. But it was Stan, the oldest boy, that he loathed the most. Stan the factory worker, the bard of the work-ing man with a wrench in one hand and a dogeared Thomas Hardy novel in the other. Stan, who fancied himself a renaissance man because he was as comfortable at Fine Print Used Books as he was on a bar stool somewhere on the main street. He took English Lit courses by correspondence, coached rugby and fought like a shrew. People were scared of him, scared enough that no one he'd punched or shoved ever pressed charges. He had a smart mouth and was another one who'd read a sampling of the law and *knew his rights.* He was arrogant like his father, and had the same tussled blond hair and girly blue eyes, his face saved from being feminine by a deep scar on his cheek and a broken nose. He liked cars. Stan Hill and his old man kept a BMW and a VW Jetta. Both cars were painted up in ridiculous non-factory colours. Both made a racket when Stan or his father whipped around town in them. Both had tinted glass and decals on the bumpers: motor oil brands and stupid slogans like *Pedal to the Metal* and so forth.

He'd scooped up Stan Hill's dopey little brother, Jarrod with ease at Skyward, just behind the petting zoo in an area marked PLEASE KEEP OUT.

"Jarrod, would you come with me? I need to talk to you about your older brother."

He told Jarrod he had to make a stop at his house first. They drove there in silence.

"You look thirsty. Did you want a drink?"

Jarrod looked over as if he'd just woken up.

"Nah, I'm okay."

The boy was a detached little creature. He didn't ask, *What did you want to say about my brother?* Or, *Is my brother okay?* He even sat in the car aimlessly, if that was possible. When they reached the house, he said to Jarrod, "You may as well come in rather than sit there."

The garage door rolled shut and he entered the house with Jarrod sleepwalking close behind him.

The boy's facial expression changed when he saw a huge bag of cheese twists on the counter and the fridge loaded with beer. He tossed the junk food to the boy like a featherweight football. He took out two beers, popped the tabs and said to Jarrod, "Did you want one?"

"Yeah, but I'm underage and you're a cop so you could arrest me for it."

"You sound like your brother, telling people what they think and how it is. Whatever you do, don't emulate him." He gave Jarrod a beer and said, "Drink it or I'll arrest you for not drinking it, and for being like your brother."

He gave Jarrod a playful tap on the shoulder and the boy actually smiled. They sat at the kitchen table and sipped their beer. Trying to make conversation was painful, and so he said, "You and Stan seem to hate each other."

"Well you just nailed it. Motherfucker thinks he knows everything."

"No one knows everything."

"Try telling him that."

"He drives like an idiot."

"He does everything fast and like he's pissed off with it. My dad's the same."

"Does he have a girlfriend?"

"No."

"Maybe that's why. He does *everything* fast."

Jarrod laughed and then crammed some cheese twists into his face. "These are good," he said.

Enjoy them while you can, he thought, but just nodded and moved his beer, leaving a wet ring on the table.

"You don't get on with your dad either?"

"Nope. My dad calls Stan, but he never asks to talk to me."

"What about Stan? Does he talk to you?"

"Not really. Only to ask where I'm going, or to threaten me."

"Threaten?"

"Yeah, he's always saying stuff like he'll beat me to a pulp or fuck me up."

"What does your mother say?"

"She wants me to go to Snelling Academy, so she's hoping my dad's business works out down in the States."

"Snelling, that's the place up north, the nature and environmental program."

"You get your high school, but you also get different choices. They have an eco-program, and environmental program, like that."

"What about Stan? He works. He won't contribute to his younger brother's education? I would have thought he would sign on for that, being such a well-read man."

"Stan? Not really. He just wants to go down and work for my dad."

"They only care for themselves."

"For sure."

"What about you? What will you do if you can't go to Snelling?"

"I'm not sure."

"Will you just hang around with Clancy?"

Jarrod stared at his lap and shrugged his shoulders. His fingers were coated in orange cheese dust. He wiped them on his pants. He appeared to zone-out for a moment, and then he looked up and said, "Why did we come here again? You said it was something with Stan?"

He smiled at the boy and reached over to the bottom drawer, near the dishwasher. "I have a message from him, actually."

He tugged out the ligature. Jarrod made a face and tilted his chin upwards to get a better look at it.

"Ah, that's perfect, keep your chin up like that!"

"What? What is that?"

As he drew the ligature tight he closed his eyes and saw a bright red speech balloon, like the ones they used in superhero comic books. It said: "AAAAARGH!"

He laughed and pulled as tight as he could.

He dumped Jarrod Hill into the room without engaging the stairs. He'd died as lazily as he'd lived, slouched in a kitchen chair, blank-faced; an exhausted and weak grasp at the plastic-coated cable around his throat, his orange fingernails barely digging into the cord as it sunk into his flesh. And then complete resignation. His body fell to the sub-basement floor with a thud worthy of a sack of turnips.

He slept the heavy sleep of a justified man that night, but awoke the next day confused and convinced that the murder of Jarrod Hill had been a strange dream. He went to the sub-basement, wound the stairs down and confirmed that he'd strangled the boy. He removed the oxidized chain and Saint Christopher medal from Jarrod's neck and dropped it in the container with Dale and Will's jewelry and accessories. He loosened the floor panel and set it against the wall. He began the trip back and forth from the backyard shed to the basement, hauling bags of earth and limestone, and sweating as he worked. He dropped the floor panel back in place, he powered up the fan, and cleaned the house, mindful to be thorough in the kitchen and hallway. He chuckled and hatched a plan to get the game show intelligent Stan Hill and the TV detective wannabe, the self-important Detective McVeigh, in a battle of wills. Both fancied themselves smarter than the average townie. Both thought themselves untouchable.

McVeigh had begged and borrowed his way onto the CIB. He had no business there. He'd proven that with his first assignment. A teen girl had been found critically injured, head trauma, in the space between her home and the home of her neighbour, a man who lived in a 2,200 square-foot home on his own. The girl had recently broken up with her boyfriend of two years, and McVeigh chased and hounded the boy; an attempt to make him crack, and own up to the brutal attack.

Sgt. Glendon had talked to McVeigh. So had Gonzalez—a detective with quadruple McVeigh's experience. Their advice for the new detective? Talk to the neighbour. He's odd, reclusive, ventures out of the house only at night. He needs to be at the top of the list.

"He is strange, but I know it's the ex-beau," McVeigh had insisted.

Three days after she had been found, collapsed, bleeding and wedged between the two homes, the girl was well enough, cognitive enough, to speak to the police. She recalled her creepy neighbour watching her by the poolside as she swam and sunbathed earlier that day. He had been in his back window, binoculars in hand.

"Stop staring at me, pervert."

"Don't flatter yourself . . ."

The exchange of insults continued for a few seconds, and then he slammed the window shut. Later that night he appeared from out of the shadows as she walked to her garage to get an air pump for her stability ball. His breath was alcohol-laden and he slurred and stepped uncomfortably close to her, and warned her not to spread rumors, or disrespect him. She remembered shouting, or at least trying to shout as he grabbed her. And then she awoke in the hospital. McVeigh had been criticized for that. The word was he'd be punted back to a community patrol car. He needed to redeem himself. What better than to solve the disappearance of three young men?

He turned on the windshield wipers, though the rain had stopped. He liked the wipers and could watch them for several minutes, just as he could watch the hands of a clock for a full hour. He turned up the heat. German and British cars all seemed to have powerful fans, and the interior was soon hot enough that he was sweating. He sat and held his breath for as long as he could while sweat trickled down his back and fell from his forehead. He liked setting small, private challenges, some just off the top of his head, others more dangerous. He once found a wasp nest in his shed. He left it there and over the spring watched it swell to something that resembled a dehydrated brain. One afternoon, he entered the shed and stripped to his boxers. He took a broom handle and thumped the nest, releasing a swarm of wasps, that pinged off the walls and rose to the ceiling, and then rained down on the lawnmower, the wheelbarrow, the gardening tools, and on him. He winced and stood his ground, took as many stings as he could, while doing his best to brush them off his face and neck. When he'd finished, and was covered in reddish-pink bumps, he put his clothes on and opened the shed door. The majority of the insects rushed into the spring air, but hundreds stayed. He splashed gasoline on the nest and then struck a match. The nest burned like dry, rippled cardboard. He watched wasps writhe as the flames consumed them. Before the flames spread to the shed ceiling and framework, he shot the fire extinguisher and doused the nest in white foam. On the way to the back door his neighbour Rex hollered over the fence, "Barry, are you there?"

"I'm here, Rex."

"Did you have a fire?"

"Yes, I just burned a wasps' nest, not to worry."

"Oh, okay, yeah that's the best way. Have a good one."

"You as well, Rex."

He went inside that day and rested until he no longer felt dizzy, and then he took a bath and rubbed himself down with antiseptic cream. *Rex*, what a moron. He seldom saw Rex and his rat-faced wife, Karen. The seven foot fence between the two properties ensured that they were heard and not seen. He'd once started mapping out how he might kill and dispose of Rex. Rex sang in the backyard and would sing not only the vocals to his stupid pop songs, but also make a strange nasal noise that was supposed to be the guitar. Plus his name was *Rex*. In the end he decided not to murder a neighbour.

The air inside the car was now arid and he released his breath and found it difficult to catch it again. He was dripping with sweat, but would not lower the window, or turn down the heat just yet. He lifted his head and thumped it down on the top of the steering wheel several times until his eyes watered. A thought entered his mind: that he hadn't a kind bone in his body. And yet just weeks ago a young woman had told him he was, in fact, a kind person. He'd worked the afternoon shift and responded to a domestic dispute. The husband, Donovan, had assaulted his young wife and stormed out just before he'd arrived on the call. He radioed the husband's name, DOB and vehicle plate number to the dispatcher. The dispatcher broadcast the information while he sat with the young wife and talked to her. She was by turns weepy and sympathetic towards her husband, whom she loved, and then angry and convinced he should be charged and convicted of domestic assault, take his punishment like a man. She'd had an inkling it had been a mistake to marry Donovan. His daddy was rich. He'd bought them the house as a wedding gift. He'd given his son one of his Mercedes for his birthday. It wasn't new but it was top of the line. She talked all about their marital struggles, and lamented the fact they were occurring so early in their relationship. He crossed a line and held the young wife's hand, squeezed it and looked into her conflicted eyes. He knew it would be okay, so he reached out and touched her face as well, and she smiled.

"You're such a kind man, thank you for sitting here with me."

"That's alright. I'm happy to do it."

He wrote down his notes while she made coffee. He also walked to the front hall.

"Elaine, I am in your front hall because my portable radio will have better reception here."

"Okay, Barry. Do you take cream or sugar?"

"Yes, both, please."

He also took a Mercedes fob from a large crystal bowl that sat atop a mahogany table in the front hall. There were two packs of gum, some loose change, a pen-light and some Subaru keys in the ornate bowl. He stuck his finger in there and mixed the contents around, and pocketed the key fob.

He sat in *that* Mercedes now and gave up. He switched off the fan and opened a window, gasping and feeling as if he were falling, or taking the huge dip on a roller coaster. The Mercedes gas gauge was at a quarter tank.

He thought about how he'd stepped away from it all and been with Sheila. It had seemed like something, at first. He drove for a few minutes and let the cool air rush into the car. It formed a glistening layer of condensation on the gauges and radio. He parked in a huge grocery store lot and shut the engine down, reclined the seat and looked at the car's perforated ceiling.

"Never had a friend, never been in love, never liked sex, really, never had joy, at least not the type you see on TV," he said. He laughed and then sat up. He couldn't recall Sheila's face. That had been happening lately. He would try to recall something that should have been etched in his mind. The layout of his kitchen, his mother's hard-working hands, his ex-girlfriend's face. Had she been his girlfriend? She was just some woman, from work. A perfume-scented load of white noise, insecurity and superstition. They had gotten to know each other after doing a few shifts together, discovering they had both been profoundly affected by the death of their fathers. And after acknowledging the sexual tension that hung inside the cruiser and whispered at them, he had bought her dinner, and taken her on a picnic, and had sex with her on his couch three times, in his bed twice and then standing behind her in his shower a few times. She seemed to particularly like that. She had called what they shared a *relationship*. He supposed that in some ways it was. And now he couldn't remember her face.

Chapter 25: Sharp

Ryan lifted his foot off the accelerator for a moment.

"Shit, broke a bootlace."

"Do you want me to drive?"

"No it's okay, but I'm gonna head over to the Square."

"Are they still open?"

"The shoe place is. If I move it."

They parked at the plaza and Sharp waited until Ryan had gone inside. He tried Ingrid again. This time he left a message.

"Hi, it's me. I'm wondering where you've gotten to. I hope everything's alright. Listen, Ingrid, I know you're feeling a little cut off right now. Sometimes you don't know how these things will go until you try them. If you want to move back to town, we can. I don't care. It won't be long and we'll be running our own place. This train derailment, I'm not sure if you've been watching the news, but it's cleared up, we were covering off three different patrols, so I might be a little late, alright? We'll see you soon."

He hit the END button and dropped the phone in his pocket. Ryan wandered out of the plaza and Sharp watched him arrive at the cruiser and hop in.

"Six bucks for laces. Can you fucking believe that?"

He collapsed his long frame as best he could, ducked his head to the steering wheel to re-lace his boot.

"Why don't you get out of the car and do that? Save yourself a trip to the chiropractor."

"I'm good. It looks unprofessional, doing it in the parking lot."

He was going to ask Ryan if he thought that police officers' boot laces were above wearing and breaking in the eye of the public. Sharp shook his head and didn't bother. He wouldn't have been responding to Ryan, he would have been responding to an *entire system, a philosophy.* Ryan was just an infinitesimal part of it. They were taught that, inoculated with it the moment they arrived at the police college. Protocol and procedure supplanted everything. Sharp had worked with cops that wouldn't eat in public. They brought their food back to the cruiser and pulled behind plazas, factories and school yards after hours to eat a sandwich. Phelps would hold his bladder until they got to the station in order to avoid using a public washroom. Sharp remembered a story Granddad Victor had told about walking the beat in the UK. His grandfather had needed to take a leak. He was on the outskirts of town and so he found a spot behind a house at the end of the close, but the lights came on and out walked Tom, the homeowner. Granddad Victor knew Tom. He was a tailor in town. Tom struck up a conversation and Granddad Victor had to cut him short and explain his urgency.

"I'd have you in, Vic, but Mary's just put the children to sleep and both of them are under the weather."

"Not to worry, I'll just duck in behind your Alder here and throw a slash."

Sharp's Grandfather stepped behind the huge tree and relieved himself while Tom stood with his back turned talking about the weather.

Sharp smiled as he recalled the story and was going to tell Ryan about it, but his young partner was swearing at his bootlaces and managed to thump his head on the dash once he'd finished what he was doing. He rubbed the back of his neck, looked to Sharp and said, "I'm ready."

Sharp thought about driving, but Ryan had done well, held his own.

"Alright, so let's take one more drive around and see if we run across that Mercedes."

"You think he's still in the region?"

"I don't know if the suspect is, but I'll bet he's dumped that car somewhere in the area."

CHAPTER 26: WARFIELD

She took side roads to avoid being seen. She kept the roof lights off. The radio was busy, frustration in the voices of her colleagues as they pitched in to keep the re-entry into Courtland under control. She was tempted to shut off the noise, and hoped against hope that leaving her post would go unnoticed. She'd been positioned on the northern perimeter. It was quiet up there. Most of the residents would access their homes from the east and west. It did not take long for her luck to run out. She heard a unit come over the radio and ask if it was okay to open the east roadblock. Another came over and said *affirmative,* as he was now seeing residents driving into the area. A cranky and hoarse Sergeant Glendon took over and asked who had given the word to let people back in. Sheila turned the radio down, but not off.

She heard Glendon call her car number, 719. He then asked for her by name. She considered ignoring his call, but radio silence would touch off a search for her, unnecessary concern piled on an already tough day. She felt her pocket for the key, looked at the radio and slowed down, picked up the mic and responded, "719."

Glendon was tired and angry. "719, what is your 10–20?"

"Responding to a report of a suspicious person," she said, lying through her teeth. She glanced at a street sign, and said, "On Falconbridge."

"You've left the north post?"

"Affirmative. Received the report from—"

"In future *you wait* before clearing a detail and you *book* on the call with the dispatcher. I want you 10–19 when you're done with that call."

Sheila took a deep breath, and then switched on the roof lights and gunned it to Barry's place.

His house was in darkness. She had hoped to arrive and find the porch light on; warm yellow light glowing behind the curtains and blinds in the front room. She would walk to the door and ring the bell, and he would answer. It would be awkward, but they would be civil, if not friendly. She would ask how he was doing, and he might be in one of his moods; a forced smile and mono-syllabic answers that would suggest he was simply tolerating her. She would give back the key and then explain that she had intend-ed to surprise him one day. But she knew better. There *were* no lights, no movement. The house seemed dead. She stood on the doorstep and took the key in her hand. Her fingers trembled, her body felt electric as she missed twice but eventually slid the key into the lock, turned it and heard the click of the deadbolt. She walked in and closed the door gently. She prepared to be attacked, not by him, she knew he was out, but by shock and betrayal. She turned on a light and walked to his bedroom door. She continued to turn on lights and made an effort not to blink. If she blinked she might not have her eyes. She'd get stuck in darkness. There was something there for her, waiting. His bedroom door was locked; a simple brass knob and kwikset lock. She braced herself, her hands either side of the frame and kicked with her heel. The door splin-tered and popped on the third crack of her boot. The king bed was made, the room impeccably clean. She opened some of the dresser drawers to find undershirts, socks and boxer shorts folded and stowed uniformly. There was a locked cabinet, a squat, wooden piece that sat against the wall beside the bed. She sat on the bed and stared at it. She left the bedroom. The door to the basement was locked. She leaned against the wall, keeping her eyes wide open. How had this never occurred to her as strange?

"*Everything* is locked," she said.

She left the house and went to the cruiser, hit the trunk release. She was opening the trap to access the spare tire when she became aware of movement behind her. She straightened and turned. The neighbour stood there, a goofy look on his face. She couldn't recall his name, Dexter? Rex? Max? Barry disliked him. He was wearing pajama bottoms and a coat that sat askew on his shoulders. He'd thrown it on in a hurry.

"Hi, is everything okay?"

"Yes, I'm Barry's partner. I'm just picking something up for him. He needs it. He's tied up with something, at the station," she said.

She was aware she sounded completely unconvincing.

"So, he's still a cop? We were thinking of buying him something, like a retirement gift."

The neighbour looked towards his house. Sheila saw that his wife was watching from the front window.

"Yeah, he still is."

"I told him I'd buy a car from him. I'm in the market. I guess he's just dabbling right now."

Sheila smiled and waited for him to leave, but he stayed put.

"He had a pretty sweet Audi last month, but he sold it."

"Oh, yeah, he did," she said. She had no idea what he was talking about.

"Well, when he's ready I'll buy from him. We were just confused about when he's leaving, retiring. It's kind of nice to have a cop living on the street. We'll miss that."

"He's a private guy. I'm sure he'll tell you when he's ready."

"No kidding. He's a man of few words."

The neighbour looked back for his wife, who was gone from the window.

"Well, it's chilly out here. Just wanted to make sure everything was cool."

"I'll tell Barry you were asking after him."

He pulled his coat tight and left. Sheila waited until his back was turned before lifting the tire-iron from the slot near the spare tire, tucking it inside her jacket and closing the trunk. She went to the cruiser's passenger seat, took her portable, her hands trembling significantly enough that she could not clip it on her belt and run the mic cord up her jacket and lock it in place. She jammed it in her pocket.

She turned off some of the lights inside. In the bedroom she jammed the tire-iron into the seams around the drawer and pushed and twisted, the weight of her body behind each shove. The drawer's face split and she heaved the iron back and forth until there was another cracking noise and the drawer popped open. She got down on her knees and drew her gun, placed it in within close reach on the carpet. She was aware of how stupid that might seem to an onlooker, but she felt better with it out of her holster. There were papers and articles, most of them bound with bull clips. She sorted them with trembling hands. Some of them had title pages, but the words would not register, would not stick, they seemed to ricochet off her comprehension.

Asphyxiation

Strangulation

Poisoning

She snatched one of the documents and flipped through some pages.

. . . *the length of time a person can survive with a completely blocked airway varies, but typically* . . .

. . . *more ease in handling the corpse prior to the onset of rigor mortis* . . .

. . . *the amount of ventilation required will depend upon numerous factors* . . .

. . . *the odor caused by decomposition can be mitigated* . . .

Sheila closed her eyes, clenched her teeth, and gagged. She tried to open them, but it was too late. She kicked her leg as if trying to escape a physical threat. The hem of her pants lifted above her ankle and she felt the hot friction of the carpet. She saw Barry. He was wearing a blue nylon shell jacket. It was nighttime and he walked an aisle of parked cars with a small flashlight in his hand. He looked towards Sheila and his facial expression was one of complete satisfaction. Behind him, music and white light reaching high against the black sky, nearly washing out the full moon. She could also see radiant light—amber, blue and red—and she sensed the violent motion of an amusement ride; children laughed and a Ferris wheel seemed to hurl their laughter skyward. A man's voice blasted over the P.A.

"We have a winner, folks!"

Sheila took her gun and looked for the tire-iron with feverish, hazy vision. The light and contrast of the real world seeped back slowly. Items in the room regained definition: the headboard, mirror and closet door handle. She ripped open the closet. She found only clothing, neatly arranged on hangers.

She walked to the basement as if walking to her death. *If I'm wrong, my life is over.* She was aware that she was whimpering as she jammed the iron into the basement door and worked it frantically. She popped it easily, her throat tightening and involuntarily whining at what she saw.

"Stop it," she said to herself.

The basement was finished: carpeting, a couch, a reclined leather chair, pot lights, gas fireplace. There was *no* ongoing renovation. Behind the comfortable sitting area she found an unlocked door and entered. A pull-string controlled the lone light bulb and she yanked it on. She became aware of a humming noise. The furnace ticked and then exhaled as it fired up. Sheila crouched and pointed her gun. She lowered her weapon when she realized it was only HVAC noise. Beyond the furnace and beside the breaker panel, a door. Locked. She tried to use the iron, but the door was shut tight. The seal or gasket made of a heavy, inflexible plastic; the door itself was solid. She ran her hand along its surface. It was a light metal, possibly fiberglass. She wound up as if holding a baseball bat, and swung. Metal would dent. Fiberglass would splinter. Wouldn't it? She released a home-run swing. The door neither dented nor cracked. It may as well have been concrete. She looked around the tool bench. Beside it, a mop, broom, shop-vac and, mercifully, a sledgehammer. She picked it up and placed it beside the door. She stood back six feet, aimed her gun and fired. The first round penetrated just above the deadbolt. The report deafened her right ear. She fired again, missing this time and leaving a twisted rip a good nine inches above the lock. She sunk four more rounds near the bolt, the last one striking it and creating a massive spark, and then a popping sound. She heard the bullet slam into something behind her, ducked an eternity too late, and realized she was lucky not have been hit as it caromed off the walls. The deadbolt was still in place, but deformed, and loose. She could shift it slightly with her thumb and forefinger. She took the sledge and wound up, striking the wall first, but then finding a rhythm and pounding the door, the knob and the bolt. She swung in a fury. Her blows sounded like thunder, shook the house. Sweat dripped from her brow when she finally dropped the sledge and did her best to kick the open the door. It didn't take much. The door, now warped, let go with a high-pitched groan. She was so tired, frightened and jacked on adrenaline that she tried to take the first step without turning the light on. Her right foot found nothing but air and she yelled, used her left forearm and elbow to jam the outside of the door and push backwards. Her weight shifted to her left thigh, down her leg, landing at her ankle. She lost her balance and fell on her ass.

She had never been so glad about falling down, especially once she had gathered herself, held the frame and felt for the light switch. There were no stairs. She had come within an inch of tipping forward and winding up eight feet below. She was so angry she shrieked and delivered a hammer fist to the light switch.

"You fucking freak!"

There was a handle, an old crank style thing that would have been charming at the local nursery or orchard, but the sight of it here made her want to vomit, and she swallowed hard and watched a single drop of sweat fall onto the floor below. A fan hummed and the air moved like a whisper beneath her cold hands as she turned the crank and watched, an admixture of horror and relief rushing through her, as a wobbling steel staircase fell into place.

Chapter 27: Stan Hill

It wasn't always so cold and distrustful between my mother and me. When Jarrod was much younger, she would call me Stan the Man. He was only little and when he was down for his nap, we would dance in the living room to her old Teac reel to reel that my father had hooked up to the stereo. She played a lot of 60s and 70s stuff, a huge range, from British Invasion to the Doobie Brothers. My mother liked to dance and she'd twirl around and swing her hips with a cigarette in one hand the the power cord to the vacuum cleaner in the other. I remember the town *being* something back then, alive and growing, thriving. My father had a good job. He was one of the only guys in the neighbourhood with a company car, an old Mercury Sable with the ugliest cloth I'd ever seen on a car seat. My mother was alert and happy. It wasn't until Jarrod got older, towards his teens, that things changed. She got quiet and forlorn and my old man got restless and fed up. In retrospect I was never sure, was it the waning fortunes of the town, or would things have skidded badly regardless of where we'd lived?

It was the first mother, the one that used to dance, that I wanted to talk to the day they impounded my car, but as we sat at the dinner table that night, eating in silence, I realized she was long gone. She kept her head down and ate tiny bites of food. I had become accustomed to the vacant look in her eyes. She appeared dazed and I wondered if she was hopelessly addicted to the pain-killers she'd began taking when she hurt her knee a few years back. I mean, there's addiction and then there's *addiction,* in my opinion.

What little small-talk she'd made seemed to have evaporated soon after Jarrod disappeared. I knew she missed him and she was worried about him. What mother wouldn't be? As I sat there picking at a slab of cold meatloaf, I wondered how she'd be if I wound up in prison. I wondered how *I'd* be if I wound up in prison? With my temperament I'd either kill someone, or be killed inside a year. I'd been working on my temper, turning the other cheek as much as I could. The last few months, the stink and heat of that factory, and the lure of Florida were making it tough not to erupt. She looked at me and then at my plate, still half-filled with food.

"I'm sorry, Stanley," she said.

"What else did you tell the cops? I need to know."

She shook salt onto her food and then pushed it around with her fork.

"I just thought you might have seen something. I know you kept an eye on him, that's why I made that call. I'd had some wine. I was upset. We're not all like you, you know, all rough and tough and sure of ourselves."

She started to cry. She gathered herself enough to say, "If you went missing, I would still worry, but I know you could fend for yourself. I'm not so sure about Jarrod."

"The cops are on me. They're convinced I have something to do with it."

"I *never* said that. I just said that you and your father turned your back on Jarrod, you know, once you figured it out."

"Figured out *what*?"

"He's with Clancy. They've always had more than a friend-ship. Your father didn't like it, and I know that you don't either. It makes you angry."

"Says who? When have *we ever* discussed this?"

She didn't answer.

"I couldn't give a shit what he does in his bedroom. What I didn't like was that he never lifted a finger around here. He's not in school, he has no job, he steals things and lies about where he is."

"You hate everything about him and I thought the police should know, that's all."

I got up and went to the kitchen counter, fuming.

"So, you told them what, exactly? I need to know this, Mum!"

She wiped her face on her dinner napkin and wouldn't look at me.

"What?"

"I told them that you had been following Jarrod—"

"To make sure he wasn't fucking up his life any further, *yes*!"

"I said that if you were following him you might know something."

"Like *what*?"

"I don't know! Like perhaps you helped him leave, or threatened him to leave."

"No, I didn't! Jesus, Mum, look at me. This is serious."

She lifted her head. Her face was empty; her mind was off somewhere else.

"Do you really think I'd do that?"

She cried harder. She made a choking sound, and then said, "How am I supposed to know?"

She placed her face in her hands. I went around and hugged her as best I could. She was rigid and pulled away from me slightly.

"First Jarrod and now you. You're going to move away and live with that father of yours. Everything's falling apart," she said.

"Mum, I have to get out of here. This place has me stuck in first gear."

"I know. I won't stay here either. I might take an apartment over in Peacefield. It's nice there."

"He'll be back, Mum."

"No, Stanley, he won't. There's two other boys missing. So, if you don't know where he is, then someone's taken them."

"They left. They wanted out of here. You don't find it coincidental that he vanished after you gave him that money?"

"That wouldn't have taken him far."

"Exactly. He'll be back. Have you seen Clancy lately?"

She blew her nose and leaned her head back. "No, not for a few days."

"I'll bet he's gone, left to join Jarrod. If you call the drycleaners tomorrow, Rachel Clancy will tell you I'm right."

My mother looked at the phone and then at the wall clock.

Later, my mother stood at the kitchen sink, tossed back some pain-killers and chased them down with wine from a cardboard container. She came into the living room and touched my head as she walked to the stairs and then climbed them up to her bedroom.

"Mum, I need you to call the police and tell them we had this talk, okay?"

"It won't help. I've already tried talking to Constable Palmer and he said that they have a process. He can't stop it now."

"Tell them I had nothing to do with it."

"It wouldn't matter. He's very stubborn."

"He's a dick, and you know it."

"I know you dislike him, but I think that's because you're alike. You're both very headstrong and opinionated. You're bound to clash."

I sat and thought hard about a rebuttal, but I was tired, saturated with it all. I thought about my car. Jarrod had been in it several times. I thought back to a time, maybe a couple of months ago, when I had driven him down to the clinic. He'd had a nose bleed and I wondered about what the cops would find; what they might assume; what they might do with that information. They could twist things. They were accountable, just like anyone. A guy like me comes along, no love lost between me and them . . .

I went to the kitchen and poured myself some wine, drank it back. It was horrible, like a mouthful of perfume, and I spat away half of it and caught myself winding up to pitch the glass against the wall. I picked up the phone and made a call of my own. My Uncle Jimbo answered on the first ring. I said hello and asked if my father was around.

"Sure thing, Stan, he's just on the balcony having a cigar. I'll get him."

I pictured my old man on the balcony of his condo, puffing on a cigarello, sipping on a cold can of Pabst; the breeze off the water hitting his face. It just about cut me in two to think about that. Jimbo said something and my father laughed as he took the phone.

"What's up, Stan?"

I didn't know what else to say and I actually had to control some panic in my throat. So I kept it short and simple. I took a breath and said, "Hey Dad, I think I might be fucked."

"Stan, I want you to listen to me. You haven't done anything. I know that. I want you to pack a bag and I am going to call a buddy of mine, his name's Max Stertkamp, he's a lawyer. Get a pen and take down his number."

Chapter 28: The Pursued

He knew that he would sound the final alarm by visiting the Hill residence. McVeigh had now been after Stan Hill for some time, but could not put the finishing touches on the case. True, it was circumstantial, but not impossible. He knew, in the end, that any charge would fall off the rails, but the entire mess would cause Stan a world of trouble, and cement McVeigh's reputation as a lightweight. Two very worthwhile endeavors.

He arrived at the Hill residence and tucked his pistol down the small of his back, pulled down his hoodie to cover his waistband. He crept along the side of the home and towards the garage where there was a radio playing, and likely where he would find Hill working on his absurd bright green car. He rolled up the door, anger boiling in him, his hand instinctively reaching back for his gun. He could shoot Stan Hill point blank and then flee and enjoy the ensuing trouble, or he could kill the punk and turn the weapon on himself. But there was no Hill and no car in the garage, only boxes, packing tape and a few articles lined up on the concrete floor. The radio sat atop a shelf over a workbench. It was playing that awful grunge music, and he shut it off. There was a bottle of water beside the radio. He felt it and it was cool. He went to the side door of the home. Mrs. Hill answered wearing baggy jeans and a sweatshirt. She had a red bandanna tied around her head. She did not recognize him at first. She regarded him with fear in her eyes and grabbed the storm door handle—as if that would stop him if he'd actually decided to rush in. He watched the fear drain from her eyes, and saw a confused, perhaps nervous smile start at the corner of her mouth.

"Oh, Officer Palmer, I wasn't expecting you."

She looked at his clothes, and then at his face. The smile that had started to form quickly disappeared.

"Is this about Jarrod?"

"No."

"Are you okay?"

"I'm fine. Is Stan around?"

"No he's not. He left."

"Left?"

"Yes, for Florida, to work with his dad."

"How long ago?"

"Two hours maybe."

She remained behind the storm door with her fingers wrapped around the flimsy lock and handle. He looked beyond her. There were a couple of boxes and some packing tape.

"It looks like you're moving."

"I'm going to get started. This place will be too much for me on my own."

He took a step back and struggled with a profound disappointment over not finding Stan Hill.

"You look warm. Did you want a glass of water?" she asked. Her voice wavered.

"No thank you. I'm fine."

"Are you on duty?"

"No, I'm retiring, so I won't be back on duty."

"Oh, well that's nice," she said. She stood there, about to say something else, and then glanced over her shoulder at the boxes.

"I'll let you get back to it."

"Thank you. I'm sure it'll take me a while. I have to find a place, an apartment. Lots to do."

"So, Stan's gone for good, off to the sunshine state?"

"That's his plan. He checked with a lawyer and the lawyer called your people. Anyway, it was decided they couldn't stop him from going. I thought you would have known that."

"Jarrod isn't missing. He's dead. And Stan didn't kill him."

She tilted her head and looked at him intently.

"I know who did it, who killed him. I will be resolving it shortly."

"Oh my God," she said. She put her hand to her mouth.

"Stay here and don't call anyone. I'll be in touch."

She didn't answer him. Her hand remained at her mouth and tears began to fall from her eyes.

"I mean it, don't mention this to anyone," he said.

"I won't, I won't, oh God . . ."

He got back in the Mercedes and yanked it into reverse, tore down the driveway.

"What on earth did you go and do that for?" he yelled.

He was soon laughing and took off down the street, blowing a stop sign and causing a man on his front porch to rise from his Muskoka chair and gesture wildly. Watching people get the news was always a thrill. There was always a moment when it felt cruel and unusual, but that passed. *Besides, I was a boy when I watched it happen. I saw it with my own two eyes.*

He drove calmly for about twenty minutes and listened to the radio. His gun pressed the small of his back and so he pulled it out and threw it on the dash. The barrel hit the windshield and sent a spider web crack across the bottom. He headed northbound through a newly developed section of town, all junk food emporiums and new steel and glass buildings. He stopped at a red. He noticed them immediately, also stopped. They were headed south. Ryan was driving. The signal turned green and he accelerated gently. He tooted the horn, lowered the window and waved as he accelerated away from the intersection. He checked the rearview, saw their taillights flare and watched them pull a fast and jarring three-point turn. Sharp was in the passenger seat. Sharp and Ryan: the sparkle-eyed, debonair cop who'd obviously watched too many Bond films and believed it was still 1960; and the rookie, a tall, raw-boned farm boy from Saskatchewan. He looked like a stick insect—same IQ as well.

He took off and put some road between him and them. It was dusk and the flash of their red and blue lights irritated, threatened him. He decided he'd head toward the Skyward fairgrounds. It was all packed up and stored until next year, but it might be fun to crash the gates and set the stage. They had caught up. Ryan hung about four car lengths back. He'd put the high-beams on, the stupid bastard. He pictured Ryan's face as he bolted from the car, side arm drawn, semi-crouched and lurching forward.

"Police, get on the ground!"

And then he'd take his hood down, and the farm boy would recognize him, and experience a brief, stress-induced anxiety, and that would be enough. He could gun down Ryan in that brief time, in that moment where the rookie said, "Huh?" under his breath. Two Ryans would have been ideal. They would defeat themselves with their adrenaline and bravado. It was Sharp who bothered him, had him grinding his teeth as he sped northbound. He reached to the dash and grabbed the gun, tucked it under his leg.

Chapter 29: Sharp

They cruised an area that always struck Sharp as stressful. Too bright and busy. As little as five years ago it had been a series of broken roads flanked by old motels and struggling used car dealerships. Those old structures had been demoed, put out of their misery. Now, there were low-rise condos and fast-food chains, and a massive grocery store built almost entirely of glass. Sharp always thought it looked out of place. Ingrid had called it the food tank when they had driven past it. They arrived at an intersection, the roads recently repaved, pitch black and smooth. Sharp looked over at the northbound traffic as the signal changed. He saw a Mercedes and his mind flashed, jaw tightened as he wondered if it was *the* Mercedes. He squinted to make out the license plate. The driver honked the horn and waved as he pulled away in the opposite direction. Ryan jammed on the brakes.

"Are you seeing this?!"

"Is it the right car?"

"Fucking right it is! BBAK 219!"

They pulled a three-point turn and Ryan hammered the accelerator. The engine whined and Sharp picked up the mic.

"Can you believe this asshole?" said Ryan. His voice was digging at Sharp's left ear drum.

Sharp told Ryan to settle down, hang back, he needed to contact the dispatcher and couldn't do it with Ryan in a panic.

The streets were wet and slick. Ryan seemed rattled this time around. Earlier, before they had lost the Mercedes, the suspect had driven expertly, as if he'd been trained to maneuver a vehicle at high speeds. Now, they whipped along in pursuit through the suburbs, through wide intersections with multiple signals, fast-food drive-thrus and brightly lit stores scattered here and there. Horns blasted and tires skidded on glistening tarmac as the Mercedes ripped through the area with no regard for anything except putting space between himself and his pursuers. Gone was the finesse driving of just a few hours ago. Sharp wished *he* were driving. Ryan's skill and ability seemed to match the recklessness of the suspect's.

"Ryan, just keep him in sight. When we get past civilization here, and he hits number 5, we can get a little cozy with him. He's out of his mind. He *wants* this chase. Give him room."

"I'm gonna pound the shit out of this asshole when we do get him. And we're fucking getting him this time around."

Sharp gritted his teeth as the suspect met with a truck, moving slowly, chugging up the incline towards highway 5. He swung out into oncoming traffic, as the lanes narrowed and they left suburbia in the rearview. Fortunately, traffic was light and he made it around the truck, which pulled onto the gravel shoulder, obviously seeing the red and blue lights pulsing behind him.

"What's this guy's story?" said Ryan.

"I don't know, but if he keeps driving like that, he won't live to tell it."

Once the line of streetlamps ended and the highway darkened, the suspect's taillights surged ahead, became faded red dots. His acceleration sent a plume of mist that dropped on the windshield of the cruiser, and Ryan slapped the arm on the steering column to speed up the wipers.

Sharp's cell phone rang and he placed his hand on his pocket, but then took it away. They were reaching some serious speed and he picked up the mic to update their position.

CHAPTER 30: WARFIELD

She descended the stairs and stood at the base, the room around her sterile, and flat except for an electric buzz and the gentle movement; an earthy smelling breeze flowing toward a large vent on the far wall.

A tomb, she thought.

"Yes," she said. She wished there was someone with her. It was too late for that now.

Her radio broke the relative silence and she jumped. She heard a blast of static and an excited voice. She hauled the radio out of her pocket. Sharp and Ryan were in pursuit again. She hit the trans button and it didn't spring back to her thumb. She looked to the top of the steel staircase in wonder. She fished her pocket for a spring, something missing from the portable. She hit the button again. Useless. She tossed the radio and pulled her cell–phone from her pocket. There was a deep crack across its face and her heart sank and gut knotted as she pictured dialing, only to find it useless.

She selected the *station contact* and hit *send.* She heard the muffled ring tone as she walked on rubber knees towards a decorative brass pot in one corner of the sub-basement.

"Nineteen division, Constable Anderson." His voice was drained. A step away from talking in his sleep.

"Ralph, it's me, Warfield."

He brightened, chuckled, advised her she was in deep shit. As he talked about residents sneaking back into Courtland from the abandoned northern post, she crouched for a closer look at the contents of the brass pot: a tarnished money clip; earrings, a necklace of black beads, the stuff of cheap jewelry; a skull ring, best suited for the finger of a teenage boy.

"Are they chasing that Mercedes again?"

"Huh?"

"Stop fucking with me, Ralph! Is Sharp on that Mercedes again?!"

"Yeah!"

"Can you give me Sharp's cell phone number?"

Anderson laughed.

"He's in pursuit. I doubt he has time right now."

"Give me the number, *please*."

"Hey, Warfield, are you fucking deaf? Where are you anyway?"

"If you give me his number, right now, I will buy you two boilers at Driscoll's on Friday and then blow you in the parking lot after. No obligation, no nothing."

The phone line went silent, and then: "Are you drunk?"

"No, I *want that* number."

"Alright, alright."

He gave it to her. She tugged out her pen and wrote it on the wall. As she strained to listen, and concentrate, she noticed she was scrawling the number above a photograph, plastic-coated, faded and pinned to the wall with a diamond stud earring. In the photo: a man and woman, a couple, circa 1970. He a good-looking man, baggy suit, pomaded hair. She a slender thing, bob cut, yellow pantsuit and matching purse. And between them, a young Barry Palmer, crew-cut, double-pleated pants and dress shirt button to the top; not a day over the age of ten, smiling like he knew the most massive secret in the world.

"Warfield, you should know that Glendon is major pissed with—"

She hung up on Anderson, and despite the adequate and ghostly light around her, squinted to see the buttons on her phone.

"Oh, God, come on," she said.

It rang several times. Anderson was right. Sharp wouldn't answer in the midst of a chase, especially with this weather and with night quickly falling. She let it ring, and ring. She stopped the call and then hit the re-dial button. She walked to the corner of the room, nearest the vent. There was a one-inch seam between the floor and the wall, so she dug in her fingers and lifted. The floorboard came away and she looked at earth beneath it, and then dropped it back into place. There was a click and then a zapping sound in her ear. She could hear the muted sound of a revving car engine.

"Sharp," he said.

She would have cheered if it weren't for a sick, dizzy sensation crawling all over her.

"Matt, it's Sheila Warfield, can you hear me okay?"

"Yes, I can hear you."

He was calm and she felt better just hearing his voice. She tried not to yell, urged herself to stay calm, speak slowly, clearly.

"I know you're in pursuit. I need to tell you something and I want you to know I am dead serious."

"Okay, Ryan, Ryan, hang back, he's not going anywhere."

"Matt?"

"Okay, Sheila, go ahead."

"You're chasing Barry Palmer. It's *Barry* in that car. He abducted and killed those boys from Skyward."

She waited. The sound of the cruiser's momentum quietly surged in the background. She feared Matt Sharp's silence at first, but as the seconds slipped by, she knew that he' d processed it.

"This car's headed towards the fairground now," he said. He sounded stunned.

"Matt, he's armed and dangerous—"

"How do you *know* this?"

"I'm in his house right now. He has a tomb in the basement."

Silence. She had thought she might have to convince him, beg him to listen, prevent him from hanging up. She could hear Sharp's voice, muffled, but insistent, imploring. And then she heard Ryan, his voice pitching higher. "What the fuck?!"

Sharp came back on. "Do the others know?"

"No."

"Tell them. Call Glendon, have them call up my old man as well."

Chapter 31: Sharp

The suspect's brake lights flared and he turned right onto a narrow concession. Ryan slowed and followed, hitting the gas hard out of the turn.

"This is *Palmer*? That doesn't *seem* right," said Ryan.

"It's him. Warfield's at his house. There's evidence."

"Doesn't this end before the fairgrounds?" Ryan asked.

Sharp mined his memory for where the road ended. He checked his side mirror and then looked over his shoulder to see a carnival of red and blue lights behind him, closing the gap.

"You're right. This pretty much ends at the fair—well, it does continue past it, but he'll have to get through the gate at the east end of the property."

"He'll just smash it," said Ryan. "And it's *him*? He *took* those guys? That's been going on for years."

"Just watch the road, Ryan, hang back, he wants us to get him."

Sharp put the phone in his pocket. He felt duped. There was anger boiling up into his throat. *Palmer.* His old man had never liked him. It had been his old man that pulled the strings to get him on the traffic cars and keep him as contained as possible. When Palmer did get on a community patrol car he was a pest; he had a history of public complaints, nothing major, allegations of rudeness, inappropriate comments. But on the other hand he spent a lot of time in the community, volunteering, charity events. He'd been the MC at a Civic Awards night a few months ago, and had been charming; received plenty of laughs and applause from the packed auditorium.

They were coming up on the fairgrounds, grey, cold and chained up for the season.

"I can't believe this," said Ryan. "I mean, he's a bizarre guy, but this is *out there*, this is sick—"

The gum Ryan had been working for the last hour fell from his mouth and onto the seat. His reflexes took over and he looked down.

"Leave it!" said Sharp.

Ryan's attention went back to the road.

"He's armed then, for sure," he said.

Sharp looked at his younger partner's face. He was obviously still trying to wrap his mind around it all.

"Yes."

Sharp had no doubt. He trusted Sheila Warfield, liked her. She was alright. She thought differently and she was good with people. A little clumsy, but that could be refined. She had what Sharp's superstitious grandmother would have called *The Gift*. Sharp never said anything to her about it, but he'd noticed it. It was subtle and she concealed it reasonably well, but it was obvious to him that Sheila Warfield had something more than investigative sense, or beginner's luck.

Chapter 32: Warfield

She ran from Barry's house and jumped in the cruiser. She turned on the light bar and fought the powerful sense that Sharp and Ryan were driving to their doom. She could feel their motion, out of control, as she pulled away from the curb and tried to clear her mind and map the best way to catch up with them. She decided she would notify Glendon once she got closer. She avoided the main roads and grabbed the fourth concession, which would take her over to Number 5. She would be hard pressed to catch them now, but the compulsion was so strong she drove like it was her sole purpose. She hit 180 and marveled at how much ground she was gaining. Once she was on Number 5, she could shoot up there and perhaps be within ten or fifteen minutes of the rest of the pack. She could hear on the radio that the provincial police had joined the chase. At least she'd be there. She might be able to help. She thought again of Sharp, the fact that he might be in harm's way, and it sickened her. She squinted at the black road and told herself this was professional concern—nothing more.

She saw its antlers first. *God almighty, what is that?* Her headlamps lit them up like giant contorted fingers against the dark sky. She touched the brakes when she saw the buck's face, its gleaming eyes. Its back legs worked against the wet tarmac and it moved like a carousel horse, running but going nowhere. She shouldn't have braked. She could have eased up on the accelerator and put two tires on the gravel shoulder. Now she was in a damned speedboat and she spun and caught a glimpse of the deer's tail as it ran to the field that surrounded the road. It had escaped death, but now she was barreling backwards across the gravel shoulder and down an embankment at about 80 KMH. When her cruiser hit something it began to spin around and face forwards, and she felt a surge of hope, but then it but flipped over and rolled. Sheila watched the space around her twist and blur, and her insides seemed to shift. She came to rest upside down, a deflated airbag in her face, her seatbelt just managing to restrain her. She placed one arm against the cruiser's ceiling, tucked her chin to her chest and released the seatbelt with her free hand. It wasn't graceful. She dropped and wasn't aware of striking her head, or injuring herself, but she felt her consciousness flee, and float. *I'm okay,* she thought, *I will just rest on the ceiling . . .*

She knew she had blacked out. The cold was digging at her. It had already carved away the dexterity in her hands. They looked like claws as she reached up for a handle, but the driver's side door had buckled and jammed. The radio was broken, its controls cracked and wires protruding from the bracket that held it in place. She used her knuckle to turn up the volume and it made a buzzing noise she'd never heard before. She slid along the ceiling, mindful of glass near the back of the vehicle. She opened a back door on the passenger side and crawled out. The cruiser's headlights were still on, dull and yellow, but there. She had been out for a while, but not for hours. The grass outside was long, frozen and it crunched as her weight broke its freezing rain shell. She stood slowly, expecting to be doubled over by pain, a yet to be discovered injury that might see her perishing in a cold field. She was amazed when she stood straight, ran her hands inside her coat and down her legs. Her pants were ripped above her right knee. There was some blood, but not much. The knee was slightly numb, but she was able to walk with little pain. She took out her flashlight, pointed it towards the road and started trudging, startled by how far the cruiser had traveled, and by the fact she was still in one piece.

Her cell phone was finished. The crack that graced its surface earlier was now a deep gash. She dropped it back in her pocket and climbed the embankment. The road was black and desolate. She heard a coyote howl and checked to make sure her sidearm was still in its holster. She waited on the roadside for a moment and felt the cold and damp pulling at her, weakening her, so she walked, keeping the flashlight at her side and wondering if she should return to the cruiser and collect the extra batteries from

the glove compartment. They would be cold as well, a few minutes of life if she was lucky. She walked against traffic, hoping that
if, and when, some lonely soul drove along this stretch she could
wave and stop them. As she walked she felt dread and anger. She
pictured Barry, expressionless, perhaps smug as he witnessed the
process of an investigation, the machinations of a police station
from the other side of the desk. She kicked herself for having
become involved with him. She longed for a hot bath, not just for
the warmth it would offer, but to wash him away. She had sat and
drank beer at his kitchen table while he cooked for her, and while
a fan spun below her, helping to ventilate his homemade tomb.
She had dropped her clothes on that damned cabinet, full of articles on maiming and killing, and then crawled into his bed and
touched him, and allowed his hands to roam all over her. She gri-
maced and her chills doubled as she recalled the photo of him and
his parents. She remembered a time when they were on the
couch, late at night. They had been watching a movie and when
it ended they mixed a nightcap. They were both a little drunk,
and so she told him about her father's sudden passing. He had
reciprocated and said that his father had been killed in an accident, but it *wasn't* an accident. He'd seemed angry and spoke of
missing him, missing his presence. His mother went downhill
after his father had died. She became religious, and when that did-
n't numb her pain and guide her off her grief-stricken road, she
became reclusive. She had held his hand and and asked what had
happened to his father.

"An accident," he said. He pulled his hand away from hers.

"Oh my God, what happened?"

He stood, took his glass and went to top up his drink. He also
lit a cigarette. He never smoked inside his house.

"Barry? What happened?"

"Not now, alright? Let's just leave it."

She fought tears and looked down at her uniform, reminded
herself to act befitting of it, regardless of being on a cold, desolate
road without a soul around. She would not cry for Barry Palmer,
nor would she visit him in prison. She did not know him, despite
their time together. He was as dark as the road before her.

CHAPTER 33: THE PURSUED

The driving was easy now. He sped and didn't even think about it. The car just ripped along and he ignored the speedometer, but did smile at the gas gauge—near empty. He urged himself not to to check the rearview or side mirrors to see the cavalry gaining on him—though he was aware of lights and noise pressuring him. He was disappointed that it was Sharp. He could disparage Sharp on the surface of things, but he confessed to himself that he actually liked him, respected him, anyway. He remembered a call he'd done with Sharp a couple of years back. They'd been in the Dufferin patrol area. It came over as unknown trouble. The comm centre had received a 911 call, an open line and what sounded like an adult male, crying. They pulled onto the driveway. The small, square bungalow was tidy, well-kept with a putting green lawn. It sat in darkness. They knocked on the door. Sharp went around to the side, found a door there and knocked on it as well. He came around to the front and said, "Palmer, it's open."

Sharp entered first. There was short flight of stairs up to the main level. Palmer shone his flashlight, but Sharp just flicked on a wall switch.

"Hello? Police department?" he said.

His voice was relaxed, almost matter-of-fact. There was a longer set of stairs to the basement. The door was closed, but there was light bleeding through its gaps. Sharp stared down and pointed at the dim light seeping from underneath the door.

"Check upstairs. I'll see what's going on down there," whispered Sharp.

Palmer went upstairs, turning on lights with one hand, pointing his side-arm with the other. The home was small, compartmentalized, and sparsely decorated. The last place he checked was the front bedroom, which was empty except for an unmade single bed. He could hear Sharp talking now, and he and turned, headed downstairs quickly.

"Sharp? What have you got?"

"Slowly, Palmer," Sharp replied.

In the basement Sharp stood just inside the doorway of an old bare room with worn shag carpet and wood paneling. Horrible florescent lights hung from the ceiling, humming and bathing the room in a sickly blue light. A roll-up desk and chair stood against one wall. A man was seated at the desk.

He was wearing shorts and black dress socks, no shirt, his once musclebound torso now gone to fat. He had a hard grip on a small caliber pistol. When Palmer entered the room, he lifted it and pressed it against his temple.

"Easy, Dan, easy, you don't want to do that," said Sharp. His voice was confident, yet kind.

Palmer remained at the doorway.

"How many of you are there?" the man said.

"It's just us."

"They said I was just going to talk, that's it. I'll do it, I swear!"

"Take a breath and let's keep talking," said Sharp. "Can I update my partner here?"

"I don't care what you do," said the man.

Sharp turned to Palmer, his gaze traveling from Palmer's weapon to his holster. Palmer did not re-holster his gun as Sharp's eyes had suggested, but held it behind his back, out of view.

"You'd better not be planning anything. I'll do it!"

Sharp raised his hand, and looked at the man.

"Dan here is having a tough time. He called a crisis hot line, he mentioned he had a gun and they patched in our dispatch on the call."

"They lied," said Dan.

"They were concerned for your safety. So are we. Put the gun down. We can't talk or figure this out with you sitting there with that thing jammed against your head."

Dan pressed the gun even harder, and for a moment the two officers prepared themselves for an explosion of blood and bone.

"Dan, who is that in the photo, right there?" asked Sharp.

Dan regarded a framed picture and lowered the gun to around his chin.

"My mother and sister."

"Where are they?"

"Out of town."

"Whereabouts?"

"A couple hours. I don't want them involved in this!"

"Can you drive there, or take the bus?"

"Yeah. Don't try and head-shrink me."

"I'm not, man, believe me I'm not, but wouldn't you rather be there having a visit with them than sitting *here*, like this?"

Dan lowered the gun and for a split second the barrel pointed in Sharp's general direction.

"Okay, Dan, we talked about that. You *do that* and it changes things. You point that *at me* and we have to respond."

"I'm sorry," said Dan. He took a huge breath and said, "I don't want them worrying about me."

"They would be heartbroken, I'm sure, if you did this."

"They might not care."

"The fact that you don't want them involved suggests that you know they'd care. They'd be crushed."

Dan shrugged and then gulped and looked down at his lap. "I don't know."

"When did you see them last?"

"Last year, maybe." Dan sat up and added, "I talk to my mother on the phone a couple times a month, though."

"What about your sister?"

"She's busy. Her husband's a dentist and she works in the office. He's a jerk."

"Dentists normally are," said Palmer.

Dan seemed to like this and allowed himself a tense chuckle.

"But you get along with your sister, what's her name?"

"Denise."

"You get along with Denise."

"Yeah, she's great. She has a five-year-old son."

"So, you have a nephew?"

Sharp nodded towards a football pennant, thumb-tacked to the wall.

"You ever toss the ball around with him?"

The gun was now on Dan's lap. His grip on it less urgent.

Sharp took a half step towards the desk, and kept talking. "Thanksgiving is coming up. Imagine visiting them, bringing them a cherry pie and a football. Imagine your nephew's face."

Dan was gulping, fighting tears. He said, "I'm in a lot of trouble now. I won't be visiting anyone any time soon."

"Sure you will. We'll do what we can to help. Why don't you call your mum now? She doesn't have to know we're here. Just call and say hello, see how she is."

Dan looked at Sharp, and then at Palmer with exhausted, red eyes.

"It's a great idea. And you don't have to share the pie with the dentist if you don't want to," said Palmer.

"What about you? Do you call your mother?" asked Dan.

Sharp took another tiny step in Dan's direction and said, "I'll call my grandfather. He and I get along really well."

"That's good," said Dan, and then, "Loneliness sucks."

"Why don't you pick up that phone and call your mum?" Sharp pointed to the phone.

He closed the gap as Dan regarded the phone. Palmer aimed his gun at Dan's head.

"Here, *I'll take* that and you can make that call."

Dan did not struggle or resist. Sharp snatched the gun. Dan had the phone and had started dialing.

Sharp looked at the gun and closed his eyes for just a moment. He looked over at Palmer and smiled.

"Hi, Mum, how are you? . . . Yeah, yeah, that's good. Well, I have something to say . . . yeah, I don't want to upset you, but I haven't been doing so good lately."

And with that, Dan became a blubbering mess. Sharp walked to him and put a hand on his shoulder.

They waited outside the bedroom while Dan got dressed and put a few things in an overnight bag. Dan's mother had asked to speak to Sharp. She told him that she and her daughter would be down as soon as possible. She also told him that Dan had struggled with depression since he was a teen. His condition had worsened after his girlfriend had left him a few months ago. She told Sharp that her son was a really a nice person.

"We'll take him to Pearson General, they have a mental health unit there. If we bring him, they'll admit him. You and his sister can see him there. I'll leave my card with the nurse."

Dan's mother was thankful.

"He had a gun in his possession. We've confiscated it. From what we can gather he does not have an FAC for it, so we will have to charge him for that."

Later, in the hospital car park, while completing their notes, Palmer said, "Possession of an unregistered firearm. That's it?"

Sharp ignored him. His head was down and his pen scratched against his notebook.

"He pointed it at us, threatened to shoot himself. We should book him for everything we can. Book him for being a fat moron."

Sharp looked up from his notes.

"What for, Palmer? Did you see that guy? He's a mess. His life is miserable enough. Why add to it?"

"He pointed that fucking gun right at you."

"It was a twenty-two. My vest would have eaten it no problem."

"So that's it?"

"You want to fight me on this? It's your call as well. So let's fight about it. You saw the guy. He wasn't going to shoot anyone, not even himself. He's mixed up. He's a headcase. Now he's in the Pearson psych wing crying like a baby in his mother's arms. She'll watch him like he's ten years old now. No real future. No dignity. Let's just leave it at that."

Palmer rolled down the window, lit a cigarette, and watched a light rain fall on the pavement.

"Alright," he said.

Palmer felt something slip inside him. He would not kill Sharp. Compassion. Sharp had it, just as he had it. He did have compassion. You'd never know it by his choices and behaviour, but he had compassion. It just lived deep, deep inside of him.

Tears in his eyes hindered his vision. He tore along without considering what might drive or step in front of him, and how it would be nearly impossible to stop. He was confused about his tears. There was a great sadness pushing in his chest. It seemed to be locked inside, fighting to get out. His thoughts rushed through his head with speed that matched the reckless pace of the stolen Mercedes. They felt like confessions and he hated them:

My father worked a lot. He worked hard. He was hard to know.

My mother would drag me to visit his grave and she would bring cut flowers to lay at his headstone.

She would weep, even years later when I was in my teens. His death was still a fresh wound to her.

I would weep because it was upsetting to see grief still controlling her.

I would weep at the constraints a dead father places on a boy.

And now they're both buried there, her headstone beside his.

It's a mysterious thing, a son gazing upon his parent's graveside.

Mum, I weep because I miss you. You were kind; you provided great care and comfort.

You soldiered on.

Dad, I weep, and let's face it, when a son weeps at his father's graveside . . .

. . . God knows what he's really weeping for.

I wept because it *wasn't* an accident.

He slowed the Mercedes and pulled a right turn into the fairgrounds. The car fishtailed and he adjusted the steering wheel just in time to prevent a full spin.

"A wipeout?!" he yelled.

The car bombed along the frozen ground. Behind him now, plenty of flashing lights.

He had a thought: about a quarter mile beyond the fairground, north of the service road, there was a fence punctuated

by viewing stations. There were three of them, thick stone benches with coin-operated viewfinders that looked like aging robots
positioned beside each. You could pay a quarter to stand at the
edge of the escarpment and look out at the valley below.

He slowed even more, and finally stopped at a makeshift building that covered the bumper cars. He knew Sharp wouldn't come
barreling right up behind him, and he didn't disappoint. His cruiser
stopped at least two car-lengths back. They waited each other out.
Sharp was a cool customer. So he exited the Mercedes with his gun
tucked in the pocket of his hoodie. Sharp and Ryan remained in
the car. Three other police vehicles had pulled in behind Sharp and
Ryan's. He could hear more sirens in the distance. He stood beside
the Mercedes and noticed dents and scratches along its doors. He
couldn't recall hitting anything. The passenger door of the cruiser
opened and Sharp stayed low, tucked in behind it, the entire scene
awash in the blue glare of headlights and strobes.

"Let me see your hands, Barry!"

He obliged and very slowly removed his hands from his
pockets. He raised them slightly.

"Where's the gun?"

He didn't answer Sharp. He had a thought, murky and pro-
viding little excitement: *a gunfight, a good, old-fashioned shoot-out
where I hit Ryan and some of the others and then Sharp cuts me down.
But who's to say that's how it would happen? Sharp, bless his heart, is
now standing, his chest, neck and head exposed above the car door.*

"Barry, let's see the gun, slowly, and let's end this."

Yes, let's end this.

"How long have you known it was me?"

Sharp turned his head and cupped his ear. He motioned at
Ryan, who ducked back in the cruiser and killed the engine.

"I said how long have you known it was me?"

"Not long."

"Have you been to the house?"

"Yeah, we've got people there now."

"I had you fooled. I was a fairly good cop."

Sharp lowered himself, gaining back more cover.

"You did. You were."

"You probably want to know why."

"I don't think it's even knowable, Barry."

He laughed and nodded at this. Sharp nodded back and went to say something else, but more cavalry arrived; lights flashing and lighting the evening sky red and blue, sirens killing any chance to talk further. Someone in behind Sharp said something and there was movement, panicked and destructive movement. He hopped back in the car, ripped it into Drive and crushed the accelerator. He sped along a narrow service road, passing disassembled rides and piles of canvas. He hit something, some aluminum or siding that was flapping on the side of a building. It flew in the air and came down on the cruiser directly behind him.

His headlights lit the centre bench and he glanced at the speedometer: 190. Snow and dirt flew in the air. It was like his car had triggered a windstorm. The bench was substantial enough that the car might just rip and fold around it and never take flight. He gently pulled the steering wheel to the right and the car responded. He blew by the stone bench and busted through the fence as if it were made of butcher's twine. He did not feel like he was flying. He felt the car lose its contact with the ground, and saw grey space beyond the windshield, and sensed the reality of the dark valley below.

What will be my last thought?

He remembered a school teacher. She was a tiny, wire-haired woman who always wore a green cardigan. Mrs. Ward, damn it, Mrs. Ward. It was Parent/Teacher day and his father was at the school. He was supposed to be in the gymnasium, playing floor hockey with some other boys. Instead, he was outside the classroom door, tucked in behind an alcove, eavesdropping on the meeting.

"Barry is a peculiar boy," said Mrs. Ward.

He heard his father clear his throat, and then the squeaking sound of his chair moving against the polished classroom tile.

"What's that supposed to mean?" said his father.

Chapter 34: Warfield

The sight of two headlamps in the distance was enough to make her yell and pump her fist. They were white-blue dots at first that grew quickly until Sheila could see an oncoming truck take form: small orange roof lights and then the growl of a diesel motor. She waved her flashlight and then pointed it briefly at the ground. The motor grumbled as the driver geared down. Its brakes hissed and it slowed and took the gravel shoulder on the opposite side. A tow truck, *Gateway Auto* emblazoned on its door. She knew some of the drivers; they had a contract with the department. She walked to the truck and the driver jumped out and zipped up his coveralls. There was a cigarette hanging from his lips. It was Sam. She knew him from various fire route tows and accident scenes, and at that moment it felt like he was her best friend.

"They're looking for you!" he said, opening the passenger door and helping her up into the cab. The warmth hit her like a hammer, and her eyes immediately began to water. Sam got in and tossed his smoke, rolled the window up tight.

"You okay? Where's your car?"

"Back there. I saw a buck on the road and lost it, spun down the bank and into the field."

Sam looked over his shoulder. "Man, you can't see it. I just cruised past there and didn't see shit."

Shiela looked at his radio and scanner. "The chase, what's going on?"

"Over," said Sam. He dropped the truck in gear and checked his mirrors. "It was a fucking cop . . . well, you probably know that. Drove through Skyward and right off the observation area."

"Is he dead?"

"Oh yeah, have you seen that fucking drop?"

She nodded and didn't know which emotion or thought to attach herself to. She closed her eyes and felt a jolt when she saw Sharp, his face full of fear and confusion.

"Was anyone else hurt?"

"Nope. You want to go to the station or the hospital? We can get your car when it's daylight."

She sighed and fought nausea. "The station."

"I don't fucking envy you," said Sam.

Sergeant Glendon sat with his fingers interlaced in front of him.

"I don't know whether to curse you or praise you," he said.

Sheila shook her head. Her visit to Barry's and her search of his home had been reckless, and Glendon told her so. She had broken protocol and hadn't stopped to think about rules of evidence. As it happened, Barry had driven to his death and there would be no arrest, no trial. She had endangered herself by becoming involved in the pursuit, and the entire mess had started when she left an assigned post without permission, without making radio contact. And yet the look in Glendon's eyes was one of amazement, even as he reprimanded her. He asked her how she knew. Sheila told him that she had pieced it together after talking to Barry the day before, and after taking into consideration the various cars he drove on a very short term; her conversations with his neighbours and the series of locked drawers and doors inside his house. Glendon listened and narrowed his eyes. She knew it didn't add up, so she took a gamble and said, "I can't explain it. I had some intuition; it's difficult to articulate."

"Indeed you did, but you're going to have to learn to manifest it properly, *find* a way to articulate it; communicate with your fellow officers."

"Yes, sir."

There was a knock at the door and Inspector Edward Sharp entered. His white shirt was so well pressed it looked like paper.

"Ed, shall I give you a minute?" said Glendon.

"Thanks," said the Inspector.

He sat and waited until the Sergeant had left the room.

Here it comes, she thought, *I'll be in the station answering phones and sticking bar-codes to recovered bicycles, stereos and laptops, and scanning them, lugging around files and stolen goods . . .*

Inspector Sharp looked around and saw the coffee pot a quarter filled.

"I suppose that's warm swamp water," he said.

"Yes, sir," she said.

He got up, took a mug down and poured. He took a whiff of the coffee before he sat back down.

"Are you okay?" he asked.

He surprised her. He looked genuinely concerned and had asked the question earnestly. She didn't know him. He was stern and held his head high much of the time. Some of the guys called him the Ice Man. Goodrich and Phelps had called him that right in front of his son, Matt Sharp. The younger Sharp ignored it; seemed not to care.

"I'm okay. I apologize for the way I handled things."

The Inspector ignored her apology.

"Some of the others think he was begging to be caught. I suppose that's obvious in hindsight."

He sipped his coffee, whistled quietly, and then pushed the mug away.

"CIB are over there now. He had things locked down and there was a supply of stone tiles, just bought, enough to finish the floor of that room. They found papers, documents about exhumation. They also found correspondence from a car dealership in BC; seems he had been talking to them about working there. Who knows with a man like this? He might have disappeared. And we certainly weren't following the right trail."

The Inspector sat back and watched Sheila as if she might morph into a strange creature.

"You look exhausted. I want you to get that knee examined."

"Yes, sir."

She closed her eyes and massaged her temples. In the two seconds she had them closed she saw Matt Sharp with a look of shock on his face, fists clenched at his sides, eyes alert with fear.

"Sir, can I ask if Matthew is okay?"

The inspector stood and raised his chin, adjusted his tie.

"He's at home. Safe to say he's been better. He's okay, though."

She wanted to ask if he was certain about that, and when was the last time anyone actually saw him, talked to him.

"The Chief wants to talk to you. Rest up though, you can see him when you've gathered yourself. A day or two."

Inspector Sharp left the room. An involuntary sigh of relief left her lips and she hoped he hadn't heard it.

She went to the hospital, and then she went home to rest. She sat in front of the TV watching colours and movement, but unaware of what was actually on. She slept fitfully; Sharp's face, his eyes and a feeling of dread glowed inside of her. She awoke at dawn, picked up the phone. She wanted to talk to Phelps, Anderson or Goodrich.

Hanson, one of the station duty operators, answered.

"Hanson, it's Sheila Warfield."

His voice dropped, a conspiratorial tone. "Hey, you alright? You knew it was Palmer all along? That's what they're saying."

"No, not all along, but I put a few things together."

"Still can't believe it. I didn't know him well, and he was a strange cat, but who would have figured? They'll probably offer you a spot in CIB."

She hadn't considered that. She had thought if anything they'd keep her locked up in the station where she couldn't sneak into a murderer's home, tear it apart and then drive her cruiser off the road like a girl. She needed Sharp's address. The need was pressing her from the inside. Hanson was a decent guy, but he wouldn't give out an address or home phone number. He was talking in her ear and she wasn't paying any attention. She thought of calling Sharp's cell number, but assuming he even answered it what would she say? She wanted to actually see him. She wondered who was in the guard room.

"Hanson, is there anyone in the guard room, or down in the gym?"

"Not sure. Anderson, from your crew, was still here a few minutes ago. He might have taken off by now."

"Can you patch me through?"

She waited and bit her fingernails while the phone rang.

"Detective McVeigh."

Sheila held the phone away from her ear for just a second.

"Hi, Kyle, it's Sheila Warfield."

"Uh huh," he said. He sounded disinterested.

"Is Anderson around?"

"He's here, why?"

"I need to talk to him."

McVeigh dropped the phone. She heard him say, "Ralph, it's for you. It's *Warfield.*"

Anderson came on.

"Can he hear you?" she asked before Ralph Anderson could start with his sarcasm.

"Hey, Warfield, I've been up for thirty-two hours, I was just about to head home."

"Can you go somewhere private and call me? It's important."

He released a dramatic groan and muttered, "What are you offering this time? I have to tell you, I dig lingerie and whipped cream."

"Come on, Ralph, don't be a asshole."

"Fine."

He took her number and she waited with the phone in her hand, ready to press the talk button as soon as it rang. She remembered doing this as a girl, back in high school. She'd been watching TV on the couch with her boyfriend, Brad. They had been kissing, and he had suggested they throw a blanket over them. They kissed under the blanket; his hands roamed and she followed his hands with hers, frequently batting them away from her thighs. She saw Brad's father. She'd only met the man once, informally on his driveway, she on her bicycle and him washing the family car. And yet there he was emerging from the darkness as she closed her eyes. She saw that he was at a hospital, or a clinic. There was a women in scrubs near a metal table. Sheila could smell the disinfectant in the room. She saw a stainless steel scale near the woman's foot. A strange looking thing. It had a large, rubber surface. She saw some unusual anesthesia masks, conical and in a range of sizes. There was a chart on the wall that contained details on animal nutrition. There was a dog whining, a plaintive sound. She understood then. She pulled her face away from her boyfriend.

"What's wrong?"

"I'll be right back."

She threw the blanket off and went to the hallway. She did not want the phone to disturb her parents. She held it in one hand while she went to the kitchen for a bottle of water. The phone rang as she reentered the living room. She whispered *hello* and a deep voice asked for Brad. She handed him the phone.

She opened the water and watched Brad's face go from curious to concerned. The call was short; Brad stood and handed the phone back to her. What had been a warm, promising evening had become a grim one.

"I have to go."

"What's wrong?" she said.

She resisted a strong urge to tell him she already knew.

"My mum's on the way to pick me up. Our dog's really sick. He's at the emergency animal clinic."

"Oh my God, I'm sorry to hear that."

Brad looked around for his coat.

"Yeah, he's old. He hasn't been doing so well lately."

The ring of her own telephone yanked her back to the present day. She answered it immediately.

"Yeah, it's Anderson."

"I need a favour."

"I am so tired right now. What is it?"

"Can you give me Sharp's address? I know basically where he lives, but I don't have the number."

"Why do you need his address? Don't tell me you have a key to *his* place as well."

"Ralph!"

"Yes?"

"Come on, I need to talk to him."

"Alright, alright. Man, I'm having problems seeing my Blackberry. I'm asleep on my feet here."

The line went quiet. She wondered what was taking so long. Maybe he'd fallen asleep.

"Are you still there?"

"Where would I have gone, Warfield? If I hang up on you you'll just track me down. I'm searching my contacts, I just have to find it."

"I appreciate this," she said.

He exhaled and cursed under his breath, and then said, "All joking aside, if I give you this and there's any fucking repercussions—you stalk him or end up hiding in his fucking attic—you will, one hundred percent, be giving me that BJ. I'm not kidding."

"Okay. I'll still buy you those boilermakers."

"Fucking right you will. Okay, here it is, you got a pen?"

She took her time, drove carefully, hands at ten and two, her banged up SUV in the right lane, part of a convoy of careful drivers that obeyed the speed limit and hit their brakes every five seconds. She relaxed and reached a better cruising speed once she hit the country roads. Her eyes were wide open, glued to the road. She could not see Sharp, but sensed that he was distressed. She was stricken for a moment by a surge of disappointment, a contrite slap in the face.

"Just leave him alone," she said.

She pulled off the road. He lived another half hour away. She thought she should call and at least warn him she was coming, and felt her pocket for her cell, only to remember it was broken.

She found his house after driving past it twice. It was tucked away behind a line of trees. A gingerbread house with a long lane way and a frozen manmade pond in front. Sharp's car was parked near a matching garage, the most quaint garage she'd ever seen. She pulled up and shut off the motor, and waited. She considered leaving, but urged herself to buck up. She lowered the sun visor, opened the little underside mirror and checked her face.

"You're so stupid," she said.

The front door was beautiful, constructed of thick wood and inlaid glass. She knocked gently, and then slightly harder. She heard movement and felt a knot in her stomach. She had never met his wife and it occurred to her she might not be very

welcoming. In fact she might be downright rude when she discovered a five-foot-ten, slightly round-shouldered, underweight
but otherwise presentable twenty-four-year-old blond on her
doorstep, inquiring after her irresistible husband. The door
opened and Sharp himself stood there. His handsome face
appeared confused at first, and then back to neutral, back to his
usual cool.

"Warfield, what a surprise."

He looked over her shoulder as if she might have someone
with her.

"I'm sorry to bother you. Anderson gave me your address,
but I hassled him for it. It's on me."

"That's alright, come in. It's been an insane couple of days."

He had always been easy to talk to, but now, in his house, in
his jeans and plaid shirt he was even more approachable. He
pointed to a couple of leather chairs. She sat in one and he took
the other.

"Can I get you a coffee or tea?"

"I'm okay. I won't stay long. I thought you might be in danger, or distressed. I mean obviously everyone's stressed about
things, but I thought you might be, that something, that maybe
there was a threat beyond—oh God, I sound stupid—beyond
pursuing Palmer."

She felt completely hopeless and wished she could melt into
the chair. He nodded and looked around the room. She followed
his gaze. The home was nice, but spare. She had imagined it
would be more stylish, filled with furniture. She remembered a
shift when he was training her; he'd mentioned he loved antiques.
She looked around the place for retro items, ornaments, lamps,
conversation makers. Anderson had told her that Sharp's wife was
an artist, a painter, and yet the walls were quite bare. There were
nails and hooks, but there was no artwork.

"Why would you think that?" he said. He seemed tired, and
his tone of voice suggested suspicion.

"I don't know. After I went off the road, by the time I got
out of the cruiser and Sam found me on the roadside, I knew it
was all over and yet I still had this gut feeling."

Sharp studied her briefly and then resumed his gaze at the walls.

"I got home and my wife had moved out—not just an overnight bag and some make-up. She's done that before. She hates confrontation, detests what she calls the 'atmosphere' after we've disagreed, so the odd time she'd go and stay with her friend. This time she rented a truck apparently."

He pointed at the bare walls and then dropped his hand in his lap. He let out a nervous chuckle. "This time it's a more permanent arrangement. She left a letter."

"I'm sorry to hear that," she said.

She couldn't look at him, so she stared at the hardwood floor.

He remained silent. Sheila felt her face flush. She should have stayed home. She did not know him well enough to sit and hold his hand, assuming that was what he even wanted, or needed. She wished she did know him well enough. Right now she was just another inconvenience, piled on top of what was no doubt the most upsetting twenty-four hours of his life.

"I should go. I just thought I'd come by and make sure you were okay."

"That's nice of you."

She stood, and as she did she realized she hadn't removed her shoes. There was a small puddle on the floor near her chair. *Idiot,* she thought, and turned toward the door ashamed, but pleased beyond belief that he was safe.

Chapter 35: Stan Hill

I have a routine now. Man, it didn't take long. I haven't broken it since I got here. I get up and go for a run in the morning. The sun is usually coming up and cutting the haze. I can run towards the water and hear its massive swishing and lapping, or I can run up to the Cleveland Street District and take in the dormant shops and bistros before they open up. The air is warm, damp but strangely fragrant on most mornings, and arid and clean on others, but either way it feels good to breathe it—gone is the reek of rust, decay and that Godforsaken factory. When I'm finished my run I go back to the condo and shower up, put the coffee on and then take a mug to my father who is usually taking his turn in the bathroom, his face slathered in shaving cream. We smile at each other like brothers, never mind father and son. It's evident that this is going to work out just fine. My father loaned me some money and I bought a car, a 2006 Saab 9.5. The thing has never seen salt or snow. An older couple sold it to us. It's immaculate and I can't believe my luck each time I jump in and crank it up.

I haven't thrown a punch since I've been down here. Haven't talked to a cop other than to pay a speeding ticket, and I even told him to have a good day. I met a girl, Barbara, my first month here. My father says not to get too carried away with her—learn the business first and then worry about chasing skirts—but Jimbo covers for me and lets me go early to see her a couple times a week.

She's different. She can carry a conversation and she has a smoking body to go along with the brain. So I let Jimbo cover for me. I'm not missing out on time with her. My job isn't the most exciting, but I'm working with Jimbo and he's bringing me along. He's a more talkative, less patient version of my old man, but he knows his stuff and he's giving me his time and energy, so

I shut up and listen, and learn, and enjoy the intense heat of the sun; the satisfaction of a job well done; the ride of a sweet European-made car; the cold, crisp beer; the insanely good feeling of warm sand in my toes.

I think of my brother more often than most would imagine. I wonder if he would have straightened up down here. If he would have been more productive, responsive, open to encouragement, and even a little tough love if we'd come down here together. One thing is for certain, he would have lived and not fallen prey to that freak.

I worry about my mum and put aside money each pay so I can fly up and see her. My father is sending her money to help her out. We've offered to bring her down here, but she's not interested. She says that she and my father didn't work out up there; why would it be any different down here? It *is* different though. But I can't worry about her. I live my new life, give thanks for escaping that northern shit-show that *was* my home. And I laugh that McVeigh had to eat humble pie. He was demoted; back in uniform and writing traffic offenses. I was going to send him a postcard: bright sun, warm sand, tanned bodies. My father squashed it. He put a hand on my shoulder, offered me a beer and reminded me to stay the course, have a cigar and go out on the balcony, enjoy the sights: a huge sky, blue-green water and lots of bright bikinis around. He lifted his hand and gave me a slap on the back, and told me to control the controllable.

Chapter 36: Sharp & Warfield

Sheila arrived at the station an hour early. She parked around front, in the small lot reserved for visitors and admin staff. She looked at the ignition key, hesitated before shutting the motor down. She could pull out of the parking space and go for coffee, or try the new smoothie and juice bar around the corner— Goodrich had said it was great. Her belly was nerve-riddled and her mouth was bone-dry. She turned the ignition key, sighed as the motor shuddered to a stop. She left the radio on. And then she recalled a time when she had sat listening to the radio for twenty minutes and her shitbox SUV wouldn't start up again. She'd had to call for a jump-start. She turned the radio off and sat in silence. She watched the parking lot, but there was not much to keep her entertained. She looked over at the row of reserved parking. The Chief's and Duty Inspector's cars were both parked, backed into their spaces. The Deputy Chief's spot was empty and she recalled that he was away on a snowboarding trip that he'd cut short because of the fallout from the Barry Palmer mess. She searched her vehicle for some mints or gum and found only a packet of soy sauce. She got out of her SUV and shut the door, which bounced back open, so she slammed it harder and promised herself she'd look around for a better ride, something that didn't have a warped door and small rust holes around the back fenders. She emptied her pockets, old tissue, car park receipts and the soy sauce at the trash can just for the sake of doing something.

When she began her walk back to her shitbox, Sharp's Jaguar rolled in. If he noticed her, he didn't acknowledge it. He cruised by and parked three spaces down from her. She watched his car's taillights turn off and she could hear the rumble of music coming from the inside of Sharp's car—evidently he did not live in fear of a dead battery.

She looked at her vehicle, and then at Sharp's gleaming royal blue car with leather seats and the smell of whatever he wore intoxicating the air inside. She stuffed her hands in her pockets and walked over. She tapped on the passenger side window and he looked up from his cell phone, placed it on the dash. The car's locks made an electric popping sound and he waved for her to hop in.

She decided she would keep things professional, stoic, if possible, but the first thing out of her mouth was, "My God you smell good, or maybe it's your car, or both."

Sharp laughed and said, "I'm not sure. I use a pretty expensive leather polish in this thing." He took a sip from a bottled water, then added, "So, you're here for the meeting with the Chief and my old man. You're early."

Sheila felt her stomach tighten.

"Yeah, I hope I'm not in shit, not too much of it, anyway."

"No, not that I know of," he said.

"That's good. Did he mention anything?" She pointed towards Inspector Sharp's car.

"He's mentioned plenty, but I think the news is good, well, decent, depending on your perspective. We'll get more details once we get inside."

"You're in the meeting?"

"Yes I am, if that's okay with you, of course." He laughed.

"I didn't mean in like that." She checked dashboard clock. "You're early too."

He looked over his shoulder to the backseat where he'd tossed his gym bag. "I was going to go downstairs and ride the stationary bike or something—"

"Oh, I'm sorry. I'll go back to my car, or go inside and straighten my locker—"

"No, stay here. We should talk."

She was anxious about what he wanted to discuss with her. She also wanted to ask if anything more had happened with his wife, but she kept her mouth shut. She pictured herself trembling or twitching, though she didn't think was really doing either. *Get a damn grip, already*, she thought.

"I'm sorry if I'm jumpy. I've never met with the Chief and the Inspector at the same time."

"Relax, it will be pretty casual. Or as casual as things can be with my old man in the room."

"So you know what it's about?"

"Yes, I do."

"But you can't say. You want to wait until we get in there."

"Oh, I can say. Do you want to know?"

He smiled at her and sat back in his seat.

"Of course I do," she said.

"I enjoyed training you, working with you, Sheila. I miss those days."

She felt flattered and was certain she'd turned red. He put his water in the cup-holder and said, "The second time we worked together, we did that radio call down on South Shore Road, the boy who was in his mother's car while she unloaded groceries. He dropped the thing into neutral and it rolled down the drive and into the road, hit that hydro truck."

"Yeah, he was lucky. Two seconds earlier and that truck might have T-boned him."

Sharp nodded and said, "We cleared that call and there was that dog, wandering around, nice dog, obviously lost."

He picked up the water and sipped at it. Her mouth had become terribly dry.

"Do you remember that?" he asked. Sharp looked at her and smiled. "You don't by any chance want one, do you?"

"One what?"

He held up the plastic bottle.

Sheila cleared her throat and ran her tongue around her mouth, searching for moisture.

"I'd love one," she said. It came out like a whisper.

Sharp chuckled.

"I have a whole case in the trunk."

He got out of the car. She heard him rooting around back there. She couldn't have forgotten that call with the dog if she'd tried. Her family had a dog just like it when she was growing up. It had tugged at her emotions to see that dog, almost an exact match, wandering the boulevard, its worried little black eyes peering up at each passing car. If it hadn't been so well-groomed she would have considered taking it home, but it obviously belonged to someone.

She had been driving that day and it had been a busy shift. Sharp had said he'd radio dispatch to contact animal control and she'd said no, don't call animal control, not yet. She pulled over and exited the cruiser. She went down on one knee and called the dog over. It was a lovely creature, licking her hand and offering its paw. It seemed glad for her friendly voice. Her dog had had the same good nature. He'd been easily distracted and too trusting, counting everyone as his friend.

She'd felt heat in her throat and the beginning of tears as she kneeled and talked to the dog, so she told herself, *Don't even fucking think about it. You're on duty right now.*

She blinked away the tears, squeezed her eyes shut. That's when she saw the girl; the open gate; the white clapboard doghouse; the grey brick house with 724 in chrome numbers over a dark green garage. She heard the girl's voice: "Marcus! Marcus! Come on, boy!"

She heard the girl hollering for her mother and saw the panic in her little face, not knowing whether to go and search for the dog, or run inside and get her mum. The girl stood in the yard and cupped her hands around her mouth, yelled for her dog to come back. And then, mercifully, Sheila saw a street sign, blurred, but definitely *Mac* something. Sheila hooked her hand in the dog's collar and said, "Come on, Marcus."

She was right. Marcus was indeed its name. The dog became even more riled and was licking and nuzzling her, looking her straight in the eye. She led Marcus to the cruiser and opened the back door. Prior to lifting Marcus inside, she slipped his collar off and dropped it in her pocket. Sharp had been jotting down some notes but lowered his notebook and watched her and the dog. The sight of her grabbing the mutt's hind legs and helping it into the back seat brought a smile to his face.

"Is he under arrest?"

"Let's just run him home."

"Is it close by?"

"Not too far."

"Why'd you take his collar off?"

"So I could read the tag, find out where he belongs, plus he'd snagged it on something, damaged it, so it was pretty well ready to fall off."

Sharp put down his notebook and reached back to stroke the dog's head. "This is your lucky day, buddy," he said.

She became nervous as she drove, pretending to know where she was headed, but trying, as casually as possible to read every street sign. *My God, please, it's* Mac *something. It can't be too far. He's not panting and he's alert. He can't have wandered far.*

"Are we taking the scenic route?" Sharp asked. He reclined his seat a little in order to lean back and pat the dog's head. "What's his name? Marvin?"

"Marcus."

She was holding her breath as she drove and contemplated telling Sharp that she was just guessing. But she couldn't possibly tell him the truth.

"I think she just likes having you in the car. You like it too. Dogs like car rides, right?" Sharp was scratching Marcus's head, chatting away to the dog.

MacTier. She saw it and hit the brakes a little too hard.

"*Jeez*, maybe you should drive, too," Sharp said to the dog.

She found the house and Sharp waited while she took Marcus up the driveway. He stayed in the passenger seat and watched a curly-headed little girl bolt from the house and hug the animal.

The girl's mother followed and Sheila Warfield stood with her and talked, each smiling and frequently stealing glances at the girl reunited with her pet.

Sharp was back in the Jag, sitting beside her, holding out a bottle of water. Sheila felt as if she'd been in a trance.

"Do you recall that day?"

"Yes, I do."

"I remember that call well. *Really* well. There was *no tag* on that dog's collar," said Sharp.

Sheila felt lightheaded for a moment. She looked Sharp in the eye and he did not avert his stare. She unscrewed the cap and drank.

"You busted that hold-up man, the lightweight who was knocking off banks with an empty gun. Goodrich said you arrested him out of the blue. You two had the guy at gunpoint and Billy was already rehearsing what he'd say to the disciplinary tribunal, but *you* wound up being right."

Sheila nodded—she couldn't disagree with anything Sharp had said.

"You came to the house," he continued, "which I appreciated. You knew Ingrid was gone."

"I didn't know she was gone, not exactly."

"Okay, fair enough, but you knew something was up, and that *something* compelled you. I won't even *start* with Barry, other than to say he hoodwinked everyone. No one even had a hunch. It adds up now, of course—now most people see him for the complicated, murderous prick he was—but you knew beforehand."

Sheila wanted to talk, but didn't know where to start.

"So why don't you tell me what's going on?" he said. "I mean, I think I have an idea."

Sheila looked out at the parking lot, shrugged her shoulders, realizing that was about the most stupid thing she could have done.

"So, full disclosure," said Sharp. "I resigned yesterday, tried to, anyway—"

"Why?"

"I had a plan. We'd had a plan, Ingrid and I. I was going to pack it in—five years, five years max. We were going to buy a bed and breakfast, move off the grid just a little, run it and live happily ever after. She left for someone else, so that's not going to happen. This is more than a marital spat."

Sharp took off his seatbelt and allowed it to snap back into place.

"So, I'm not going to be running a bed and breakfast on my own."

"I think she made a mistake," said Sheila.

"Doesn't matter. It's done. So my old man was apoplectic when I told him I wanted to resign. He took it personally. We sat and talked for two hours. He asked me to reconsider, give it another chance. He offered me a spot in CIB. I thought about it, and my immediate reaction was to tell him no way. But reality started to sneak up on me. What the hell am I going to do if I quit? I mean really? It would be different work in CIB, out of uniform, working cases with a beginning, middle, and hopefully an end, away from the bump and grind of the community patrol cars. I called my grandfather and talked it over with him. He gave it the thumbs up."

"I remember you telling me you were close with him."

Sharp smiled. "I am."

"So you're meeting here today to accept the job."

"Yeah, that's why I'm here. The thing is, McVeigh is being demoted. Gonzalez, he's a good guy, but he won't work one-on-one with anybody, and the others are swamped. They need someone else, so I put your name forward. *That's* why you're here."

Sheila was thrilled, flattered, and shocked. The news gave her a strange lift and she knew it would take time to sink in.

"The last day or two have consisted of me at my old man's place, or on the phone with him, and with him on the phone to Chief Boyle."

Sheila glugged her water. Her mouth was back to normal, her gut no longer packed with nerves.

"I'm a rookie. How would this work? This is going to piss some people off."

"Yeah, you'd be a trainee. You'd retain your constable status, but as far as the CIB work goes, you'd be in training, probationary. And as far as the others go, we'll let my old man deal with the foot-stompers."

She thought this over.

"This is too good to be true."

"You have a good track record. You make arrests."

"I was trained well," she said.

"We worked well together, no question. And we can do it again. But, before this gets the gold seal, I need to know what happens, how you *know*."

Sharp pointed to the clock.

"We have half an hour. I'll shut up and you tell me what you can."

"Have you told your father that you think I'm—"

"No I haven't. I haven't and I won't breathe a word of it. Whatever you tell me stays in this car."

"Okay."

He waited, drummed his fingers lightly on the steering wheel.

"You're procrastinating, Warfield."

"Okay, okay."

Sheila looked out beyond the dash towards the station building. She shifted in her seat to face him as best she could. She remembered being in the airport departure lounge back when she was a girl, fear and darkness descending upon her. Sharp narrowed his eyes and waited. She figured she'd better start telling her story, and felt grateful that Sharp was there for the telling.

ACKNOWLEDGEMENTS

Thanks to my editor Chris Needham for keeping this novel on track and for all of the support and creative freedom he provides. I believe I owe him at least twenty beers by now. . . .